Caffeine Nig

BREATHE

David Ince

Fiction aimed at the heart
and the head...

Published by Caffeine Nights Publishing 2015

Published in Great Britain by
Caffeine Nights Publishing
4 Eton Close
Walderslade
Chatham

Kent

ME5 9AT

www.caffeine-nights.com
www.caffeinenightsbooks.com

British Library Cataloguing in Publication Data.
A CIP catalogue record for this book is available from the British Library

ISBN: 978-1-907565-88-5

Cover design by David Ince
Artworked by Mark (Wills) Williams

Everything else by
Default, Luck and Accident

BREATHE

a novel by
DAVID INCE

Before becoming a writer, David Ince spent ten years working as a graphic designer. He completed his undergraduate degree at Falmouth College of Art, and later completed a part-time Masters Degree in photography, a purely self-indulgent reaction to the rigors of budgets and deadlines.

In 2010, David focused on his ambitions as an author and screenwriter. He completed a second Masters Degree in Creative Writing in 2011, and in the same year was one of a handful of screenwriters selected internationally for the North Sea Screen Partnership Script Development Programme. He pitched at the 2012 Berlin Film Festival, and later won a place on the Screen South Creative Business Base Script Development Programme.

David's debut novel, *Bubble Goes Bang* was published in 2013.

Alongside the writing, David applies his design and photography experience to the art of film-making. He is an award-winning editor for the short film *Samsa Wandelt Um*, and was director of photography on the short documentary *Happy and Glorious* (directed by Alex Kelly), which was nominated for Best Documentary at the 2013 Flicker Fest in Australia.

David has written, directed and edited more than half a dozen short projects, and has six feature film scripts in development. David is currently working alongside the prestigious Screen Arts Institute, building relationships in the UK film industry, and writing his new novel *Capture Release.*

Acknowledgements:

My thanks go to Darren Laws and the team at Caffeine Nights. Emma Grundy-Haig, for highlighting a few things that I suspected but couldn't articulate. Vanessa Stevenson, for unflagging faith. Carl Jeffrey, for the on-going conversation (twenty years in and we still have so much to discuss). My parents, Sonia and George, who operate the most exclusive taxi service in England, and most importantly my wife, Emma Ince, who has given me more than I deserve and without whom I would never have made it this far.

For my wife

1979

With his face smeared in camouflage paint and wearing his khaki shorts and T-shirt, and with his bronzed spindly legs and wiry arms, the Field Marshall is almost impossible to see. He races through the long grass flanking the narrow path, knees bent, keeping himself as low as possible. He dives for cover, rolling elegantly over his shoulder, barely feeling the backpack at all, coming up onto his knees poised behind a tree and hidden from the Infiltrators.

Without shifting his eyes from his prey, he signals behind, a hand gesture copied from old black-and-white war movies.

At the signal, the General Major scrambles to his feet and sprints from behind the fallen tree, bent double, his home-made crossbow pointing low for safety. He races past the Field Marshall, advancing another twenty metres along the path before diving and rolling, not as fast as the Field Marshall, not as graceful, coming to a poised stop behind a wooden bench. The General Major signals behind.

The Field Marshall sighs. The General Major is slow and careless. In his bright red shorts and *Star Trek* T-shirt he couldn't be more conspicuous. His mum's red lipstick and blue eye shadow smeared haphazardly across his little elfin face is more clown-like than paramilitary. If the Infiltrators happen to glance behind them, they will almost certainly see him hunkered down behind the bench. Frankly, the General Major is a bit of an embarrassment. But the Field Marshall doesn't have any other comrades to replace him with. Other boys tend to keep their distance.

It has been a long summer, and a long time under siege. "Defending the Realm" has proved a challenging game. Brazen attacks by other gangs of kids have been met with direct confrontation, while stealthy incursions by adults have forced them to develop guerrilla-style tactics. Lengthy days in the blazing sunshine, from just after breakfast to just before teatime, has tested their commitment. But even this late in the season, their determination in defending the Realm is undimmed. The novelty of the game is yet to wear off.

The Field Marshall springs out from behind the tree. He is fast for an eleven-year-old. Very fast. He races beyond the General Major, advancing within ten metres of the Infiltrators. He comes to an abrupt stop behind a large, dense bush. Excellent cover. He turns and with a different hand gesture signals for the General Major to form up on his position.

The General Major comes scooting through the long grass and power-slides to a stop. The Field Marshall tuts in exasperation. The General Major is too loud, unsuited for this kind of stealthy pursuit. The Field Marshall is suddenly aware of the age difference between them. Two years doesn't sound like a lot, but it is. He frowns at the boy, then lays flat on his stomach and wriggles out from the bush. He bends the tall grass with his gloved hands and takes a look.

The Infiltrators are walking arm in arm, their bodies turned inwards towards each other. They are following the grey line of the path cutting through the grass, little clouds of dust spiralling up from the sun-baked dirt beneath their feet. The girl is in her late teens and petite, her slim body revealed by her clinging turquoise dress. The guy is in his early twenties, with long black hair and bushy sideburns, his lean body burnished by the sun, wearing only a tight pair of black shorts. Their laughter rings clear against the buzz of crickets and the breeze in the trees. They seem oblivious to their trespass, strolling casually through the Realm as if they were entitled to be there. These types of enemies are the most common, individuals or couples who show nothing but contempt for the zoning restrictions. Sometimes the boys let them pass through the Realm without issue; sometimes they just like the look of them. But not today.

"They couldn't give a shit!" the Field Marshall whispers.

"Maybe they missed the latest prop-ganda campaign," the General Major whispers back.

"No excuse. Article 17 of the Medway Charter states that ignorance won't get you off the hook. These two are in clear breach of the charter."

"You mean we have no choice?"

"We have no choice."

Brows knit together with mock consternation. Outrage rises at the affront of these two *militants* who dare threaten the safety and tranquillity of the Realm. They must be stopped. Infiltrators must be taught a lesson. An example must be made. Nobody is allowed to set foot on this hallowed ground without written permission from the Field Marshall.

"What's our strategy?"

"They'll take the path to the south, into the woods."

"How do you know?"

"Sideburns has caught the horn. He's touching her arse. They'll find a quiet place to *do it*, and that's where we'll strike."

"What if they don't? What's our con-tin-gin-see?"

"Then we'll have to move fast, We'll get to where the path goes by the Watchtower and ambush them there. But that won't happen. Trust me. They'll go into the woods."

The Infiltrators are approaching the fork in the path. The boys hold their breath in expectation. At the gentle sound of the girl's laughter the Field Marshall whispers:

"There they go. Told you."

The Infiltrators take the left-hand fork and follow the path into the tightly packed trees.

The General Major shifts his weight, poised to break cover, crossbow held at the ready.

But the Field Marshall touches his arm. "Wait. Lets give them a few seconds."

The General Major is about to argue, but then doesn't. Earlier that morning the Field Marshall gave a briefing extolling the virtues of caution and patience. The General Major tries hard to be good.

The Field Marshall looks up as a bird wheels and calls overhead. He tracks its flight, inscribing a graceful arc across the deep summer sky before vanishing into the canopy of a tree. He glances behind at the long grass dropping steeply down the bank to the field where the horses sometimes graze, the furthest part of the Realm. On the other side is Star Lane, the narrow winding road that acts as a buffer between the Realm and the Dark City beyond. The roof and round tower of the converted Oast House juts upwards, the rest of the old building hidden by a cluster of trees. Now a pub and hotel, it is neutral territory sometimes used for negotiations, when representatives of the Realm and the Dark City have need to meet and discuss mutual interests. On the far side of Star Lane, a dense maze of streets and houses shimmering hazily in the late summer heat unroll towards the sparkling strip of the river. The Dark City makes for an interesting view. The Field Marshall often spends time looking out at those streets and houses, wondering about the people who live there. He wonders how easy it would be to cross the border, to become an Infiltrator himself. This year the Realm has felt too small, its defence too easy. The Dark City holds the promise of greater adventures.

"Come on," whines the General Major.

"Repeat after me," commands the Field Marshall. "This is our land!"

"This our land!"

"All those who trespass will be punished!"

"All those who trespass will be punished!"

"In the name of our fallen brethren!"

"In the name of our fallen brev-ren!"

"Who embodied the spirit of our people!"

"Who imbobbid the spirit of our people!"

"Who fought with bravery and without fear!"

"Who fought with gravy and without fear!"

"Who held the line in the Battle of the Banks!"

"Who held the line in the Battle of the Banks!"

"Who succumbed to vastly superior numbers!"

"Who suck-umed to vastly super numbers!"

"And then they were Dead!"

"And then they were Dead!"

"Leaving only us!"

"Leaving only us!"

"Move out!"

"Move out!"

The two boys cut swiftly across the path and into the woods, plunging into gloom. The canopy above is thick with leaves and a dense lattice of branches.

The General Major is on point about ten metres in front of the Field Marshall, creeping along the narrow path as it winds through the trees, scanning for flashes of colour – turquoise dress or golden skin. The occasional squirrel scoots away and up into the canopy overhead, startled by the boys as they sneak along from tree to tree. The General Major moves on tiptoes, taking delicate little hops over broken branches and piles of dry leaves. So intent on trying to be silent, he misses the flash of colour just up ahead. But the sound of laughter brings him up short and he drops instantly to one knee and holds up a clenched fist.

The Field Marshall sighs again. He'd been aware of the Infiltrators for several minutes already. He can hear them talking.

"There," whispers the General Major.

Just a few metres away, the couple have stopped in the middle of the path, arms around each other, kissing deeply.

The boys are frozen statues, hidden in the undergrowth, breath held, watching, as Sideburns slides his hands up the girl's long smooth thighs, raising the hem of her dress and revealing...

"Nice," breathes the General Major, so low the Field Marshall barely hears him.

"Confirmed."

The girl smiles at Sideburns, her slender fingers stroking upwards along his spine. They turn and continue walking, holding each other tightly, their pace reduced to a crawl. They take another left fork, the path bearing downhill and past the enormous tree with the rusty nails hammered into the trunk.

"They're heading for the Runway." The General Major whispers.

"Yes."

"How do they know about the Runway?"

"They must have been here before. Slipped through the net in the dead of night, or come in through the minefield."

"It's possible."

"It's brazen."

The General Major looks at his friend. "Brazen" is a new word, one he hasn't heard before. But he likes it.

"Yeah. *Brazen*."

The couple amble out from the trees into the open space of the Runway. It was a road once, long ago. Where it came from or where it went to the boys don't know. Nor do they care. Now all that remains is fifteen metres of crumbling concrete, burst by industrious weeds and stingers and lined on either side by tall trees. The rusting hulk of an ancient car is slowly being digested as the woods gradually creep inwards, its colour long vanished beneath a patina of rust, brown stains creeping out from where the wheel-less axles rest on the concrete. Vines and stinging nettles leer out of the broken windows like crazed revellers on a midnight joyride. The sun above the narrow gap in the canopy is harsh and bright. A slight breeze briefly troubles the tops of the trees; the leaves momentarily whisper and then fall quiet. In the distance, a persistent drone of industry is just audible, floating over the trees from the newly constructed industrial estate on the far side of the woods.

The boys crouch in the undergrowth along the edge of the runway, using the trees for cover. The Infiltrators, out in the middle of the open space, are kissing once again, bodies pressed together, working their way across the road to rest up against the old car.

"They're really going for it," breathes the General Major.

The girl's hands plunge beneath the waistband of Sideburns's shorts. He slides the straps of her dress down from her delicate shoulders, her heaving breasts revealed then smothered by his eager mouth. The boys watch, spellbound, something neither has ever seen before.

She squats down, her hands pulling at the front of his shorts. She pauses to admire for just a moment, looking up at him, before smiling wide and taking him in.

"Jeez," breathes the Field Marshal.

The General Major doesn't hear him. Squatting in the undergrowth, hidden by nettles and weeds, his attention is acutely focused; the crossbow now in his left hand, his right tugs at the button on his shorts, releasing his child's prick, bobbing enthusiastically through the piss hole in his Y-fronts.

"Christ!" the Field Marshall whispers.

The General Major is pulling on his "boy", watching the Infiltrators with a look of rapture on his luridly coloured face.

"Pack it in," the Field Marshall orders.

The girl comes up from her knees and Sideburns spins her round and bends her over the rusting bonnet of the car. Her squeal of laughter turns to a sigh as he slides his hands up the backs of her thighs, lifting her dress up and over her hips. She turns her head and looks back at him, her smile all the invitation he needs.

"What are we going to do?" The General Major's eyes are still fixated on the spectacle, his voice a-quiver with excitement.

The Field Marshal considers the tactical situation, his sharp mind calculating options and risk: Sideburns is a much older and formidable opponent, while the girl is much older but very small, no bigger than the Field Marshall himself despite a difference of at least seven years. Sideburns is the risk. The girl is not. He must be contained quickly and decisively. The girl can be toyed with.

"Focus!" the Field Marshall whispers. "Put your dick away. When I make my move come forwards with the crossbow. Your target is the girl. Do not shoot. Just make sure she doesn't run."

The General Major responds to the authority in his friend's voice. At times like this, when action is imminent, something seems to solidify in the Field Marshall. He becomes hard and menacing. His big-for-his-age frame appears to grow further still. His voice deepens and becomes emotionally flat, issuing his orders in a matter-of-fact tone that even some adults hesitate to question, like when they encountered the tramp sleeping rough under the trees.

The Field Marshall reaches for his scabbard and unhooks the strap securing the large and wickedly sharp fishing knife that he stole from his father. He draws the blade and casts his eyes about the ground for a suitable rock. Finding one half buried, he wiggles it loose.

The General Major's eyes go wide at the sight of his friend. With the knife in his left hand and rock in his right, the Field Marshall looks every inch the combatant. The ruthless intention carried in his expression is somehow emphasised by his child's face, a vision that would make a grown man shudder. But the General Major trembles with excitement instead of fear, as a seductive feeling of power blooms within him, because whenever the Field Marshall gears up ready for war, no one can stand in his way.

The girl is trying to contain her gasps. Sideburns is deep inside her, one hand reaching forward, his fingers in her mouth. She bites down on him, stifling her cries just in case some errant dog walker is close by. Sweat runs down Sideburns's back as her teeth send pain shooting through his fingers. He gasps and grins, reaching round with his other hand to squeeze her breasts. He bites her neck and she squeals even louder.

So lost in the moment are they both, neither one hears the Field Marshall as he sprints from the cover of the trees directly behind them. He crosses the short distance in just a few seconds, leaping high in the air and raising the rock up above his head, bringing his entire bodyweight to bare on the blunt, flat chunk as he comes back down. His feet hit the tarmac beside the fucking couple at precisely the same instant the flat side of the rock crunches down onto the back of Sideburns's head.

The impact throws him forwards and he crushes the girl down onto the bonnet. She shrieks in pain and surprise.

He does not.

Instead, Sideburns sinks to his knees and collapses back on the concrete, his cock still erect and nodding in the air.

The Field Marshall grabs a fistful of the girl's hair and harshly yanks her backwards off the bonnet of the car. She trips over her fallen lover and lands heavily on her naked arse, staring up at the young boy standing over her, knife in hand.

"You're trespassing," announces the Field Marshall in a voice so cold the girl can almost see the expelled air puffing out around the words.

The General Major is out from the trees, the crossbow trained on the girl, his erect nine-year-old prick jutting stubbornly from his pants.

"What the fuck are you doing?" There is outrage in the girl's voice as she attempts to rise, her attention switching from the boys to her unconscious lover, not yet comprehending the merciless nature of her assailants, thinking this is just some schoolboy prank gone horribly wrong.

The General Major smacks her in the face with the butt of his crossbow. His small body and young arms are still too weak to inflict much damage, but the decisive action is enough to douse the flame of fury burning in the girl's heart. She gasps in shock, her hands going to her nose to stem the blood.

The Field Marshall unslings the backpack from his shoulders. He unzips it and pulls out a length of rope.

The General Major is staring at the girl's exposed breasts, watching as the blood seeps through her fingers, dripping off her chin and splashing onto her chest. The girl struggles to pull her dress back up.

"Don't move," the General Major says.

"Fuck you!" the girl spits back.

The General Major hits her in the face again with the butt of his crossbow. There is a crunch and the girl rocks back onto the ground. As she falls her legs open and the General Major's gaze instantly alights on the darkness where they meet.

"If you move again I'll gut you like a fish." The Field Marshall's voice suggests a statement of fact far more than a threat.

The girl slowly comes back onto her knees and looks up at the boys. Blood runs freely from her broken nose, and down between her breasts, soaking the blue dress bunched around her waist. Black bruises are already circling her eyes.

The Field Marshall crouches down beside Sideburns. He slaps his cheek to see if he'll wake up. A gory halo is slowly spreading around his head. His bronzed muscles have gone slack and the black shorts around his ankles look pathetic and sad.

"We don't even need to tie him up." The Field Marshall turns his attention back to the girl. "Now what shall we do with you?"

He tries to pull her arms behind her back. She resists and the General Major kicks her sharply in the ribs. At the instant of impact her body goes limp and she gasps and the Field Marshall yanks her arms behind her and quickly loops a length of rope around her wrists with seemingly practised ease.

"Now then," he says, pulling the knot tight, "what shall we make you do? General Major, any ideas?"

"Let's watch her do him."

"We've seen that already."

"Yeah but let's see it again."

"You heard the GM. Fuck him."

The girl looks from one boy to the other, arms taut behind her back, squirming furiously at their feet as she tries to free her hands from the Field Marshall's rock-solid knot.

"But you're just children," she says quietly, almost to herself. Tears are rolling down her cheeks and cutting tracks through the blood around the lower part of her face.

"Let's see you do it."

"Do what?" Sobbing now.

"Do it with him."

"I ca—" she begins but is cut short as the Field Marshall shoves her with his boot and she sprawls against her unconscious lover.

"General Major, shoot her in the foot."

"Yes sir." The General Major takes aim and fires. The arrow is sharp, and although the crossbow is not exactly powerful, the arrow still penetrates and draws a little blood from the top of the girl's foot, before falling off to the side.

She screams.

The Field Marshall bends down and punches her in the face, a brutal, solid impact that bursts her lips and rocks her head back onto the concrete.

"Do it." His voice is oh-so cold.

The girl, slipping into shock, crawls over her lover's unconscious body, her thighs parting, her knees biting into the concrete on either side of him.

"Sit up so we can see you."

With her hands bound behind her back, the girl struggles upright.

"He... He can't," she whispers.

"Pretend."

His voice sends shivers down her spine and she does as instructed, her eyes tightly closed, tears leaking down the ruin of her face, hips grinding ridiculously against the unconscious man between her legs.

After watching for several seconds, the boys fade silently back into the trees, leaving the poor girl, hands bound and all but naked, battered and bloodied, dry humping her useless lover on the old road hidden in the woods.

The boys sprint between the trees, following a well-established path of retreat. They arrive at a massive, ancient oak and nimbly ascend through the branches, higher and higher until lost among the green canopy, perched confidently on thin branches some thirty feet off the ground, rocking in a gentle breeze.

Here they debrief another successful mission. So far this summer, three groups of kids, one tramp, an elderly lady walking a dog and now the lovers have suffered the consequences of unwittingly crossing into their territory.

The tramp is still there, buried in a shallow grave beneath the bush where they first discovered him.

He was older than they thought. With brittle bones.

But they weren't to know.

Part 1

1

Sebastian spies the old guy shuffling down the street. He's clutching a carrier bag in both hands like he's afraid someone might steal it. He's walking in the gutter, freezing rainwater sloshing over his old-man shoes. For some reason he reminds Sebastian of his grandfather, long since in the ground. Something about the stoop and the trilby, seen from behind as he catches him up.

Sebastian flashbacks to Grandpa, sat forever in that old hard-backed chair by the window, calling out through the net curtain when he was just a kid playing football in the street. He'd call Sebastian into the parlour, as Ma used to call it, holding out a wrinkled hand with a few coins and send him off down the pub for two bottles of ale.

"Dark, mind," he'd always say. "Not light, y'hear?"

Sebastian would pluck the coins from his palm, worn and weathered like leather and wood.

"Keep the change boy," he'd say.

It was Grandpa who picked him off the slabs when he was jumped by the arseholes from up the street. Sebastian remembers his hard grey eyes, bright lights in a face that seemed incomprehensibly old.

"You gonna let them beat you, son?" His nose was just inches from Sebastian's face. "Don't ever run, because you can't. Always stand. Always fight."

He gave Sebastian a swig from that day's bottle and sent him back out. Sebastian took his cricket bat. That was the first time he got in trouble with the police. He was twelve years old.

But this old guy in the rain, shuffling along the gutter beneath the yellow streetlights, furred up arteries in his legs preventing his knees from bending like they should. Where's he going at this time of night, in this kind of weather? The rain's already thickening into sleet, and the radio said a blizzard was on the way. Sebastian glances at the dash, looking for a clock. But this shitty old car doesn't have one. It must be older than me, he thinks. Whose idea was it to give me this heap?

Sebastian pulls up next to the old guy and rolls down the window.

"Hey mate, where can I get a cuppa?" Whatever he's got in that bag stinks to high heaven.

"Eh?"

"Cuppa tea mate?"

"Uh, okay yeah. That'd be nice, cheers." The rain drips from the brim of the old guy's hat, his face beneath is dark and pitted, awareness in his eyes vague and fleeting. He's shivering. Poor old sod.

"I ain't offering you one. I'm looking for a café or something." Sebastian feels bad that he can't offer the guy a lift.

"Eh?" the old guy says, eyes darting around. He's already forgotten what was asked.

"Don't worry. You have a good night, yeah." Sebastian drives away and rolls up the window, watching in the rear-view as the old guy stands in the rain.

The night is street-lamp yellow and glistening wet, freezing cold. Only a few people are out and about, hunched and hurrying through the shadows from one island of light to another. Cruising along in the car, Sebastian can see it: everyone's afraid of everyone else.

This part of town, the run-down busted part, highlights the great social lie of the last few years. There was never a booming economy down here, never mind a crash. That all happened out by the river, where the wealthy could buy into the glittering dream. Here there's only what's forgotten in the dark when the spotlight points somewhere else, a chaotic mix of poverty, drugs, grievances and depressions. You travel to these satellite towns, these seething webs of urban chaos, and you get to know.

A skinny prostitute loiters on the corner, swamped by the threadbare coat around her shoulders, eyes and cheeks just dark holes in a face so pale you'd think she was a ghostly effect in a Hollywood B-movie. There are piles of rubbish swept up by the wind, heaped against graffiti-covered walls. Broken windows. Jagged glass. Some blocked by chipboard or corrugated-iron, a futile attempt to stop the addicts from turning the empty buildings into junkie warrens.

Beyond a squat and run-down pub, leaking light and noise into the night, is the rusted ironwork of a railway bridge, crossing over the street and slicing between the buildings on either side, so close you could jump from a window onto the tracks. A bunch of lilies are taped to a flaking pillar. Streetlights stain the petals yellow, bowed under the weight of the rain. Someone met their death at this bridge, a random assault, a mugging, a car accident.

Sebastian wonders about the person who left the flowers as he drives slowly by. Was it a parent, child, lover or friend? Would anyone leave flowers for him if the time came?

Up ahead is a petrol station. He checks the gauge and then swings in between the pumps. He'll need more juice to get his arse back up to London.

He kills the engine and pats his pockets. Wallet. Phone. Asthma pump.

There's a group of teenagers larking around by the shop, swigging from cans of beer and eating a kebab. They go quiet as he gets out, turning to him with a mixture of contempt and menace. Sebastian makes some immediate judgements: White Beanie is the dominant one, what would pass for an alpha male among this little rogue's gallery, his body language leaking aggression into the night. Blue Cap is the arsehole of the gang; he's fat and has the spiteful look of the chronically bullied. Black Cap and No Hat are your basic sheep, swagger and paper-thin ego over jagged insecurities, all of them.

They can stare.

Sebastian fills up. Fuck it's cold. The petrol pump in his hand is freezing and his lungs begin to itch. The snow can't be far away. The smell of petrol is sweet and sharp. When the pump cuts out he racks it and locks the car.

Sebastian walks directly towards the rogues, making eye contact with each one of them. They part and let him through, staying silent. Perhaps they're not as dumb as they look.

Inside the station he looks for a coffee machine but finds zip. He pays the Indian guy behind the counter and on the way out a girl comes in, brushing past him casual as you please, white umbrella in one hand and perfume lingering.

Outside, the rogues have lost interest in Sebastian. They're looking through the glass at the girl instead. He pauses a moment as he unlocks the car, looking too. The girl inside is paying for cigarettes. She comes back out and the rogues try talking to her, but she doesn't look at them. She doesn't look at Sebastian either. Beneath her umbrella, strolling up the road, she looks like a model straight out of some glossy magazine: long legs, broad hips, shimmering black halter-neck dress, naked back tattooed with coloured stars. She looks too well fed to be a prostitute, but no other would stroll around by themselves in such clothes. She must be on drugs not to feel the cold. The rogues are wolf whistling and yelling. Sebastian gets back in the car and pulls the door shut.

He takes out his mobile and checks the time: just after midnight. He's still got an hour before he needs to make the delivery.

Sebastian flicks through his contacts and selects Kenosha's landline.

"Who's this?"

"Sebastian."

"Seb, dude. Thought you weren't around until the early hours."

"I'm not. Still got the cargo in the back."

"Where are you? Down in Dover?"

"No, I'm in town. The guy down there turned up bang on time."

"Well come over dude. I'm not doing nothing."

"You not working tonight?"

"Nah. I had one appointment but I rescheduled for you."

"Thanks man. Appreciate it."

"She's a regular, middle-aged and sagging. Difficult, you know."

"Yeah terrible. I still think you've got the best job in the world."

"Sometimes it really is. But then other times – fucking, you would not believe."

"Can't you pick and choose?"

"Doesn't work like that. I take a booking and off I go. Never know what I'm getting myself into. No pun intended."

Sebastian laughs.

"So what're you doing now?"

"Looking for somewhere to get a cuppa."

"No chance. 'Fraid we ain't that cosmopolitan down here. You could try a pub."

"Nah. Don't wanna leave the car. A bit nervous about this one to be honest. After what happened last time."

"Wasn't your fault."

"Don't think they saw it that way."

There's a pause, and then Kenosha says, "Don't it worry you, what you do?"

"Yeah, it does. But the money's brilliant, and as long as I don't know anything I can live with my with conscience."

"Do you really need the money?"

"Who doesn't?"

"You could do something else."

"Like what?"

"I don't know. Something that isn't illegal."

"Look who's talking. Anyway mate, I'll let you get back to whatever you're doing. I'll come over after I've dropped this bag off.'

"You know the way?"

"Think so. I'll call if I get lost."

Sebastian gets the car started and drives out of the garage, past the rogues who stare at him with their dull little eyes.

Up ahead is the model, sashaying down the path, delicately perched atop black high heels, head lost in the dome of her white umbrella. He rumbles past and then pulls over. It's obvious he's stopped for her. If she comes to the window without any prompting he'll know she's a working girl.

She saunters casually by, the rain bouncing off her white brolly, just her inflated lips and strong jaw visible, a curl of black hair. She ignores him completely, so he winds down the window and calls out:

"'Scuse me."

She stops and turns, tilting the brolly back a little so she can get a look at him. From back at the petrol station the rogues yell and call.

"What?"

"Is there a café round here?"

"A café?" She comes closer, her eyes darting towards his seatbelt, looking to see if he's still strapped in. He's less of a threat if he can't dive out and make a grab for her.

"There's no café round here." Her pretty face is confident and calm. "What you want a café for?"

"I can't go to bed yet. Need something to do for a while."

"Yeah. Well there's plenty of pubs but I don't know any that'll let you in now. You could try a club." She glances over the car, her eyes coming to rest on the duffle bag in the back seat.

Something about the size and shape, or maybe the canvas is wrapped tightly about the contours of what's inside, either way it spooks her, disquiet flaring in her eyes.

She takes a step away from the car.

"What's wrong?" Sebastian makes sure his hands are visible.

"I can't help you." She turns and walks back towards the petrol station. The rogues continue to call, then fall silent when they realise she'll soon be upon them. Sebastian drives away.

He turns on the radio. This car is so old it doesn't even have a CD player. But the stations are tuned in, and he turns up the volume to hear a melancholic piano and a brooding soulful voice. The song, "Into My Arms", is one he knows well. His old Ma fell in love with it before she died. Where she heard it he has no idea.

Sebastian flashbacks to the song on repeat, looping endlessly as Ma poured tea. They were in the claustrophobic little sitting room at the front of the house. The parlour, as she liked to call it. The brass clock on the dark wooden mantle filled the room with its precise tick-tock, counting down the seconds towards the inevitable, or so it seemed to Sebastian. The smell of polish. The warmth of a teapot. A biscuit selection on a decorative plate. Familiar, but not comforting.

For a short while it was different when he got back from the army. For a couple of weeks he was glad to be home, glad to be back with her in the old house, the old stomping ground. But she fussed like he was some invalid child, treating him like some terminal patient. Moving back in after life at the barracks wasn't worth his sanity.

It upset her when he moved out again. Later when he went round to visit she fussed worse than ever. He never did get used to the idea of being a guest, treated in the same fashion as some cousin she hadn't seen for years. Too formal. He'd pop in for a cuppa and she'd break out the best china, wanting to mark the occasion as if it were a big deal. Maybe it was to her, but it didn't seem right.

Sebastian has heard that people can go a bit strange at the end, as if they instinctively know that death is looming. Maybe subconsciously, she knew her time was almost done.

A fox brings him back to the night. It sits in the road watching him approach with its cold yellow eyes. Sebastian slows the car, waiting for the fox to run. But it just stares at him, transfixed by the headlights. He brings the car to complete stop.

The buildings on either side of the road are a mixture of dark brick and cheap prefab, fading into darkness above the line of streetlights. Some windows are boarded, others simply smashed.

Sebastian glances in the mirrors. There's not a soul on the street. He turns the radio down. Sleet patters lightly on the roof.

He looks back at the fox, and for a long moment they stare at each other.

Then suddenly the fox turns, looking intently down the street, its slippery body poised and glistening, curved spine vibrating with tension, ready for flight.

Fifty yards further down, a couple of streetlights are out and the darkness there is inky black. Sebastian is tempted to turn the car a little, put the headlights into that patch of shadow, but he doesn't want to break the spell.

The fox springs into life anyway, darting towards the car and vanishing below the line of the bonnet. In the mirror he can see it sprinting back up the road.

Sebastian is about to put the car in gear and drive on when a woman walks out from the shadows. She is tall and rangy, wearing a long black overcoat. Dirty blond hair plastered flat to her scalp, hanging down past her shoulders. Her step is weary, trudging through the sleet. She looks up, and stops walking when she sees the car. Her face is long and drawn, tension writ large across features that would be attractive if not so miserable.

She comes towards the car. No doubt she wants a lift, and Sebastian feels bad about having to turn her away. He can't risk anything happening that might jeopardise the delivery. He leans across the car to roll down the passenger window. But she simply opens the door and gets in.

Her boldness throws him off balance and before he can say anything she shuts the door behind her. The thump is solid and somehow final. She looks across at Sebastian, her eyes slightly pleading. The windows are already starting to steam up. Water drips onto her coat from her hair.

"What the fuck are you doing?"

"Please, just drive," she says.

Apprehension squirts through Sebastian's heart like acid. She looks like more trouble than he can deal with. Strangers, hitchhikers – there's just too many variables, too many unknowns.

"Hey look, I'd love to help, but I've got to be somewhere in just under an hour and really…" Sebastian lets his sentence trail off.

"I don't want to cause you any trouble. I just need a lift."

There is something dark beneath the pleading in her voice. The downtrodden ambiance is genuine, but it's not the whole story.

Or maybe he's just paranoid. After what happened the last time he made a delivery, it's not so surprising.

Maybe she's just a girl caught out by the rain.

"Can't you get a cab? I can call one for you now."

"You're not from around here are you?" she says. "London. Right? I can tell. Guess cabs just happen along every minute in the big city. Bet you just stick out your thumb and there the fucker is. Take you anywhere you want to go. Well, good for you. But this isn't London. Here cabs are fucking expensive and few and far between."

He should go round to her side of the car and drag her out. He could lean across her and open the door, try and boot her out onto the road. But this isn't as easy as it looks in the films. Or he could simply smack her in the face and push her out the door.

But he can't do any of that.

She slouches down in the chair, slips off her sodden trainers and puts her bare feet up on the dash. Her toes are almost blue. Eyes closed and the tension in her face unwinds a little.

"Didn't realise I was so far out in the sticks," Sebastian says.

She starts laughing.

"Oh my God, I'm so sorry. I get in your car uninvited and just go off at you. I'm not a crazy bitch, I just need to get home and get some sleep."

"How far away do you live?"

"Not far. You'll get to where you need to be in plenty of time."

"Where I need to be could be miles away."

"Then you're going to be late no matter what."

Just under an hour's grace, he thinks. She wants a ride? No worries. Calm yourself Sebastian. Just take her to where she wants to go, then say goodbye and let her out. Nothing to do now anyway, except sit in this dumb car and watch the sleet for the better part of an hour. Be charitable. Sort her out, make the delivery, get paid, then go get wasted with Kenosha. Stop worrying. It'll be the death of you.

"Alright, alright."

Sebastian puts the car in gear and together they roll forward into the night.

2

Isobel's knees are pressed into the pillow on either side of his face. Her eyes are closed, her hips moving with an urgent rhythm. Beneath her, sprawled on his back, is Andrew. His hands roam her body as she straddles his face, squeezing her breasts, encircling her throat.

She's known him only a few weeks, but already she is fucking him like she has fucked no other, loosing her inhibitions and revealing herself completely. She's had affairs with other men in the past, but never one so intense so quickly. She feels reckless just at the thought of him.

Grimy light from the streetlamp outside highlights her narrow body, her pale skin taught and jaundiced in the yellow gloom as she thrusts herself into his mouth. Beyond the window dark clouds swell and knit together, the darkness deepening as the rain pours forth. Snow later, or so the weatherman said.

She can feel his eyes on her body, and it excites her. His fingers grip the insides of her thighs as she gasps her orgasm at the ceiling.

The flat is mostly silent, just the creak of her single bed and the sound of their flesh. The red digits of her alarm clock say 22:05. In the other room across the hallway, the remains of a Chinese takeaway litter the carpet and a forgotten bottle of wine lies unopened on the sofa. Isobel was expecting an early night; her shift at the hospital starts at dawn. But when she heard his voice through the intercom her breath caught in her throat and she buzzed him in. A moment later Andrew knocked on the door. Casually dressed in grey slacks and a white shirt, brandishing an expensive bottle of wine, he strolled into her flat. His sudden arrival set fire to her passion and she pulled him to the sofa. As she reached for his belt the question went through her mind: Why can't I resist him?

Andrew is unremarkable except for a degree of apparent kindness, which cannot run deep, as every time he fucks her he is cheating on his wife. He is neither particularly handsome nor significantly intelligent. But there is something intangible lurking behind his eyes, some kind of strength that transcends the ordinary, lending him a magnetism that Isobel cannot resist. She has always found commitment and stability attractive qualities, ever since her first lover as a teenager. But now, at thirty-four, she has loved and lost enough to know that married men rarely leave their wives. After the last time she promised herself: never again will I get involved with a man already spoken for. But life has a way of subverting the best intentions. Despite the intensity of her need, Andrew is destined to be just another notch on her bedpost, another body keeping her company on the road to some longed-for happiness.

Only once has Andrew talk about his wife. He described a kind but indifferent woman who neither cared for nor despised him.

"It's not like we don't get on. But we hardly see each other and I think she's glad about that."

Isobel had the distinct impression he was trying to justify cheating. Not to her – she was incidental – but to himself. The kind of self-pitying logic only a man would entertain. In those moments she felt contempt for him. After he'd left she decided to call it off. But a few days later, at his invitation, they hooked up again.

The wind is on the rise, bellowing around the eaves, lashing rain against the windows. The sickly yellow light from the streetlamp outside paints his body as he kneels above her. Isobel slides her hands over his strong abdominals. In his mid-forties, he has the physique of a much younger man. His strokes begin smooth and slow and she uses her tongue to help him along, all the while watching his face. She can sense when the moment arrives and she opens her mouth to receive him. He is hot and bitter to taste. But she likes it.

Andrew lies down beside her, and Isobel leans in to kiss him, but he pulls away. He glides his fingers along the length of her spine. In moments like these, Isobel envies his wife. Sex can be found elsewhere; Isobel has never struggled to satisfy her desires. But this kind of gentle intimacy was something unfamiliar, and with Andrew it felt genuine. His affections beyond the carnal were unforced and honest and Isobel found herself wanting them more than anything else.

"I told my wife I'd met someone."

"What did she say?"

"She laughed."

"Was she angry?"

"I don't think so. I don't think she cares."

"Is she seeing someone else?"

"She has in the past, but I don't know about right now. Our marriage is pretty dysfunctional."

"Is that how we'd end up, if we made a go of it?"

"Probably."

"Sometimes I think about it. A house somewhere, maybe abroad, in the sun, near a beach."

"Sounds like a dream."

"That's all it is. I wouldn't be good for you."

Andrew rolls over and looks at Isobel, her face in the dim light cast in shadow, making her seem distant, insubstantial.

"Why do I get the feeling there's something I don't know about you?" Andrew studies Isobel's face, searching for her eyes in the gloom.

"You can't stay."

"I know."

Isobel drifts off to sleep in Andrew's arms, hoping that when she wakes, he'll still be there. But it's just a dream. It wouldn't be safe to let Andrew get too close.

* * *

The shrill ringing of the telephone cuts through Isobel's sleep. Her eyes flicker open and she reaches out for Andrew, but finds only emptiness next to her, not even the lingering residue of his heat in the sheets to keep her company.

The telephone.

She goes to grab the handset from her bedside table, but then suddenly hesitates.

Dread climbs her spine, one vertebra at a time, black bitten nails capping long chilling fingers, digging deep into her nervous system.

Isobel knows who it is.

A face she's never seen, but a voice she cannot forget. It's been many months since the last time he called. Just long enough for her to indulge a fantasy that something terrible had happened. Something fatal, a catastrophic car accident, or maybe a gang-related shooting. Her imagination has conjured a dozen different scenarios. The detail doesn't matter. All she wants is for him to be gone, out of her life, once and for all.

But now Mr Punch is calling again. She doesn't need to answer the phone. She knows it's him. She can feel it. She'd gotten too comfortable, and now he's back, pulling her strings.

Isobel shivers, suddenly cold. The telephone is still ringing. Any normal person would have given up by now. But Mr Punch knows she is home. Is he watching her from a house across the street? Hidden behind net curtains in the dark, spying on her through some kind of night vision scope? He has the resources, she knows. Was he watching earlier, when Andrew was kneeling over her face?

The faint taste of semen in her mouth suddenly turns acidic and bile squirms up from her guts. She's never felt so vulnerable, naked in her dark apartment, alone.

It'll be worse if she doesn't answer the phone.

With trembling fingers she plucks the handset from the bedside table. She presses the button and puts the phone to her ear.

"Isobel."

Her heart sinks. Always there is that tiny fragment of hope, holding out for a wrong number, a long-lost cousin, anything but those dead tones speaking the three syllables of her name. Foolish optimism. Her fingers tighten around the handset.

"Isobel. It is time."

Mr Punch with his mechanical calm, his flat monotone, unmistakably organic if not exactly human. She knows what he wants. For sixteen years it has been roughly the same. And each time she does as instructed, it is another loop of rope around her wrists, binding her tighter.

A perfect circle of coercion.

Isobel is tired to her bones. Long shifts at the hospital, late nights with Andrew. She wants to weep, but there is no point. All she can do is go with the flow, resign herself to whatever will follow. Captives have few options. The bars of her prison are intangible, but no less secure.

"Get your shit together. You know the score. I'll call you back in five."

The connection is cut, just the dial tone beeping in her ear. For a long moment she stays statue still, then she turns off the phone and sets it back on the bedside table.

Isobel allows herself fifteen seconds. She hugs her knees, closes her eyes, permits one loud sob before she hitches in a breath and takes control.

She gets up out of bed. The apartment is cold. She doesn't turn on the light. She explores her wardrobe until her fingers find denim, an old pair of jeans that ride low on her hips, a thick jumper to keep her warm. A hanger pings off the rail and clatters to the floor, scaring her witless. Lastly, she shrugs into a long black overcoat.

Concealed beneath the bottom drawer in the bedside cabinet are her tools for these missions. The hardware has evolved somewhat over the years, arriving every now and then in an unmarked envelope. The wireless earpiece is flesh coloured and discreet, hidden completely by her long blond hair. The receiver, small and thin, fits neatly in the pocket of her jeans. From the cavity beneath the drawer she picks up the gun, releasing the clip and checking it is loaded. She pulls the slide and chambers a round, engages the safety. The gun goes into a pocket of her coat. She heads to the door, pausing in front of the mirror. All she can see is a black shape in the darkness.

Isobel's fingers curl around the gun in her pocket, acquired some years ago, unbeknownst to Mr Punch. At least she hopes. The one he sent her was only a replica. But this one holds the promise of liberation. If she ever finds out who he really is, if she gets a name, a number, a face, catches sight of him behind her on a night like this –

a moment of decisive action, then release from his clutching, death-stained fingers.

But after sixteen years, he has not made a single mistake. She is as clueless about his identity now as she was the first time he called her.

She leaves the apartment, shutting the door gently behind her. As she walks the corridor to the stairs the earpiece buzzes into life.

"I don't have a visual."

Isobel taps the top button of her coat, a surveillance camera with an inbuilt microphone. She spent one rainy afternoon sewing it on last autumn. Mr Punch sees what she sees, hears what she hears, and whispers his instructions directly into her ear.

"Head towards the river, via the park."

Out in the street Isobel turns her collar up against the freezing cold. She sets off with her head down and shoulders hunched. Sleet drifts down from swollen clouds. Isobel splashes through puddles along deserted streets, past rows of terraced houses, divided by narrow alleys. She walks beneath the streetlamps, avoiding the deeper shadows. Her dark coat, waterlogged, weighs heavy. Freezing water drips down her forehead into her eyes. She is misery incarnate, but there is at least one poor soul more unfortunate than her tonight: the person she is being sent to meet. Her hands are stuffed deep into her pockets, the weight of the gun tap, tap, tapping against her thigh as she walks. She feels it always, the life-altering, world-shattering power of it. Holding it makes her feel queasy.

But this caution smacks of hypocrisy.

The weight of the guilt is something she has learned to live with over the years. She's had no other choice. The first time was an accident, or so Mr Punch has led her to believe. But since then she has been manipulated and coerced, some would say complicit, and each time she obeys it increases his power over her. Such a despicable cycle – interrupted one day, or so she dreams. The sudden crack of the shot, brains erupting from the back of his head, his body toppling forward, dead at her feet. The only death she wishes for, the only one she wouldn't feel guilty about.

"Left here. Through the park."

Why the park? If she is to head towards the river, the quickest route is down Barnsole Road to Livingston Circus. From there it's just a short walk to the high street and Dock Road, which curves down to the river. The park is out of the way. Not by much, but in the efficient world of Mr Punch, anything that isn't a straight line from A to B should be avoided. No, he must have a reason for sending her to the park. Surely he isn't planning on two in one night? Isobel doubts she is up to it.

"What's in the park?" she speaks out loud, seemingly to herself. She must look like a mad woman.

"A surprise."

"I don't like surprises."

"I don't care. This is necessary."

His words fill her with dread. The voice in her ear feels so close, as if a separate entity was at large in her mind, something destructive, devoid of human emotion – a devil on her shoulder.

"Whatever it is I don't want to do it."

"Of course you don't. But I enjoy your reluctance. It's the only reason you're still alive."

Isobel shivers. She doesn't know what's worse, the possibility of her death at the hands of this madman, or the idea that he derives some sick pleasure from using her this way? His soulless monotone speaking of joy is almost too frightening to contemplate. It is easier believing him to be some kind of elusive gangster, using her to facilitate business-style executions. But an agenda based on emotion makes him more than just ruthless. It makes him insane.

Cutting across Cleave Road now, alongside a row of garages. One is open, the metal door pulled up and slid back into the roof. Darkness inside, absolute, and something else, something that scrapes across the concrete floor as Isobel passes by. A chair being moved? Something being dragged?

Isobel hurries past, nerves fluttering, fingers curled tightly around the gun in her pocket. Cleave Road meets Park Avenue directly in front of her, the two roads intersecting at ninety degrees. The old trees loom high, the park a broad wall of darkness at the end of the street.

A crash from behind and Isobel jumps. She spins round to see a television exploding across the road. She tugs at the gun in her pocket, but the bulky shape is caught on the lining of her coat.

A man appears from the open garage. He is naked to the waist, his pale narrow body tattooed and scarred. He walks into the road and kicks the smashed television. Glass and plastic skitter across the wet tarmac. He follows after it, stamping down with worn, heavy-duty work boots. The man hawks up from the back of his throat, a deep gurgle that Isobel can hear above the sleet pattering down, and then spits on the television. He turns his sunken eyes to Isobel, black pits in the wreck of his face, framed by curtains of lank dark hair.

"Fuck'ye look'n at?" Misshapen words spat through broken teeth. There are letters in a gothic typeface tattooed on his shrunken stomach, the word might be German, black fading to green, outlines softened over time. His skin looks shrink-wrapped around his crooked skeleton, thin to the point of emancipation. Isobel watches the sleet-melt running through the depressions between his ribs, little rivulets like the tributaries of a river. She wonders about the television. What did it do to him?

"Ignore him. Go to the park." Mr Punch whispers in her ear.

With her hand still holding the gun in her pocket, Isobel walks away. She crosses Park Avenue quickly and walks down towards the gate. She looks over her shoulder, but the man has disappeared back inside his garage.

The thought of entering the park on such a dark and miserable night fills her with dread. The gate is old, rusty, but so wet it doesn't squeak when she pushes it open. She means to follow the path around the edge of the park, keeping undercover among the trees and close to the fence and the road.

Great trunks loom black and monolithic in the dark, rising up and breaking apart, skeleton limbs straining towards the low-slung clouds, tinged orange by the streetlights of the town.

Isobel reaches out to the trees for balance, the darkness here so deep and disorientating. The tree bark is slick beneath her freezing fingers. She walks cautiously, eyes struggling to penetrate the darkness.

"No, don't hide in the trees. Cut straight across the grass. He is waiting on the swings."

Isobel's heartbeat quickens.

She walks out from the trees into the open. With her pulse in her ears and growing apprehension biting at her heels, Isobel moves slowly forwards. The park is perhaps a quarter of a mile across, and with her slow progress it is a couple of minutes before skeletal shapes appear out of the darkness: a climbing frame and seesaw, a slide that must seem huge to five-year-old eyes. The children's play area is close to the centre of the park, right out in the open.

A sharp clink rings out against the silence, as of metal striking metal. Isobel stops, eyes searching the gloom, finding movement: a hunched shape, darker than the surrounding night, swinging gently.

"Go over."

The clink comes again – a piercing, sinister sound, like the blade of a knife tapping against the steel frame of the swings.

"What's going on?" Isobel whispers.

"Go over."

The black shape is rising now, coming forwards to meet her – a stooped figure, Puffa jacket grossly enlarging his upper body, skinny legs in drainpipe jeans poking out from beneath. His white trainers are the brightest thing in the night. The collar on his jacket is pulled up around his neck and the baseball cap on his head is pulled low, the peak all but obscuring his face. He walks up too close, forcing her to retreat a step. He tilts his head back and peers at her from beneath the peak of his cap.

"So less 'ave it, den." His voice seems to swell around the syllables, moronic and urban, as distinctive as the upper-class twang but hailing from the opposite end of the economic spectrum.

Isobel is at a loss.

"Well giz-us it, den." He shifts his weight from foot to foot. Clearly he is expecting something from Isobel, but what exactly she has no idea. Slowly, as discreetly as possible, she starts to withdraw the gun from her pocket, freeing the grip, leaving the barrel hidden. In the darkness she doubts the guy will notice. Knowing that she can draw down on him gives her a little confidence.

"Whatever you're expecting, I haven't got it."

The guy huffs and turns away. Then he turns back, shoulders swinging. The baseball cap hides his face but Isobel gets the impression of long sour features, divided down the middle by an ungainly ridge of nose.

"He sed yid fuckin' 'ave it, yeah? Fuckin' sed." His voice rises as he speaks, then drops quiet as if remembering suddenly that he is here in secret. Isobel can sense his frustration. The scenario has already broken from the script he imagined.

"Ah pay tha' cunt 'n he sed yid 'ave it. Ah fuckin' pay tha' cunt, yeah?" The guy moves closer, forcing Isobel to take another step back. Then he suddenly backs away, muttering under his breath, before squaring up to her again.

"Wer yi godit 'id? Yi fuckin… He sed yid fuckin' 'ave it, yeah?"

He reaches for her now; Isobel backs off and draws the gun but the guy is fast, closing her down, the weapon batted from her hand before she can get it raised, and now he is falling upon her.

"Wer yi godit? Wer yi godit yer bitch, wer yi godit 'id?"

The peak of his cap shoves against her forehead as he pushes his face into hers, odourless breath hot against her cheek and implausibly the smell of some branded aftershave. His hands reach for her neck and she momentarily flashes upon a memory of Andrew, his hands constricting her throat as she straddled his face and came in his mouth.

Isobel's feet slip from under her and she screams and falls, and all the way down the guy is on her.

"Ah fuckin pay tha' cunt. He sed yid fuckin' 'ave it."

Isobel struggles, nails clawing for his face, knocking his hat aslant. The guy tries to pin her down with one hand, ripping at her coat with the other. He leans in, trying to force his tongue into her mouth and she whips her head to the side.

Just in time to catch a flash of movement, someone running, incredibly fast, completely silent, in her field of vision one moment and gone the next, and so close, running right past them as they fight on the grass.

The guy on top of her is suddenly still.

It takes Isobel a moment to realise. She panics and struggles violently from under her attacker, leaving him face down on the grass.

The knife in the back of his neck looks absurd.

"Did you see me?"

She sits on the grass, breathless, using her legs to push herself away from the dead man, eyes fixed on the knife poking out from the base of his skull. "What…?"

"I just saved your innocence. Maybe even your life."

Isobel struggles to her feet, stumbles away, but then stops and turns back.

Down on her knees, she searches for the gun that was knocked from her grasp, eyes straining against the darkness, fingers sliding through slimy grass un-mowed since early autumn.

Her hand bumps into something solid. The gun. She grabs it, relieved. Back on her feet, running, while in her ear Mr Punch is laughing hard.

Isobel sprints across the park, her heart pounding and the gun clenched in her fist. She slams up against the fence on the far side.

Where is the gate?

She runs right, left hand trailing along the fence, and there it is. Banging open with a resounding clank and she is through, back out under the streetlamps, tarmac under her feet, just a stone's throw from the Municipal Buildings. She runs down Canterbury Street towards the shopping precinct.

* * *

"It's been a while, Isobel. I don't want you to grow complacent. What happened back there was a reminder, to put some fear back in your step. Just in case you'd forgotten me."

"Who was he?"

"He was nobody. A means to an end. He thought he was buying drugs, instead he paid for his death."

"And that was you who killed him?"

"Maybe, maybe not. It doesn't matter either way. What matters is that you head down to the river. There's someone you need to meet."

The high street is mostly deserted, the shops silent, glass fronts protected by thick metal grills. Isobel walks over the glistening block paving; shimmering lamplight reflections make the ground seem insubstantial. An all-night laundrette, its grimy glow bursting into the sleet from discoloured windows. A woman sits watching a machine clatter and bang against its silent neighbours, her eyes glazed, hypnotised by the rapid twist of clothing spinning against the porthole door.

Isobel follows a stooped old woman towing a bag on wheels up the street. She has just left the laundrette. A clean bed sheet spills from the top of her bag, trailing on the ground, soaking up the sleet.

"Look at it," Mr Punch whispers in her ear. *"These fucking people."*

"There's nothing wrong with these people. Only with you."

"I am what I am. I make no excuses. You shouldn't either. You're just as culpable."

"You're a psycho and I'm a victim."

"Is that how you see yourself? I'm surprised. All I've ever done is present you with a choice. Blackmail, coercion, murder? No, these things are mere details. You choose your path, Isobel – to submit or not."

"You're a coward."

"You have no idea what I am."

Despite having no information about him, Isobel has nevertheless constructed a mental image: a well-built man, taller than average, wearing dark conservative clothes, sitting in a black Chesterfield armchair, posture maintained. The scene lit by an inadequate table lamp. He is shrouded in shadow, his features obscured, the weak light only picking up the silver studs in the chair and the suggestion of his face.

This portrait is about all her imagination has managed to conjure, except the name she has given him: Mr Punch.

The obvious questions are the ones that preoccupy her the most: is he tall and powerfully built? Or skinny and weed-like? Perhaps he is an invalid confined to a wheelchair, like a James Bond villain. She just doesn't know, but nothing would surprise her. His misanthropic views, occasionally poured forth into her ear during one of these night excursions, chill her to the bone. But it's not often he gives her anything beyond instructions, his choice of words usually tame, almost polite.

Isobel crosses into Dock Road, leaving the high street behind. The occasional car goes rifling by, and as she walks past the sports field she can hear the desperate sound of two people fucking somewhere in the dark. Further along, the nightclub is all light and noise, crowds in the car park full of bombast and the comically huge doormen looming like jailers at the main entrance.

Down near the river Isobel turns away from the main road into a darker, narrower street. The buildings here are tightly packed and disintegrating. This is the urban reality the council tries so desperately to hide, the combination of overpopulation and economic decline.

There is glass all over the pavement and a tramp fast asleep in a doorway, almost buried beneath cardboard and newspapers, just the pale oval of his face visible in the gloom. Some of the streetlamps are broken and she walks through patchy shadows.

"Stop."

His sudden instruction makes her jump.

"Wait here."

"What am I waiting for?"

"He is close."

Isobel leans against a rough brick wall, and watches the sleet falling fast in the lamplight. Movement catches her eye, a fox nosing through rubbish heaped in a doorway, and Isobel idly wonders where in all this concrete and brick would a fox find a home? It climbs into a swollen cardboard box and she can hear it rummaging. Dislodged glass bottles go rolling out across the pavement, and the startled fox leaps from the box and out into the road. Headlights appear from up the street and the fox is rooted to the spot, looking towards the twin orbs of light as they come bearing down. Isobel, leaning against the wall and wrapped in the shadows, looks on as the car slows and comes to a halt.

"That's convenient. If not for the fox you'd be flinging yourself into the road to get him to stop."

Isobel pushes off from the wall, calm now. She is oddly comforted, back on familiar ground, knowing exactly what Mr Punch expects from her.

As she moves the fox turns in her direction. She walks up the path towards the car and the frightened animal disappears, scampering silently up the street.

"Stop." Mr Punch commands as she emerges from the shadows. *"Let him get a look at you."*

She pauses a moment, looking into the dark interior of the car, trying to make out the face of the man she is about to condemn. As she moves closer the passenger window begins to unroll.

"Open the door and get in."

The man starts to speak, but Isobel just opens the door. His words abruptly cease, and she climbs in, relieved to be out of the sleet and the cold.

The guy, stunned by her boldness, stares at her stupidly. He is in his early thirties, cute in a rugged sort of way.

"What the fuck are you doing?"

"Please, just drive."

His confused expression would be comical, except Isobel knows a bullet will ruin it sometime before dawn.

Pity.

3

Isobel is staring out of the window, watching the sleet drift down from the clouds. The streets are dark and indistinct, the buildings and alleys wrapped in shadows. Every few seconds comes the *swish-thump* of the windscreen wipers. The sleet is falling faster, and the temperature is dropping. The wipers leave little ridges of slush on the screen.

She looks across at Sebastian. He is a big guy, his head nearing the roof, his face intermittently revealed as they drive along under the streetlamps. His large hands grip the steering wheel firmly. He's cautious in case the roads are slippery.

Isobel spies the lights on the radio, the station frequency highlighted in the liquid crystal display. She turns up the volume, some gruff-sounding troubadour singing melancholy lyrics about love gone wrong. How much can you tell about a man based on the music he listens to? Sebastian seems like a serious but decent guy.

"What're you doing out tonight?" she asks.

He looks at her briefly, his eyes snapping back to the road after just a second.

"Running an errand. What're you doing out tonight?"

"Nothing much."

Isobel observes his expression; so sceptical it is almost funny, like a bad actor on television. So we're both being evasive. So what? At this point it's academic anyway. His fate is sealed.

"Bit late for a walk isn't it?"

"I'm a night person."

"You work at night?"

He thinks I'm a prostitute. Isobel smiles. "No, I work during the day. Got an early start tomorrow, in for eight o'clock."

The car is steaming up and Sebastian cracks his window. He tries a number of different buttons and dials on the dash, looking for the one that will turn on the fan and clear the windscreen.

Isobel is suddenly curious.

"Did you steal this car?"

"No, but it's not mine."

"So you did steal it."

"Borrowed it. With permission."

"Who owns it?"

"No idea."

"What did you say you were doing again?"

"An errand."

"What sort of errand?"

"The secret kind. I could tell you, but then I'd have to kill you."

They pull up at a set of traffic lights. At this time of night they change almost immediately, but Sebastian takes the opportunity to study her for a moment. Her coat is covered in mud and grass stains. Isobel can see the questions flashing behind his eyes.

"What do you do for a living?" she asks, putting off his inquiry.

"I was in the army," Sebastian gets the car rolling again.

"Was?"

"I'm not any more."

"You look a little young to be retired. What did you do, fuck the general's wife?"

Sebastian glances over at her. Isobel flicks her eyebrows up and down. Sebastian grins.

"I should have done that."

"Hey, never run from a sure thing."

"I'm hopeless at running. So is that your philosophy on life? Never run from a sure thing?"

"Hardly. My life is just the same old routines. Work and play."

"What do you do for work?"

"I'm a nurse."

"I know who to come to when some general shoots me in the arse."

Isobel smiles.

"And what do you do for play?"

"Pick up guys. You want to turn left up here."

Sebastian slows the car and flips the indicator.

"What did you do in the army?"

"Not much. Surfed a desk mostly."

"You ever kill anybody?"

Sebastian glances at her. Streetlamp light slides across his face, catching briefly in his eyes, and Isobel, for just a moment, sees something dark and unnerving. He may not be that easy to subdue. He may even fight back.

"Why would you want to know that?"

"So I know how good a soldier you were."

"I never saw combat."

"Why not?"

"Because I'm not very good at running."

"Surely that's a good thing for a soldier. Stand and fight, right?"

Sebastian doesn't answer and Isobel suspects she's touched a nerve.

"Well, look on the bright side," she says. "At least you still have your arms and legs."

"You're a funny girl tonight, Isobel."

Her features pinch at Mr Punch's intrusion. She looks to Sebastian to see if he noticed anything.

"You're a bit, you know, messed up, right?"

Then Sebastian's mobile phone beeps with an incoming text message.

"You're popular."

"It's a mate of mine. You'd like him. He's a gigolo."

"Really. Does he live in town?"

"You want me to hook you up?"

"Get a name."

"What's his name?"

"Kenosha."

"What?"

"Kenosha."

"What kind of name is that?"

"One he gave to himself, I guess."

"You need to turn right up here."

They turn into a narrow one-way street. The tarmac is studded down the middle with square speed bumps. Parked cars line either side and the terraced houses are barely ten feet in width, packed in tight, front doors right on the pavement.

"Where are we going?"

"Make another right at the end."

Sebastian flicks the indicator again and turns into a short, narrow hill, leading down to the esplanade and the dark, fast-flowing river. To the left is a long empty row of parking spaces; to the right manicured lawns and sparse flowerbeds lead to the river wall.

"Pull in just up here."

Sebastian eases into one of the parking spaces and pulls on the handbrake. Across from the car a long wooden pier interrupts the high river wall, stretching out into the swift current. The streetlights illuminate the first few metres, slick wooden boards reflect the orange light, but beyond that it's as if the pier leads off into the void.

"Don't tell me you live somewhere down here." Sebastian turns in his seat to face Isobel. She is staring back at him.

"Have you ever thought about how you're going to die?" she asks.

"What?"

"Your death. It's the only thing guaranteed to happen to you."

"What kind of a question is that?"

"I think about it a lot. About all the different possibilities, from the obvious ones like cancer or a car accident to the not so obvious like falling down a mine shaft or being eaten by a shark."

"You're crazy."

"I think about death all the time. It's an occupational hazard. But you know what?"

"What?"

"It makes me realise how much fun there is to be had in living. You just have to know how to make the most of it."

Isobel bends down and slips on her soaking trainers.

"Don't take me seriously," she says, straightening up. "My job makes me think about life in a different way to most people."

"Maybe I should meet more nurses."

"My shift starts at eight tomorrow. Drop by and I'll introduce you. Although none of the others are as interesting as me."

Isobel holds Sebastian's gaze, waiting for him to reply. But he just looks at her, and so she says:

"Well, thanks for the lift. It was nice knowing you…" Isobel leaves the sentence hanging.

"Sebastian."

"Right."

"And you?"

"Isobel." She holds out a hand. Sebastian takes it, feeling her cold fingers lightly grip his own. It would appear oddly formal in the tight confines of the car, but their hands linger, the touch lasting longer than a formal farewell would permit. Then Isobel shoves open the door and is gone into the night. The door swings shut with the same solid clunk.

* * *

Sebastian puts his hands on the steering wheel and sighs deeply. A slight smile graces his face, but then he turns and looks over his shoulder at the bag on the backseat. He shakes his head.

He is just about to release the handbrake when there is a tap on his driver-side window. He jumps in shock and uses the sleeve of his jacket to rub a patch in the condensation. Isobel is standing there, shivering in the sleet.

Sebastian rolls down the window. Before he can say anything, Isobel leans in and kisses him.

Her hand finds the car key in the ignition and turns it. The low grumble of the engine dies instantly and Sebastian breaks the kiss, pulling away.

Isobel grins at him. She cups the back of his head and pulls him into another kiss, this one longer, deeper.

Then she snaps the key from the ignition and steps back away from the car.

It takes Sebastian a moment to realise what Isobel has done.

"Give that to me."

Isobel smiles.

"You're going to be late, Sebastian." She takes another step away from the car.

"I'm not playing games."

"I am." Isobel turns and saunters away towards the pier.

Sebastian unclips his seatbelt and flings open the door. He gives the bag on the back seat a worried glance, then sprints after Isobel.

She runs, her old coat streaming out behind her. She flies over the grass and runs straight through one of the flowerbeds, heedless of the mud squelching beneath her sodden trainers. The freezing cold sleet whips into her eyes but she doesn't care. She races onto the pier rearing out over the swift black river, leaving the streetlights behind and plunging into darkness.

Sebastian is fast on her heels, his footfalls thumping along the slippery wooden boards.

Isobel reaches the end of the pier. There is nowhere else to run. She turns her back to the railings and confronts Sebastian. She holds up the keys.

"Give them back." His breathing is ragged. Isobel can hear a faint whistling as he struggles to pull air into his lungs.

Her hands drop to her jeans, undoing the first two buttons and sliding the keys down between her legs. The metal is cold against her skin and she shivers.

"You'll have to get them yourself."

"Isobel, I really have to be somewhere."

"Then you best hurry."

"Why don't we meet later? I'll do what I need to do and then…"

"It's a one-time offer Sebastian. We'll never see each other again." Isobel leans back on the railing, spreading her hands along the freezing rail, pushing up little piles of slush.

Sebastian looks back over his shoulder at the esplanade, at the row of streetlights and the gardens and the old little car all by itself in the parking bay. There is not a soul on the street.

"Come and get it."

"I don't have time for games."

Sebastian moves closer.

"Come. And. Get. It." Isobel says softly.

"Isobel, please."

"Are you begging me, soldier?"

Despite himself, Sebastian laughs.

He is very close now, looking down at her. Isobel wonders if he can hear her heart pounding away. It'll enforce the ruse if he can.

His hands reach out to her waist, fingers popping the remaining buttons. Sebastian slides her jeans over her hips.

The cold is intense. Isobel reaches for his face and kisses him, then guides him down.

"Down you go, soldier boy."

Sebastian sinks to his knees. He plucks the keys from the jeans bunched around her ankles, and puts his mouth between her legs.

Isobel feels nothing. His touch is gentle and under different circumstances she would no doubt be stimulated, but here and now all she wants to do is get this over with and get herself home. She cups the back of his head with one hand, pulling him in tighter, and with the other she pulls the gun from her coat pocket, raising it high above her head. Sebastian senses her movement, pulls away and looks up, searching for her eyes in the gloom.

Isobel slams the butt of the pistol down into his temple and knocks him senseless. He falls back unconscious on the slippery-wet boards of the pier.

*   *   *

Isobel is breathing hard, hands shaking. She looks around at the night. The sleet is thickening, turning to snow. The river roars at her back; everything else is deathly silent. She puts the gun back in her coat pocket and hitches up her jeans, trembling fingers struggling with the buttons.

"You are too good at this, Isobel. You've lost none of your charm."

"Go fuck yourself."

Isobel kneels down beside Sebastian. His eyes have rolled up into the sockets. She touches her fingers to his face.

"What will happen to him now?"

"You know what will happen. Someone will find him floating in the river."

"I mean now. What do you do to them after I've gone?"

"Getting curious as you get older? That's not good for you. The less you know the longer you'll live. Now get his keys, get in his car and drive. The others are only moments away."

"Where am I taking the car?"

"I'll tell you when you're moving. Now go."

Isobel hurries away, leaving Sebastian's unconscious body lying on the wet boards of the pier.

She gets in the car and slides the key into the ignition, acutely aware that she is leaving him to die. She is just as responsible as whoever finally pulls the trigger. The guilt that swarms around her heart is tempered with anger. Each time she does this, it increases Mr Punch's hold over her. For being an accessory to countless murders over the years, she would be facing life in prison. And Mr Punch has evidence – photographs and videos placing her at the scene. That bitter anger is not directed at him, but at herself. If only she were strong enough to walk into a police station.

But she isn't.

"You have three choices, Isobel. You can obey me, you can run or you can go to the authorities. The first option means you will live. Chose the others and you'll be killed, slowly and horribly. You'll be raped first. It'll be recorded, and after you're dead a roomful of psychos will get off on watching you suffer. I might even send a copy to your Mum. If you want this to stop then you know what to do. But you won't do it. I'm not the coward, Isobel. You are."

She turns the key and the old car splutters into life. Isobel backs out of the parking space. She takes one last look at the pier. Sebastian is hidden by the darkness at the far end.

Isobel drives away.

4

Sebastian lost his virginity to a girl down the street. Her name was Annabel and she was seventeen years old. Sebastian was a year older. He'd known her most of his life. They had been neighbours since they were kids.

When he was four and Annabel was three, he used to tell her she stank. Sometimes he'd creep up behind and scare her witless. If she cried he used to think he had won. When Annabel was nine and he was ten, he convinced her she would grow up pretty if she kissed him everyday. Every morning on the way to school, when they turned the corner of their street, she would give him a quick peck on the cheek. After a few weeks he convinced her it would work better if she kissed him on the lips. This happened for a few months until Annabel confessed to her friends. They told her she was stupid and she hated Sebastian for a whole year.

But he must have done something right, because at sixteen she was beautiful.

Throughout their teens they didn't see so much of each other. Annabel went to an all-girls grammar, while Sebastian was at the local comprehensive. One summer they bumped into each other in the street, as neighbours will. Annabel was preparing to leave for university; Sebastian wasn't doing much of anything. They started chatting and he reminded her of the kissing incident. Annabel thought it was funny.

That night they climbed through a hole in the fence and went strolling around her school field. Not long after they were fucking. Towards the end of the summer, shortly before Annabel left for university, her parents went abroad for a week.

Sebastian and Annabel took full advantage of the empty house and it was the first time Sebastian had ever fallen asleep with a girl.

One morning he was teased from his slumber by Annabel straddling him, her naked body golden in the early morning sunlight, her eyes closed, her hands on his chest. She was fucking him slowly, discreetly, in no rush to climax, trying not to disturb his sleep.

Waking that way was the most perfect thing that had ever happened to Sebastian. Even now, years later, he still dreams about Annabel's hot slippery cunt enveloping his cock, her small hands, her nails digging into his chest, the creak of the bed, the soft mattress beneath his back, the weight and rhythm of her hips.

Sebastian opens his eyes.

Bliss. Perfection.

Annabel above him, her eyes closed, long black hair hanging in her face.

Wait.

Annabel was a redhead.

Who is this woman impaled upon him?

Sebastian snaps to his senses, sleep rushes out of him, leaving in its wake a hard pounding clarity.

Annabel was nothing more than a dream.

Shock and disorientation slams through him and his body spasms, trying to lash out at this woman grinding down on him, but his hands and feet are tied fast. His bucking body causes the woman to bounce up and down. She moans in response. Sebastian screams through the gag in his mouth. The woman opens her eyes and looks down on him through curtains of black hair. Her eyes are clear, focused, filled with sadness. Sebastian goes quiet as he meets her eyes. The woman tries a smile. Not sexy, not playful, but reassuring, tinged with pity.

Sebastian looks away, turning his head to take in the room. Something about the impersonal nature of the furniture, the benign colour scheme and the single mediocre art print high on the wall. It must be a hotel, somewhere cheap, somewhere transitory.

His hands are strapped to the headboard, a belt biting into the flesh of his wrists. He's not so sure about his feet; his ankles must be strapped to something, probably the bed legs. The rag stuffed in his mouth makes it difficult to breathe. His lungs itch.

That maddening, terrifying fucking itch.

Sebastian tries to control his chaotic heartbeat. He snorts in oxygen through his nostrils.

The woman's black hair has fallen back in front of her face. She has small breasts and a bushy, untamed cunt. She is packing a little weight around a body that would have been desirable ten or fifteen years ago. She's raping Sebastian in the most disinterested way, neither in pleasure or desperation.

He yells through the gag and snaps his head from side to side. She flicks her hair back. Her expression is one he will never forget, somewhere between utter boredom and utter disgust.

Sebastian struggles with the belt around his wrists, but he's roped down too tight. He glares at her.

It is all he can do.

She looks down on him, her hips grinding away smoothly, small hands weakly grasping his chest. Something close to sympathy swims up behind her flat grey eyes. She looks off to the left and then back to Sebastian. She does this a couple of times, flicking just her eyes, her head remaining still.

The meaning cuts through Sebastian's turmoil and he turns his head to see what she's trying to indicate: a laptop on the dresser. On the screen is a live video feed of two people having sex. It takes Sebastian a moment to recognise himself, tied down, eyes bulging, nose flaring as he struggles to draw enough air to inflate his traitorous lungs. The camera in the laptop is watching them. Is it recording? Is it broadcasting? Suddenly the woman's disinterest makes sense. This isn't for her benefit. She's performing for someone else.

Someone is watching this.

She throws her head back, mouth open in a perfect *oh*, her hips piston faster and she fakes a loud and dramatic orgasm. She falls forward. Sebastian is suddenly surrounded by her fresh-smelling hair, her naked shoulder close against his mouth. Her lips brush against his ear, whispering so low he can only just hear her.

"When I leave, two men will come in and kill you."

Sebastian has trouble focusing on her words. His head is thumping, either from a lack of oxygen or from where that bitch Isobel hit him.

"I'll do what I can but it won't be much. I'm sorry." She gets up and crosses the room to the laptop. She closes the lid, shutting it down.

Sebastian is struggling against his bonds, the muscles in his arms and shoulders twang taught and he bellows in pain and frustration through the gag. His eyes bore into hers and she looks back with compassion. She gets dressed and stows the laptop in a rucksack.

Sebastian can see the conflict, her face betraying such anguish that he feels no malice towards her. She wants to set him free, he knows she does, he can see it in her eyes. But she's frightened too. Someone has got her very scared – the same someone watching over the webcam?

But she's packed the laptop away so no one can see them now.

Sebastian tries to get her attention, yelling around the gag. She holds a finger to her lips, then points at the door and silently mouths, "Right outside." . She shrugs on her coat and shoulders the rucksack. Taking one last look at Sebastian, she makes up her mind. She crouches at the foot of the bed and frees his ankles. Then she loosens the belt that ties his hands. Sebastian is struggling to get free as she whispers, "I can't do anything else. I'm sorry."

She cracks the door to the room and slips through the gap.

Outside in the corridor, Sebastian can hear people talking. Is she trying to stall them? He gets one hand free and rips the gag out of his mouth, hauling in a great draught of air as he goes to work on the last belt around his wrist.

He hears laughter – brief, mirthless – floating in through the gap in the door.

Sebastian squeezes his hand through the loop, the leather crushing his fingers together and abrading the skin.

The door swings open.

Sebastian leaps across the bed towards the door as a man strolls through. His bland face registers a moment of surprise, seeing Sebastian, naked, flying towards him.

The assassin pulls a silenced pistol from inside his jacket, but Sebastian is already too close. He grabs the assassin's wrist with his left hand and headbutts him in the face. The gun goes off, the bullet striking the laminate just beyond Sebastian's toes, and splinters lash up across his feet and legs. The thump of the shot is loud despite the silencer.

Sebastian swings the assassin around and kicks the door shut at the same time. The second assassin, just behind the first, collides with the door, slowing him down for just a moment.

Sebastian throws the first assassin against the wall, keeping his gun hand pinned. He's strong, and struggling. Sebastian knees him in the groin as hard as he can. The guy's body goes limp, and with his survival instinct in overdrive Sebastian strikes out at his throat, punching with everything he's got.

The crunch is sickening. The assassin drops like a stone and Sebastian plucks the gun from his hand as he falls. Hc turns and pulls the trigger as the second assassin bursts through the door. His head jolts away from the barrel and he drops to the laminate, spilling his brains.

Shock.

In the moments after, Sebastian stands with the gun in his shaking fist, looking down upon the two assassins. Then he sucks in a great lungful of air, sinks to his knees and closes his eyes.

His head is pounding, ears ringing. His whole body begins to shake, adrenalin dumping through his system. Any moment he expects others to come bursting through the door.

But after a few seconds, nothing happens. Sebastian opens his eyes and looks at the men he's just killed. The first assassin is slumped against the wall, eyes open, face slack. The second is sprawled across the floor, the side of his head just a wet mess pressed against the laminate. The bullet deformed his face as it burst through his skull, leaving in its wake a stretched, grinning rictus.

Sebastian looks down at his hands. The gun is in his right, his left is a clenched fist. There is no blood on him. Two men dead, and not a drop touched him. Sebastian starts laughing, then abruptly stops. Something about defeating them feels good, but the enormity of what has just happened slams through him and tears prick his eyes.

He leans forward, retching. Jesus, get a grip. I've got to get out of here.

Sebastian drags himself back to his feet. He tosses the gun on the bed, and with jelly legs steps over assassin number two, searching for his clothes.

He finds them folded neatly on the chair by the dresser. He pulls everything on, reaching into his pockets for his wallet, keys, asthma pump. He puts the pump in his mouth, hits the button twice and heaves in, holds, breathes out. The gesture is so familiar, synonymous with relief. His pulse begins to slow and his head begins to clear.

Sebastian moves back around the bed and looks down at the corpses.

Weapons. He needs the weapons. He finds another silenced pistol tucked into the jacket of the second assassin. He avoids looking at that face as he pats him down, searching for spare magazines. He grabs the first pistol off the bed. Two guns now.

He leans against the wall by the door and runs through a breathing exercise, getting control of his inhalations, slowing his heartbeat. He empties his mind, trying not to think, letting his body run on survival mode. His body remembers the training. His mind will only fuck things up. For now, all he needs to do is get out of the hotel and find somewhere safe.

He checks the clips in the guns, two bullets fired from the first and none from the second. He tucks the first into his waistband and with a two-handed grip he sights down the barrel of the second, familiarising himself.

"I can do this," he whispers. "Nobody is going to beat me."

Sebastian opens the door.

* * *

The corridor is empty. There are doors evenly spaced on both sides and lights running down the middle of the ceiling. Sebastian's senses are sharp and he's picking up details he wouldn't normally notice: the flower pattern in the blue carpet, the faint joins on the pinstripe wallpaper, the silver roman digits of the door numbers. Further down the corridor one of the lights is flickering, just fast enough for his eyes to register the disturbance. He can hear the muffled drone of a television behind one of the doors on his left. Apart from that everything is whisper quiet. He can go in either direction, and on instinct moves to the right, gun raised, cautious.

He slides up against the wall at the end of the corridor and peaks around the corner. Another corridor, identical to the first, but with a green EXIT sign pointing to a white door. Sebastian moves swiftly, his footfalls softened by the carpet. At the exit door he suddenly wonders what floor he is on. The nearest door number says 305. He's expecting six flights going down.

Through the door, and Sebastian finds himself at the top of a narrow switch-backing staircase. Glancing over the banister, he can see a narrow slice of tiled floor three stories below. The stairs are carpeted and he descends silently, back against the wall, step by step, until he arrives in the hotel lobby.

The stairwell is across from the main entrance, and through the glass door Sebastian can see the car park beyond. There's a light outside and a light dusting of snow on the ground. Flakes in the air go whirling by.

There's a guy wearing a dark blue uniform behind the reception desk, looking bored and half asleep, browsing through a magazine. Behind the desk is a television showing BBC News with the sound turned down. The clock in the corner says 03:23 as the headlines go scrolling across the bottom of the screen.

03:23? He's been unconscious for three hours.

Holding the gun down by his side, Sebastian strolls out from the stairwell. The guy behind reception looks up and goes pale. He looks towards the main entrance, and Sebastian knows there are others waiting for him out there, somewhere in the darkness. He raises the gun.

The reception guy is in his early twenties, with trendy dark hair framing an undistinguished face. He's pulling the late shift, either paid off or intimidated into keeping his mouth shut.

"How many are out there?" Sebastian asks.

"Two," he squeaks. "In the BMW."

"Where am I?"

"The Honourable Pilot."

'What?'

"It's a Premier Inn. On the A2."

"Next to the industrial estate?"

"Yeah."

"Is there a back way out?"

"Of course. But it's alarmed. The sirens'll go off when you open the door."

Could I just walk away? Sebastian wonders. Could I just open the front door and stroll round to the back of the building and get lost up in the industrial estate? Would those in the BMW even notice me?

Either way he cannot wait. Those outside will be expecting those who are dead. Pretty soon they'll be in here looking for their friends.

Fuck it. If there's a chance of walking away quietly, that's got to be the option to take. Sebastian points the gun at the reception guy. He should kill him, to stop him from contacting those outside. He should also make his way over to the BMW and kill whoever is sitting in it, covertly, in the interests of self-preservation.

But he can't. He's not that cold-blooded.

Not yet.

"If you tell anyone you saw me, I'll come back and kill you." It sounds empty, but Sebastian hopes it will be enough. He hopes the reception guy believes it.

He moves across to the main entrance and takes a peek. The car park is wide and on a slant. There is an outside light on the wall by the door and he's conscious of being visible. Other lights are dotted around the edge of the car park. Stationary cars are randomly distributed, details gradually hidden by the gently falling snow.

Sebastian spots the BMW, far back in the shadows. The wipers are on intermittent, cleaning the windscreen at ten-second intervals.

He takes a deep breath, then steps through door and out into the night. He moves right, along the wall of the hotel, in profile view of the BMW. He keeps his head down, chin into his chest, shoulders hunched against the cold. He turns his face towards the hotel wall, looking at the lighted windows, the rooms beyond hidden behind decorative curtains. Somewhere off to his left, in the shadows on the far side of the car park, is the BMW. He fancies he can hear the *swish-thump* of the windscreen wipers, can sense the killers hidden in the dark beyond the glass, watching him as he shuffles away.

"Ignore me," he whispers. "I'm nobody."

At the corner he turns along the flank of the building, towards the industrial estate. Now he has his back to the BMW. Most of the windows on this side of the hotel are dark; his brief, intermittent reflection in the glass is an indistinct shadow, black against black. The snow crunches lightly beneath his boots.

Halfway along and he starts grinning. I've made it, he thinks. The bushes at the back of the building are just in front. Beyond, the industrial estate is a maze of factories and office buildings.

But then the powerful roar of an engine shatters the illusion. Light bursts across the car park at Sebastian's back, throwing his shadow before him. The pitch of the engine changes as the BMW slams into gear and comes roaring across the car park, wheels spinning through pristine snow.

Sebastian sprints along the side of the hotel. He crosses the grass verge and dives through the bushes, crashing through branches and sprawling on the far side. He gets to his feet and looks back to see the BMW slewing to a halt. The two front doors open and the men spring out, as ordinary-looking as the other two from the hotel. They sprint away from the car, raising their weapons and firing wildly. Silenced gunshots thump at his back and Sebastian is off at a dead run. Hearing the rattle and curse of the men blundering through the bushes in pursuit, he races towards the nearest building, but there is no refuge to be found there. He needs more distance if he is to find a safe place to hide.

He can hear the rasp of his breath. He desperately tries to suck oxygen through his airways as they close in response to the freezing night. Already he can feel himself slowing, his vision darkening at the edges. The blackout isn't far behind.

He's out in the open now, some warehouse delivery area, the massive corrugated metal structure looming in front and the concrete concourse lit with yellow sodium lamps. Snow goes swirling through light, a dance of motion that would be hypnotic if only he had chance to pause and appreciate it. Sebastian blunders towards the nearest corner of the warehouse, hoping to put some cover between him and the assailants. Muffled shots thump from somewhere behind. His lungs are screaming and he's scooping ragged breaths, his mouth open as wide as it will go, but the rasp is too loud and his lungs too painful. He cannot outrun them.

Security lights blink on as he rounds the corner and stumbles across the front of the warehouse, picking out his solitary ragged figure as if in league with his pursuers. He moves through the car park at the front of the building towards another massive structure, leaving his footsteps in the snow to mark his progress. Black spots appear before his eyes.

He makes it round to the back of the warehouse and plunges into a dark narrow valley between the corrugated wall of the building and a steep grass bank. A thin strip of gravel crunches underneath the snow at his feet. It is dark here, but there's no cover and nowhere to hide. The grass bank is far too steep to climb.

"Fuck it!" Sebastian gasps as the realisation swims to the surface of his fading consciousness. He has run himself into a narrow alley with only one exit at the end.

You gonna let them beat you, son?

With his grandfather's question blazing in his mind Sebastian sprints for his life, an act that may kill him anyway. His legs and arms pump as he desperately hitches tiny little gasps of freezing air into his chest. His back is tingling, waiting for the bullet to shred his spine.

He makes it to the corner of the warehouse and bursts out of the valley, collapsing to the ground just as gunfire roars at his back. Bullets sing off the corrugated wall as Sebastian, curled into a ball on his side of the building, struggles for his asthma pump, his consciousness slipping away. Two shots of Seratide and a tiny breath in; it's the best he can manage before he's gone.

Seconds later and a faint whistling penetrates the darkness, bringing him around. It takes a moment for him to realise the whistling is the sound of his breath, but it's enough to focus his mind. He is not dead yet.

Sebastian struggles to his feet. He's done all the running he's going to do. No choice now but to face them. If they followed him along the valley then he's got the advantage. They must be moving cautiously or they'd be upon him already.

He takes another deep hit from the pump and slips it back in his pocket. He raises the gun. His hands are shaking. He wills them to be still. He remembers his drill sergeant, a compact little man called Warrington, hardened to his very bones, who despite his size always gave the impression of being indomitable, impervious to just about everything. He remembers Warrington bellowing his favourite sound bite at the top of his lungs: "Trust in your training!"

Trust in your training.

Sebastian takes a deep breath and darts around the corner, gun up in a two-handed grip. Without giving himself time to focus or doubt he squeezes off two shots, *thump-thump*, from the silenced pistol.

A short gasp, like a whisper of love in the dark, and a black shape folds to the ground.

Sebastian is back out of the line of fire, back around his corner, replaying the image in his mind. There was a second man behind the first. Why didn't the second man flank him? Why didn't he come around the building from the opposite side? Poor tactics. No strategy.

Sebastian closes his eyes. He takes in deep breaths and concentrates on his heartbeat.

"Control," he whispers. "Stay in control."

With the tactical advantage now in his favour, Sebastian takes two paces back from the corner of the building and raises the gun to head height, arm straight, the business end of the silenced barrel just two inches from the corner of the building. He focuses his attention, listening; the background hum of the urban sprawl all around, the drone of an occasional car on the A2 somewhere behind the industrial estate, the crunch of feet on snow and gravel as the assailant oh-so carefully approaches.

The last assassin has only two choices: either retreat or come forwards along the valley. He's being cautious, but he doesn't know Sebastian is this close. He'll be expecting him to run. Sebastian blinks snow from his eyelashes. The barrel of the silencer twitches in his jittery hands. He wills his breathing to slow, to soften. He visualises his airways expanding like rubber hoses, fresh clean air with a taste of spring rushing easily into his alveoli.

Footsteps in the snow, crunching softly, just inches away.

Sebastian's mind clears. Nothing exists but the corner of the warehouse and the guy pressed against the wall just around the corner, so close to the barrel of the gun, only he doesn't know it yet.

Sebastian holds his breath.

Carefully, slowly, a man's face appears beyond the edge of the warehouse. He peeks around the corner and inadvertently puts his forehead against the barrel of Sebastian's pistol. It couldn't be any more perfect.

"Don't fucking move."

The man's eyes go comically wide and his face is suddenly etched in absolute terror.

"Drop your gun." Sebastian's voice is a weak croak, but the assailant understands well enough. He swallows, sweat rolling down his temples, a subtle trembling at the corners of his lips. His back is to the warehouse wall around his side, trying to present as small a target as possible, just his head showing along with the tip of his gun barrel, announcing his arrival, as if the sound of his footsteps wasn't enough. Sebastian assimilates all these little details. *Amateur* blossoms in his mind.

"Drop your gun. Now."

The man throws his weapon away in a convulsive little jerk. Sebastian pushes him in the forehead with the barrel of his gun, shoving him back around his side of the building. In the narrow valley between the building and the grass bank, the man has nowhere to run, nowhere to escape to. Sebastian lets the man take a few paces back, out of arms reach, so he cannot try and take the gun. Not that he would, frightened little rabbit.

"Move." Sebastian drives him back down the valley, far enough to take them well out of sight of any potential passer-by. There is barely any light way back here behind the warehouse and all Sebastian can see of the guy is a trembling black shape and the faint white of his eyes.

"Lay back on the bank."

The man does as instructed, sitting down in the snow and laying back. The bank is steep, about a forty-five-degree angle, and he would have to try and raise himself up before launching any attack. He's fucked and he knows it.

"Keep your arms above your head."

"Look man, I really didn't mean…"

"You really didn't mean what? To kill me?"

Anger begins to well up inside, but Sebastian beats it down. He needs information and venting his fury is not the way to get it.

"Why are you trying to kill me?"

"I was told to. Really I didn't…"

"By who?"

The man pauses a moment. "I don't know his name."

"Don't fuck with me."

"I'm not. Really. I don't know who he is. He calls me, calls all of us and tells us what to do, but we don't know who he is."

"Why don't you tell him to go fuck himself?"

"We don't have a choice. He... Please... Just let me go."

"Why do you do what he says?" Sebastian repeats.

"I have to. If I don't something will happen to wife, my son. He... You have no idea who you're fucking with."

Snow is drifting down silently, melting off the barrel of Sebastian's gun on impact. The man is trying to be calm, but he's not succeeding very well. His quivering voice is in danger of running off into repetitive pleading. Sebastian doubts he'd be much different if roles were reversed.

"Who was the woman?"

"What woman?"

"The woman raping me when I woke up in the hotel room."

"I don't know anything about a woman. I never go inside. My job is to wait in the car with the other guy, and we wait. That's it. I don't know nothing about a woman. I don't even know the names of the other guys."

"You done this before?"

Again he pauses before answering. Struggling with guilt perhaps. This guy is clearly no hardened criminal.

"Yes," he says, "a couple of times."

"Ever had to chase somebody down like you've done tonight?"

"No. I've never killed anybody. Never even fired a gun until tonight."

"So you take orders from a guy you've never met, and do something you don't really understand with a bunch of guys you don't know, and the shared objective is to kill a man you never see, and you don't know anything about a woman, who for whatever reason was raping me when I woke up. That about the size of it?"

"Yes," he says quietly.

Sebastian shoots him in the leg.

A moment of silence, then the man screams.

"Who told you to kill me tonight?"

"I swear to fucking Christ I don't know."

He's curled up, on his side, cradling his punctured thigh with both hands. Sebastian shoots him in the other leg and he screams again.

"Who told you to kill me tonight?"

"I don't know." He is crying now, whimpering, struggling to squeeze words out around the pain. He is no tough guy. He's probably telling the truth. Most of the gangsters and criminals Sebastian knows of in London enjoyed the notoriety. They'd want their victims to know who they were. But this was something different. Somebody is working hard to stay in the shadows.

What do I do now? Take his life or let him live? Sebastian is suddenly conflicted. The logical answer is obvious, but since when has anything been logical? Sebastian is still pointing the gun at him, but his resolve is already weakening. It's one thing to kill a man when you're fighting for your life, but flat out executing someone when there is a choice, that's something else.

"What's your name?"

"Daniel."

"Roll over Daniel. Put your face in the snow."

"Please."

"Roll over."

The man struggles, crying in pain, as he rolls over onto his stomach. The blood pouring from the holes in his legs is black against the snow. Sebastian aims the gun at the back of his head, his finger on the trigger.

He wants to do it. Every instinct he has for self-preservation tells him he should.

But he can't. He's just not that kind of man.

"If I ever see you again, Daniel, I will kill you."

5

Sebastian's hands are suddenly cold. He can't stop them shaking. He puts the gun in the waistband of his jeans and stuffs his hands in his pockets. In fact he's shaking all over. They were going to kill to me, he thinks. It's a stone-cold fact.

Snow is beginning to settle on the dead man, turning his black clothes grey in the darkness. He lies face down in the snow. Sebastian doesn't want to see his final expression. The two men back at the hotel were enough.

Daniel is whimpering, still lying on the bank. His whole body is shaking and there is a lot of blood staining the snow from the bullet wounds in his legs.

Sebastian can feel his lungs drawing closed again and he takes a hit from his asthma pump. He turns and walks away, moving quickly through the deepening snow, as quickly as the stabbing pain in his chest will allow, away from the men behind the warehouse, away from the two dead men in the hotel. Adrift in the dwindling hours of the night, with blood on his hands, his whole life has just gone sideways and suddenly everything looks different.

This has all been planned. Everything calculated. The girl, Isobel, when she got in the car – that wasn't random. Then the hotel and the other woman and the laptop with the webcam. What is that? You don't do that to someone you want dead. But the assassins were there to do a job, even if they made mistakes. So the rape must've meant something to someone. But afterwards, he was irrelevant.

Disposable. Was it some kind of message? If so, who for? Nothing makes sense.

Then Sebastian remembers the bag.

Is that what this is about? Is someone after the cargo?

Sebastian is moving along a gravel path, winding around small patches of grass and trees, little green spaces punctuating the industrial landscape. There are warehouses on either side, and the occasional security light blinks on as he stumbles by, falling snow drifting through the light. He takes a smaller path, away from the lights, and plunges into the shadows. With shaking fingers he pulls out his phone.

"Hello?"

"Kenosha! Thank Christ."

"Where the fuck are you, man? Thought you'd be here hours ago."

"Kenosha listen, I need you to come and pick me up."

"Why? Thought they gave you a car."

"They did but something's happened. I need you to come and get me."

"What happened?"

"Doesn't matter now and we don't have time to chat on the phone. I'm in the industrial estate, you know where that is?"

"Yeah, of course."

"So will you come and get me?"

"No, man. Do you know what time it is? I've been sat here drinking the voddy by myself. I turned down a guaranteed shag that I'd've been paid for…"

"Kenosha shut up! Someone's tried to kill me tonight, alright? I've been a little busy."

"Someone tried to kill you?"

"Yes."

"Jesus, what have you got yourself into? You need to stop doing these delivery jobs."

"Kenosha just get in the fucking car and come and pick me up."

"Alright, alright. There's a shitty hotel on the corner near the A2. Meet me there in ten minutes."

"No way. Not there."

"Well where then? All them fucking warehouses look the same. It's a maze."

"I don't know, Kenosha – you fucking live here, you tell me."

He's silent for a moment, thinking. Sebastian waits in the dark, snow falling on the hand holding the phone, the other deep in his jacket pocket out of the cold.

"Up from the hotel, on the other side of the trees, there's a path that leads out of the industrial estate into Darland. It runs along the back of the Anchorians' sports field. I'll meet you at the Darland end, under the big tree."

"You better not be fucking about."

"Take the path and I'll meet you at the tree in about fifteen minutes."

"Alright. Thanks man."

Sebastian hangs up and gets moving, sneaking past small office buildings and enormous warehouses, delivery depots and through empty car parks. He sticks to the shadows as much as possible, avoiding the security lights. Snow crunches under his boots, and at every corner he expects either the police to come running or a gunshot.

The adrenalin rush of the fight is already a thing of the past and Sebastian feels exhausted. Apprehension bites at his heels every step of the way.

The lights from the hotel are visible through the bushes. Sebastian stays in the shadows. The BMW is still there, stopped at a curious angle, the engine idling and the doors wide.

The Anchorians' field is deathly still and ghostly white, bordered by a strong chain-link fence maybe twenty feet high. The path leading out of the industrial estate is more of a tree-lined road. There are soulless modern houses with blank windows facing the field. Sebastian wonders if anyone is watching as he moves beneath the trees. He keeps to the shadows, close to the fence.

The field on his right is unnerving, the snow-covered expanse huge and dark, and unnaturally still. He looks at the silent houses, trying to catch movement behind the dark windows, a pale face behind twitching curtains. But there is nothing.

Just spooking yourself, he admonishes. Push on and don't worry about it.

At the end of the path is a normal residential street, slightly more upmarket than the terraced rat runs he was driving through earlier. A vast old tree guards the end of the junction, skeleton branches twisting out above the fence and over the field. Yellow streetlamps stain the snow. Sebastian can hardly believe it was raining a few hours ago. The temperature must have dropped like a man punched in the throat.

Sebastian waits for Kenosha under the tree, in full view of the houses and lit up by the street lamps. He couldn't have chosen a worse place, alone on the street at nearly four in the morning. The pain in his lungs has faded to a dull ache, but the cold makes his airways feel itchy, like it always does, and his breathing sounds ragged in the silence.

Then Sebastian spies the phone box about a hundred yards down on the other side of the road. He pulls his wallet from his pocket, hunting for change.

The box has two smashed windows. Web-like cracks radiate from the centre of the glass. Inside, a thin coating of grime is lacquered over the handset and keypad.

Sebastian checks his mobile for the correct number, rolls in the coins and taps in the digits.

Ringing. Once. Twice. Then the phone is answered:

"Who's this?"

"It's Sebastian."

There is silence for some time. Sebastian watches the snow falling in the light from a nearby streetlamp.

"Are you there?" he asks.

"You were supposed to make your delivery."

"I was attacked."

"Robbed again? Seems like it's becoming a habit, Sebastian."

"This was different."

"Do you still have the cargo?"

"No."

"Who does?"

"I've no idea. I didn't get chance to ask the three men I killed."

"Three? How resourceful of you Sebastian. You surprise me."

"Yeah well, I surprised myself."

"So what do you propose to do now?"

"I don't know."

"That's twice you've let us down."

"I'm aware of that."

"It makes your position an interesting one."

"How so?"

"You're a dead man walking."

Sebastian shivers. The surety in the voice turns his blood to ice. I should never have got involved in this. Sebastian closes his eyes.

"What if I get it back?"

"The cargo? How do you propose to do that?"

"I have a lead."

"A lead?" Mirthless laughter. "You sound like a television detective."

"I'm serious."

"I'm sure you are."

There is a pause. Sebastian can tell nothing about the man from his voice. He doesn't sound like Brando in *The Godfather*, or any other powerful figure. For some reason, this blandness makes him even more threatening.

"You've got twenty-four hours to recover the cargo. The clock is ticking as of now. If I haven't heard from you this time tomorrow, the contract goes out on your life and you'll be dead by Monday morning. Are we clear?"

"Yes."

"And Sebastian?"

"Yeah?"

"Don't use this time to run. You may have called me from a pay phone, but I can find you faster than you'd believe. Deliver my cargo and you keep your life."

The line goes dead.

Sebastian hangs up the phone. It's a bitter sense of relief. Twenty-four hours isn't very long. But it's better than nothing.

He leaves the phone box, and finds Kenosha's Mercedes idling at the curb, with a thin layer of snow covering its roof.

Sebastian walks around to the passenger side and gets in, pulling the door closed. The night might be over, but there's a tough and bloody day yet to come.

6

Sebastian is sitting in Kenosha's green Chesterfield rocking chair, his fingers wrapped around a giant mug of tea. The action and adrenalin has left him exhausted. There is a dull ache in his head from where Isobel hit him; a dull ache in his balls from being fucked by that strange woman without ejaculating. His lungs feel stretched, his throat raw, like he'd just sprinted a marathon. All he wants to do is sleep.

But Kenosha won't let him until he knows what's happening. Sebastian cannot blame him for that. He'd want to know too, if he was harbouring a marked man. He'd be worried about the front door being kicked in by gun-toting thugs hungry for blood.

Kenosha sits on the edge of the sofa, glass of water held in his manicured hand, staring intently.

"Don't panic," says Sebastian. "No one's gonna kill me until tomorrow night."

"Funny enough I wasn't thinking about you."

"Oh, well that's comforting."

"Stop fucking about and tell me what's happened."

"I killed three men tonight."

Kenosha swallows.

"Seriously?"

"I let one go."

"Because, I mean, none of this is funny you know. I mean, if you're winding me up."

"Kenosha. Seriously."

"Christ, man." Kenosha flops back on the sofa, spilling his glass of water. He's more freaked out than I am, Sebastian thinks. But he's not the one swinging from the rope.

Kenosha stares out through his floor to ceiling windows at the dark night and drifting snow.

"Tell me you had no choice, right?"

Sebastian thinks about Daniel, laid out on the bank, the blood from the bullet holes in his legs running into the snow, black on white.

"It was self-defence, Kenosha. I'm not a murderer. I didn't kill the last one."

Kenosha looks at Sebastian for a moment longer than is comfortable, and then he turns away, casting his gaze back out through the window.

"So what happens now?" he asks.

"I need to get the delivery back. They've given me a twenty-four-hour extension."

"Can't you just walk away?"

"I wish I could."

"Will they kill you?"

"Yes."

"Man... So what is it?"

"What is what?"

"Your delivery. Is it drugs?"

"Dunno, but I don't think so. They never told me and I never asked. To be honest, I don't want to know."

"How could you not know what you were carrying, Sebastian? You must have some idea."

"A big holdall, padlocked shut. It was heavy. Whatever was inside was an odd shape. I picked it up from the guy in Dover, slung it on the back seat and drove here. That's it."

Sebastian sips his tea, alarmed to note that his hands are still shaking. Tiredness? Or fear? Either just as likely.

Knowing you're about to die isn't exactly soothing. What am I prepared to do in pursuit of that bag? He wonders. And what about those who took it? Who are they? What's their objective? And what was the purpose of raping me? More than anything, the enigma of that woman is what he needs an answer to most. It suddenly occurs to him that his image, naked and bound, is out there somewhere. Will the scene pop up on some porn site as an amateur sex clip? Will anyone see it? Who would believe that he wasn't complicit?

This is all too much for his exhausted mind and he stands up.

"Gonna use your shower if that's okay, then get some sleep."

"Spare bedroom's down the hall. There's an en suite."

"Thanks." He gives Kenosha a grateful look, conveying a genuine depth of feeling.

"Can't vouch for how clean the room is in there. Can't remember the last time I tidied it."

"Tonight mate, I really don't care." Sebastian walks away through the living room and into the hall, leaving Kenosha staring out of the window.

* * *

Standing in the shower, the water running hot, Sebastian closes his eyes and can feel sleep dragging him down. He's unsteady on his feet and his stomach is doing cartwheels. He doubles up and retches in pain, but nothing spews. He has listened to others talking about it, guys who served in the Falklands and the Gulf War, and they all said the same thing: you shut down and deal with it later, perhaps when you find yourself alone in the shower, and you let all the emotions go. After all, it has to go somewhere. Otherwise you wouldn't feel a thing, and then you wouldn't be human.

Despite doing the occasional run for an obviously criminal outfit of some kind, he always believed himself to be an innocent, on the right side of the law more or less. But he can't hold to such fantasies anymore.

A line has been crossed.

Sebastian leans against the tiled wall, feeling a little claustrophobic in the heat and the steam. Like all modern homes, despite its swanky ambience Kenosha's apartment is pretty damn small. The en suite to the second bedroom is tiny, the shower just big enough to stand up in and turn around. But he doesn't lower the heat, and he's not ready to get out. Not yet.

There's a knock at the door and Kenosha calls out, "You alright in there?"

"Yeah."

"Anything you need?"

"Nah, I'm good mate."

"Alright. Well, I'm off to bed. Catch you in the morning."

Sebastian flashbacks to when he first saw Kenosha, in a bar about four years ago, somewhere in Covent Garden. Sebastian had been going there on a semi-regular basis, trying to hook up with a Latino barmaid. She barely spoke English and had arrived in London from Havana.

Kenosha was sat at the bar sinking whisky and looking about as nervous as any man Sebastian had ever seen. He was dressed to the nines and as Sebastian walked past he caught a whiff of expensive cologne.

Carmita, the barmaid, was hovering and Sebastian ordered a beer, saying hello, flashing his most inviting smile. Carmita responded in kind; she was easy-going and quick to laugh, even though Sebastian was sure she only understood about half of what anyone said to her in English.

Kenosha ordered another whisky and Sebastian asked, "Going somewhere nice?"

Kenosha turned and looked at Sebastian with completely clear and lucid eyes.

"Man," he said, "I'm going to the best place in the world."

"Don't look too happy about it."

"Happy…? Oh yeah. Nervous about it too."

"What is it? A job interview or something?"

Carmita plonked Sebastian's drink on the bar. He said thanks and paid and she sauntered over to the till.

"Ha! A job, for sure. Best fucking job in the world."

"Really? They need one more?"

Kenosha looked Sebastian up and down and said, "Yeah sure. I'm sure you could do alright if you tried."

Sebastian had no idea what he was talking about and sipped his pint, taking change from Carmita's hand, catching her eye as he did so. Kenosha sunk his latest shot and pushed the glass a little way up the bar. Carmita grabbed it, frowning.

"So what's the job?" Sebastian asked.

"Having sex with a beautiful woman," Kenosha said.

"It does sound like the best job in the world."

Kenosha was starring down at the bar top, lost in thought.

"For real?"

"I was at this party last week. Some friend of a friend who hangs out with a bunch of company execs earning a million plus a year. And there's this girl there. She's, like, some CEO of an advertising agency, mid-thirties, looks like a model, but she's smart with it too."

"Sounds great."

"So we get chatting and she's way, way out of my league. And she's going on about advertising and other bullshit and then she asks what I do, right? Now, I work in a shop along Oxford Street. But I can't tell this woman that."

"So what did you tell her?"

"I told her I was a gigolo." He smiled.

"That's fucking brilliant."

"Yeah, I know. Best thing I've ever said. So the party goes through the motions and we chatted some, I made up some bullshit about things that'd happened to me on the job – you know, funny stories about sex and that. And we go our separate ways. I don't think anything more about it. Until," Kenosha moved in closer to Sebastian, his voice dropping a little as if confiding a secret, "on Monday she rang me up."

"She rang you?"

"Yeah. I didn't even give her my number. She tracked me down through mutual acquaintances. She told them, get this, she told them I'd left my keys with her at the party and she wanted to return them."

"Did you?"

"No, man. She's bullshitting because she doesn't wanna tell my friend the real reason she's calling me."

"Which is?"

"She offered me five hundred quid to go with her to an award ceremony as her date. It's something to do with advertising. But, and here's the clincher, she said she'd pay extra, for extra."

Sebastian looked at him, convinced it was a wind up. But Kenosha showed no sign of deception, only apprehension, and with him so immaculately dressed it didn't seem so far-fetched.

"Seriously?"

"Yeah man. I've got to be at her place in..." He checked his watch. "Forty minutes."

Before he left the bar that day Sebastian gave him his phone number and told him to text. His story was just too good for Sebastian not to know what happened. Kenosha said he would, and true to his word the following morning Sebastian woke to find a text message. They hooked up for a pint and Kenosha spilled the beans in hilarious and graphic detail. They'd been mates ever since.

The cooler air in the little en suite is invigorating when Sebastian steps out of the shower.

He collapses on the bed, not bothering to get under the covers. He closes his eyes and sees the woman, the reluctant rapist. Her disinterested face floats before Sebastian in the darkness. She must be in her forties; either that or she's lived a very stressful life, which seems likely. I want to know who she is. Sebastian is consumed. I want to know why.

This need is as powerful as getting the cargo back. Maybe it smacks of ego, or pride. He doesn't know. But being tied up and raped? Sebastian shudders.

But the bag must be the priority. Retrieve the cargo, otherwise he'll be dead. And then he'll never know.

With that in mind, he falls asleep.

* * *

Sebastian's eyelids flutter open. He hauls himself awake through an effort of will. There is a dull ache in his head and he is groggy and feels finished even though the day hasn't begun.

I can't believe I'm going out to fight for my life feeling like this. Sebastian shakes his head.

He gets to his feet and turns to the window. Dawn, the rising sun lost behind a blanket of low grey cloud. It's still snowing. He checks his watch. Just before seven. He's had barely three hours sleep. Perhaps it would have been better staying awake, buzzing on energy drinks and coffee.

Sebastian goes down the hall to Kenosha's room. He's all but invisible beneath the duvet on his king-size bed. Sebastian shakes him awake and Kenosha tells him to fuck off. Sebastian taps him on the head and Kenosha tries to shoo him away. Sebastian would find this funny if it wasn't the last day of his life.

"Kenosha, wake up."

"Man…"

"I need a couple of things."

"What? Time is it?"

"It's about eight."

"Man."

"Kenosha."

"What?"

"I'm going to be dead soon, you cunt. Wake up."

This gets him a little more focused and Kenosha sits up, rubbing his face.

"What?"

"I need to borrow your car."

"Um…"

"And I need a safe place to go."

"A safe place?"

"Yeah."

"I don't know what…"

"I'm going to kidnap somebody and I need to take them somewhere and interrogate them."

"Fuck, man."

"Yeah it's serious. But that's what I'm gonna do."

"Well, not here."

"I know that. I don't want you involved. That's why I need somewhere else."

Kenosha gets up out of bed, butt naked, and goes to the window. He turns back. "I know a place you could go."

"Where?"

"There'll be others there. It's a junky hellhole, but you could bust in and turf them out of a room or something. They'll be so fucked they won't even know what's going on."

"Where is it?"

"The high street. Above the shops."

"Near the hospital?"

"Yeah, not far. Couple minutes drive."

"How do you know about this place?"

"Everyone knows. This place is fucking Brown Town, even London people know about it."

"Alright. Where are your car keys?"

"Ah man, not my car. I don't want no part of this. Can't you steal one or something?"

"I don't know how to steal a car!"

"You're kidding?"

"Do you?"

"No, but I thought, you know, you're a crim."

"Kenosha, I've made a few deliveries for a bunch of mysterious gangsters. But I'm not a career criminal, and I've never stolen a car."

"What about the car you were driving last night?"

"That was left for me by the people who hired me, in a car park in Brixton. I was supposed to return it to the same place when I got back to London."

"So where is it now?"

"I don't know, Kenosha. When they knocked me out I didn't get chance to fucking ask about it."

"All right, calm down. You can borrow my car."

95

Sebastian leaves him to get dressed and goes into the kitchen. He interrogates the expensive, shiny espresso machine but without success. Eventually Kenosha comes in and does it for him. Sebastian drinks six. It's going to be a long day.

7

Isobel is fleeing from hooded figures dressed in black, all pointed teeth and sunken eyes, small hands with long grasping skeletal fingers. She remains just a fraction beyond their reach, sprinting down corridors and through rooms, corpses piled high, like sandbags against walls and doors, all grasping limbs and vacant, staring eyes.

She sprints through a reception area stacked with rotting flesh, the melted face of the receptionist congealing around a telephone handset, through operating theatres and down long halls with rows of beds. The sinister dead grin at her with their yellow teeth. Behind, the black-hooded figures are fast on her heels, stretching, raking needle-like fingers down her back.

Gasping and covered in sweat, the shriek dies on her lips as her bedroom takes shape around her. Breathing hard, Isobel collapses back on the pillow, throwing an arm across her eyes to shut out the dull grey light.

The alarm begins its ritualistic peal and she reaches out and stabs the button, knocking the clock off her bedside table with a clatter. The noise kindles a memory from a week before: her and Andrew fucking hard, their passion rocking the bed and the table next to it, eventually knocking over the clock and the vase of flowers, spilling stale water down the bedroom wall. She allows the memory to burn a little, hoping to obscure the events of last night and the return of Mr Punch to her life. After so long without him, she was starting to believe in her freedom.

Isobel drags herself out of bed. She has a twelve-hour shift ahead of her, a long and no doubt turbulent day, hard enough on a full night's sleep.

In the bathroom, she studies her reflection in the mirror – a pretty face once upon a time, lurking somewhere beneath features ruined by stress, thin grey lips turned down at the corners, eyes sunken and bloodshot.

Isobel wipes her hands over her face, hoping for the bitter-looking creature in the mirror to fade. But peeking between her fingers, there she is, staring back.

What have I become? she wonders. It is hard to see a future beyond the adrenalin-fuelled smack of her gun slamming into some unfortunate man's head, with Mr Punch's monotone whispering in her ear, while the victim lies prone at her feet.

Her only chance of salvation is the gun, aimed not at another victim, but at the unknown face from the other side of the telephone: Mr Punch, whose face she has wondered about for so many years.

Isobel turns away from the mirror, unable to look upon the darkness in her eyes. She steps into the scalding-hot shower, scrubbing herself vigorously, trying to focus her thoughts on the day ahead, her patients and colleagues, and on Andrew, who she will call tonight looking for comfort, needing him to fuck the coldness from her bones.

She pulls a fresh uniform from the cupboard, pulls on thick tights against the cold – even the wards can be chilly. Brushing her hair, putting on simple make-up, trying to hide the bruises around her eyes.

Isobel is just about to leave when the telephone rings. She hesitates. Who would call her this early? Deciding it must be Andrew she rushes into her bedroom and grabs the handset.

"Hello?"

"Isobel."

She sits down on the bed.

"What do you want?"

"Something went wrong."

"Went wrong?"

"Last night."

"I did what you said. You know I did."

"You played your part well."

"I don't understand."

"Afterwards. After you left. What was supposed to happen, didn't. There is something that still needs to be done."

"I have to go to work."

"Yes. That is what you should do. But I need you wired."

"Why?"

"Someone may come for you."

"What? Who? The guy from last night?"

"Probably."

"Why?"

"Because the others failed."

Isobel is suddenly breathless. Sebastian is still alive. Somehow he got away.

"Is he dangerous?"

"More so than we thought."

"We?"

She wasn't thinking, her mind preoccupied with unexpected concerns, wondering if Sebastian is coming for revenge.

There is silence from the other end for a moment, a fraction too long. She is about to apologise for probing when Mr Punch continues:

"He has an agenda. You are all that he has. You will stay wired. If he makes contact, I will know. You will do what he says. Do you understand?"

"Yes," Isobel whispers.

"The camera on your coat, make sure you transfer it to your uniform."

"It will stand out. The buttons are a different colour."

"It will have to do."

"I'll be late for work."

"So be late."

The connection is cut. Isobel listens to the dial tone, looking through the window at the snow. The road outside has lost its crisp perfection, scarred now with tyre tracks, the morning rush hour well under way.

Isobel puts the phone down and prepares to meet a day unlike any other, not knowing if she'll still be alive at the end of it, but knowing that for the first time, someone is making a stand.

8

Medway Hospital is a kidnappers nightmare. Sebastian cruises slowly around the site, looking for somewhere to stash the car. All the car parks have ticket access. Push the button, take your ticket and the barrier lifts. The problem is getting back out. The barriers won't lift unless the fee has been paid at the ticket machine by the main entrance.

Sebastian wonders if he could crash through the barriers like you see in the films. Maybe, but it's hardly covert, and at the very least it would fuck up Kenosha's car.

Someone has been out gritting, and the roads are wet and slushy. Snow is still falling, grass verges and car roofs piling up. People are flooding into the hospital's main entrance, bundled up in coats and hats. It's almost impossible to see faces, but he tries to scan each one nevertheless, on the hunt for Isobel.

Eventually, luck shines on him and he finds a space right near the main door in an area reserved for drop-offs and pick-ups. A sign reads: 'Maximum stay 10 mins. Clamping in operation.' It's gone eight o'clock already and his last few hours are ticking away. The need to find Isobel is fierce. He avoids the possibility that she was lying when she said she worked at the hospital. To indulge that idea is to lose hope, and he's not there yet.

For a few minutes he sits in the car, watching people go by. He's waiting to see how long the other cars stay put and scanning for anyone who might resemble a parking attendant. The last thing he wants is to find Isobel and get out of the building, only to find the car clamped.

To Sebastian's right, through the window, he observes a haggard-looking old guy wearing a thin jacket, hands in leather gloves, smoking a rolled-up cigarette next to a big sign that says 'NO SMOKING'. Clearly he doesn't give a shit, and by the looks of the people filing past neither does anyone else.

The front entrance is glass and sliding doors, with a huge awning giving shelter to the intermittent ambulances, which pull up and drop off the wheelchair- and gurney-bound. People file in through the doors, looking miserable and huddled against the weather. There is something hopeless about the whole place – the immense volume of people, the immense volume of traffic, everyone fighting over parking spaces. The place feels besieged, struggling to stave off the persistent tide of substandard humanity washing up against its walls.

Sebastian opens the door and gets out, beeping the car locked as he walks away. He breezes through the entrance, in among the crowds flowing through the door. Just inside there is a small shop selling newspapers, flowers, sweets and drinks. An old lady wearing a Salvation Army uniform is perched on a stool behind a small information desk. Stood next to her is a tall black guy sporting a security guard uniform and cap, with no weapons of any kind on his belt. Sebastian strolls over to the desk, standing right next to the security guard.

"Do you know Isobel?" he asks the Salvation Army lady.

"Who, dear?"

"Isobel? Nurse Isobel?"

She looks back at him blankly. The security guard turns in his direction.

"Never mind." He walks away.

The large reception area is heaving with people. To his left is the outpatients desk, the three women staffing it already looking stressed, still wearing their coats and woolly fingerless gloves. Every time the main doors slide open the cold rushes in with the people. Sebastian feels the air on his neck and pities the women, sat there for hours in this intermittent draft.

Rows of plastic chairs are filled with waiting patients, mostly old or obese, faces puffy red or wrinkly, their melancholic expressions like a special brand of NHS face paint. There's a shelf loaded with second-hand books, free to all in return for a donation, the collection box weighed down with chains and padlocked to stop some local nimrod stealing it. A tacky-looking cubicle selling overpriced coffee in paper cups is the only source of heat in the immediate vicinity and the tables are crowded.

Sebastian marches through this miserable gathering, scrutinising all, categorising rapidly – male, female, old, young, fat, thin – he tries to get a better look at those with the right attributes, searching for that face, those weary eyes and that long blond hair.

Beyond reception, the hospital is a grey maze of corridors and staircases, institutional-coloured paint peeling here and there, and great fat pipes emerging through grills to run the length of the corridors, close to the ceiling. Windows let onto closed courtyards, stone gardens half buried in snow, flanked on all sides by looming old brick walls, streaked with rusting drainage pipes and punctuated by slowly rotting window frames.

One courtyard is given over to model children enjoying a playground setting – fake kids in a fake playground imprisoned by institutional walls, slowly buried by falling snow, their fake grins unchanging as the snow rises up around their wooden necks. Sebastian shudders.

Dotted along the corridor walls are paintings in various styles of many different subjects, from botanical illustrations to harbour scenes, yachts glistening under a summer sun, and a multitude of World War Two aircraft flying low over patchwork green countryside. The differing quality ranges from poor to masterpiece, each painting accompanied by a cheaply produced plaque with the name of the artist and a price tag. The one subject conspicuous by its absence is people. No life studies, no Vettriano knock-offs or nudes, nothing abstract like Picasso either. Sebastian wonders if paintings of people in a place drowning in them is some kind of social faux pas; as the disintegrating wrecks shuffle past in their slippers, thumping walking sticks and spilling fat over the sides of wheelchairs, perhaps they don't wish to be jollied by some intimate scene, or maybe those riddled with disease are offended by the sight of a beautiful woman revelling in her naked perfection. Youthful health and vigour are just ghosts in these purgatorial halls, clearly remembered perhaps, but never to come again.

Sebastian flashbacks to his mother after the heart attack – her shrunken lifeless frame, muscles slack but somehow rigid.

"I fucking hate hospitals," he mutters.

The last thing his mother said to him was, "Be a good boy." It's what she always said whenever they parted company. Every day of his childhood, in the mornings when he left for school, during the holidays when she left for work, in the evenings when he went out to play in the street or if she went to bingo.

Be a good boy.

A nurse is coming the other way, sensible shoes clopping along, white uniform buttoned primly, a red cardigan thrown around her shoulders to ward off the chill. Her face is stressed and she looks hurried and worried, red hair bunched, pulled tightly back from a high, clear forehead.

"Excuse me."

She walks past Sebastian a step and then stops and turns. Clearly she doesn't have time to be chatting.

"Sorry, I know you're busy."

"That's alright." She has an interesting lilt to her voice that he cannot place, somewhere far away, maybe Hungarian, but he can't be sure.

"Do you know Isobel?"

"Isobel? No, what ward is she on?"

"I've no idea. I'm just trying to find her."

"Are you a relative?"

"No. No, she isn't a patient. She works here."

"Oh right. As what? A consultant?"

"I don't think so. I think she's a nurse."

"I'm sorry, I don't know." She turns and walks on, clop-clopping her way down the corridor.

This isn't working. She could be anywhere in this fucking maze and the clock is ticking. Sebastian is getting agitated. He decides to start at the top and work down. Finding the nearest stairwell, he climbs up, flight after flight, his boots slapping the stairs, that awful disinfectant smell. He gets to the top and walks through the door into a corridor that looks exactly the same as the one three floors below.

He stops, waits for his breathing to settle down, then marches into the first ward he comes to, passing a couple of private rooms. An old man is laid out in his dressing gown and slippers, watching a television screwed to the wall. He looks pale and dead, although Sebastian is sure he is not.

He briefly recollects the old man shuffling down the street in the rain, just before all this madness started. If I'd offered the guy a lift none of this would have happened. Sebastian tries not to dwell on this. What-ifs will not help him find Isobel.

The nurses' station up ahead is busy. An old woman totters by, leaning on a walking frame, her progress so slow that by the time she gets to wherever she's going it'll be time to come straight back again.

Sebastian gets a few inquisitive looks from the nurses but he just ignores them, walking with purpose, hoping to project an air of confidence that will communicate all the right things.

Nobody here resembles Isobel and he walks along to the next ward.

This one is for kids. As he marches through the doors a doctor in a long white coat points to a dispenser on the wall.

"Hands."

"Huh?"

"Clean your hands. We don't want MRSA in our hospital, thank you."

Sebastian pulls the tab and the dispenser squirts a clear gel into his palm. He walks away rubbing the gel into his hands. It evaporates quickly leaving his fingers feeling cold. Rows of beds filled with glum-looking kids. Some fiddle with their smartphones, others are watching television, one is reading a thin paperback. There appears to be only two nurses on duty here and they both ignore him. No sign of Isobel.

He searches the whole of the top floor and finds nothing. His heart is beating hard in his chest and his hands are clenched into fists. He's walking too fast to be casual. He's worried now about drawing attention to himself. He goes down two flights and steps out of the stairwell onto the floor below.

Here are cardio, respiratory and other impressive-sounding areas, familiar to him since he was a child seeing consultants about his asthma.

Sebastian pushes through a set of double doors into what appears to be a waiting area and finds a bunch of people who've taken root in their uncomfortable chairs. A nurse comes out of a room and calls a name. It isn't Isobel. A fat guy heaves and struggles his way off the chair and waddles into the room; the nurse shuts the door behind them. Nothing here, and he's back out into the corridor, pausing for a moment wondering which way to go.

But then there she is.

Walking towards him, eyes cast downward.

Isobel.

Sebastian's guts and fists involuntarily clench at the sight of her and he forces himself to relax. He takes a few deep breaths as she draws closer. The corridor is suddenly very clear, every movement, every sound. Sebastian's senses range out over the area, alive to every little detail; something in his mind has switched to combat mode, a state of mind he barely had chance to register the night before, but he can appreciate it now.

But now that he's found her, he doesn't have a concrete plan for getting out of the building with Isobel as a hostage. Will she fight or run? If he's lucky she'll submit. But where has he been lucky in the last few hours?

Sebastian walks towards her. Acting with purpose now, mind clear and movements lucid.

She still hasn't seen him.

* * *

Isobel, shoes still damp from the snow, top button on her uniform black and absurd, is on the hunt for a dialysis machine. The hospital only has a couple and they move around. The earpiece is uncomfortable, a constant reminder that she is not alone. Mr Punch is seeing what she sees, hearing what she hears, observing her life and pulling her strings. She feels helpless, put out like bait, waiting for some predator to snap her up in its powerful jaws, crunching her bones. Her cold feet send chills up her legs and through her spine. She's only been on duty for about twenty minutes and already she is exhausted and ready to drop.

On the second floor she wanders along, from one ward to the next, asking if anyone has seen the machines, responses coming in a variety of accents, but always the same: No, we don't know where the dialysis machines are. Her patient, a cantankerous old bastard at the best of times, will be getting angry. As she walks along, staring at her feet, Mr Punch whispers in her ear:

"Heads up."

Isobel looks up and there he is, Sebastian, the man from last night. The left side of his face is bruised, discolouration around his eye. From where I hit him? He looks about as tired as she does, but he's dealing with it much better. His face is frozen with determination, a long way from the calm and easy-going guy she met last night. Something in him has awoken, a resourceful, dangerous animal. For some reason, she isn't surprised he's still alive.

He reaches out, spinning her round and forcing her wrist way up her back, his other hand suddenly over her mouth, stifling her scream. Pain explodes through her shoulder, horrible pressure on her wrist, her fingers right up between her shoulder blades. His movement is swift and full of intention, an indomitable strength that she cannot counter. His lips are at her ear, whispering: "I've already killed three. You'll be four if you try to run. I've got two guns, and you'll be dead before you take a step."

If not for her long hair, worn down today against hospital regulations, he would likely see the earpiece. Isobel stands rigid in his grip, her heart hammering and fear sapping the strength from her legs.

"We're going outside. We're going to walk calmly. Down the stairs and out the front door. You're going to act natural. I'm going to keep one hand on the back of your neck. The other will be close to a gun. One wrong move and you're dead. After you, I'm going to shoot whoever gets in the way, and their deaths will be your fault too."

He releases her wrist and the pain in her shoulder is suddenly eased, the hand around her mouth moves to the back of her neck and he steps from behind to her side. She turns to look at him. His grim eyes drill into her head, looking for answers she probably doesn't have. Isobel doubts he'll believe her ignorance. But what can she do?

"Walk."

"Don't resist," Mr Punch whispers. *"Do as he instructs."*

His hand is huge on her neck, powerful fingers pressed painfully into her flesh, pushing her forwards along the corridor towards the stairwell. As they approach the door a couple of patients and a doctor come walking along in the opposite direction.

The patients ignore them completely but the doctor nods hello. Isobel smiles back, the expression so patently false, and the doctor's smile falters for a moment. But then he carries on past. Sebastian pushes Isobel through the door into the stairwell and they start down.

On the ground floor, they move out of the stairwell into the wide corridor. Patients go wheeling by on gurneys, sprouting tubes from thin forearms and awkward noses, some talking to the porters in blue uniforms pushing them along, gurney wheels squeaking.

They move, Sebastian right up close. Her hip bumps his, and under different circumstances this all might be quite pleasant. Isobel can sense the power in him, his innate strength radiating from his fingertips, down her spine, in total possession of her. She is caught now between two powerful masters.

Towards the end of the corridor a voice rings out from behind:

"Isobel!"

They both go rigid. His fingers on the back of her neck bite deeper into her flesh. He guides her around to face whoever is calling. Fear brings a sour, bile-like taste to her mouth.

"Isobel."

It is Emma, an auxiliary from William Henry ward, a nice girl, recently qualified and still young enough not to be cynical. Isobel cannot risk anything happening to her, and she has no doubt that Sebastian's threat is genuine.

"We found one," Emma says, trotting up. She falters when she glances at Sebastian.

"Sorry?" Isobel's voice catches in her throat.

"Dialysis machine," prompts Emma, now openly looking at Sebastian, suspicion writ large across her face.

"Oh right. Great." Isobel's heart is hammering and her hands are thrust deep in the pockets of her uniform, fingers clenching and unclenching with nervous apprehension.

Emma is looking Sebastian up and down, clearly wondering who he is and Isobel feels the situation straying from the script, Emma getting ready to pose some difficult questions. Something about the whole scene is clearly wrong and Emma is perceptive; she can sometimes make a nuisance of herself.

"Could you grab it for me and get it down to the lab? I'll be along in a sec." Isobel smiles.

"Alright."

Emma hesitates and Isobel, improvising, suddenly says:

"This is Andrew."

Sebastian goes with the flow and smiles.

"Oh right." Emma's suspicion deflates in a moment. "Hello. We've all heard a great deal."

An awkward pause as the three of them face each other in the corridor. Emma clearly expects some kind of response from Sebastian, but he stands there silent, grinning, unwilling to get into a conversation with the possibility of tripping himself up and revealing the deception, having no idea who Andrew might be or what information Isobel may have given about him.

"Okay. Well, I'll let your patient know you'll be along in a mo." Emma turns to Sebastian. "Nice to meet you."

Isobel is propelled out of the corridor into the chaos of reception. The crowd at the outpatients counter is three deep and one skinny woman, a cluster of cheap gold chains around her scrawny neck, is having a loud argument with a terrified-looking lady in a duffle coat on the other side of the desk. People come and go and mill about and through them all Sebastian guides Isobel towards the door and no one takes any notice of them. As they pass the information desk the Salvation Army lady spots Sebastian and calls out,

"Take it you found her then."

Isobel looks to Sebastian, who is smiling and nodding to the lady. The security guard is also looking, following their progress with alert eyes, suddenly more awake and focused than he had been earlier. The glass doors swish open at their approach and snow and bitter cold air come whirling in.

Another security guard, this one older and sporting a hefty beer belly underneath his thick black coat, is hovering around Kenosha's Mercedes.

Sebastian beeps the doors open and guides Isobel towards the driver's seat.

"You'll have to move this car. You've been here too long.," the guard says. "Ten minutes only."

"We're just leaving," Sebastian replies, opening the passenger door.

The smoking group by the NO SMOKING sign is bigger now, an assorted collection of illnesses and conditions, watching with interest at this minor confrontation. Sebastian nods towards the sign and says to the guard:

"Why don't you enforce that instead of wasting your time with me?"

The guard turns to look at the sign as if seeing it for the first time and Sebastian gets in and pulls the door shut.

"Drive."

"I don't have the key," Isobel says quietly. She looks at Sebastian. A confused expression flutters across his face. Then he hands the key over.

Isobel gets the car started. She pulls away, following the one-way system around the hospital grounds, giving way to people at the zebra crossing, trying to maintain a degree of calm. In her ear Mr Punch whispers:

"Stay calm. You're doing well."

* * *

Sebastian's heart is racing and the gun in his hand is unsteady. He holds it down between his knees, out of sight of both Isobel and people on the street.

Isobel is driving calmly. She seems to have a high degree of self-control. Sebastian is impressed. But then she clubbed him in the head without revealing much in the way of nerves, so he isn't really surprised. Compared to last night, this should be a breeze.

They are cruising slowly around the hospital one-way system. There's a mini-roundabout just up ahead, and an exit from the hospital grounds. Sebastian tells her to take it and to be careful. Snow is still falling and the roads are treacherous, car tracks forming valleys through the mounting snow.

He grabs his phone and taps in the number.

"Kenosha."

"Yo, what's going on? Where are you?"

"Just left the hospital. Where am I going now?"

"Fuck should I know?"

Sebastian sighs. Sometimes Kenosha can be such a nightmare.

"The place, Kenosha, the one you said about. How do I get there?"

"Ah right. You're going there. Okay. Where are you now?"

"Just come out of the hospital, round the back."

"Okay, so go all the way down to the end of that road and turn right. Follow the road round the bends, looping around the back of the high street. The Co-Op should be on your right."

"Turn right at the end," Sebastian says to Isobel. She's cruising down the road slowly, carefully. Good girl.

Kenosha continues:

"There's traffic lights round the back of the Co-Op.. Get in the right-hand lane and turn right onto Canterbury Street. This cuts up through the middle of the high street. Up past the nightclub on your left is a little turning,

Green Street. Go along there and take the first turning on your left. Are you getting this?"

"Yes, I'm getting it. Then what?"

"Then that's it. The road'll bare right at ninety degrees. Follow it along to the end and park up. On your left will be fences and gates, the back of the shops in the high street. Get through a gate and up the stairs at the back and you'll be at the flats. From what I've been told, the walls have been knocked through inside, so the place is like a fucking rabbit warren. What's in there is anyone's guess. But no one will come looking for you."

"Thanks."

"No worries. And Sebastian…"

"Yeah?"

"Be nice to my car."

Isobel is following the road around the high street. Cheap-looking restaurants on the left and the public library on the right. A sharp bend in the road and some new-build flats on the corner, then a squalid-looking taxi office and on the right the back end of the Co-Op, a concrete slab chock-a-block with delivery trucks and rolling metal doors. Sebastian sees the traffic lights up ahead and tells Isobel to turn right. She pulls the car over into the right-hand lane, wheels spinning as they plough through snow into a new set of tracks. They wait at the red light. There's a chip shop on the corner, a guy out front sprinkling salt, trying to clear the pavement around the door. The windshield wipers thump and swish, sweeping the gently falling snow off the glass. Although the details are different, the situation is so close to the night before it sends shivers down Sebastian's spine.

"Where are we going?" Isobel asks.

"Not far."

"But where?"

"Somewhere anonymous."

Sebastian is beginning to have second thoughts about the wisdom of this. He's taking a hostage into a den of junkies, with no idea what awaits him, no clue as to how many people might be in there. There could be dealers who object to his presence. But is this likely? Addicts approach the dealers, not the other way around. But even so, this location is a complete unknown. It might be best to stay in the car, pulled up at the side of the road. But will Isobel be responsive to that? A lot of interrogation is about perception. She needs to believe that he has friends and resources. She needs to believe he is powerful.

The lights change green. Isobel is a little heavy on the gas and the wheels spin before biting. They drive up between the two halves of the high street, people waiting to cross on either side, dressed up against the weather, kids off school hurling snowballs through shop doors at the people browsing inside. The nightclub on the left is shut up and silent, the gaudy lights and neon sign dead in the grey daylight, and just beyond, the turning into Green Street.

"Left here."

Isobel swings the car into the tight little junction.

"Take the first left."

She makes the turn and sure enough, just as Kenosha said, the road bares round to the right, running along the back of the shops, flanked by a line of smashed and rotting fences, the flats above with broken and boarded windows.

Sebastian tells Isobel to stop and she guides the car over to the verge and switches off the engine.

"Give me the key."

Her hand is shaking when she passes it over. Good. Sebastian wants her to be afraid.

"Get out."

Isobel opens the door. Sebastian gets out at the same time. The gun is still in his hand and he makes sure Isobel sees it. He locks the car and nods towards the nearest gate on the other side of the narrow road.

"What's in there?" she asks. Her eyes are fearful, peeking out between curtains of blond hair hanging in front her face. She is shivering in her nurses uniform, arms crossed against her breasts. Sebastian has no sympathy, she set him up and put his life in jeopardy, but her vulnerability brings home the full implications of what he's set in motion.

What am I prepared to do if she doesn't talk willingly? The thought flashes through his mind, making him hesitate. How far am I willing to go?

Sebastian nods towards the gate:

"Move."

The gate is held erect by one remaining hinge, rusted black. Beyond, the backyard is full of weeds. Nettles poke out from the corners and rubbish and discarded junk is heaped all over the place. Just inside the gate, half buried in the snow, is a large pile of used condoms. Some pro must bring her tricks here during the night. A couple of shopping trolleys, a smashed computer and a filing cabinet, a bin bag full of swollen paperbacks – everything gradually buried, flake by pristine flake, as the snow falls silently from the gunmetal sky.

Sebastian follows Isobel, moving across the yard. At the back wall is a single flight of metal stairs, like a fire escape, leading up to a rickety-looking gantry running along to the door of the flat above. Sebastian prods Isobel with the silenced barrel of the pistol and she moves, climbing carefully, the snow-covered metal dangerous beneath her sensible shoes.

"Are you sure you want to do this? If you kill me here you'll never get away."

"Shut up and keep going."

They reach the top of the stairs and move along the gantry to the door. Below, all the neighbouring yards stretch out in a squalid line.

The door to the flat is solid wood, green paint bubbled and peeling, with the handle held in place by only one screw. The frame around the door is damaged, the wood split and splintered, as if someone in the past had wildly attempted to crowbar their way in. There is no window in the door, and Sebastian has no idea what may lurk behind it.

Isobel reaches for the door handle. Sebastian half expects it to be locked, but the handle turns and the door creaks inwards. Isobel looks over her shoulder at Sebastian.

"Go on," he says, with as much confidence as he can muster.

Isobel steps over the threshold. Sebastian follows, closing the door behind him.

9

They stand just inside the doorway, a thin corridor stretching before them. There is something rotten inside this flat, putrefying, turning the air thick and sickly. Sebastian's eyes adjust to the dim light – peeling flower-patterned wallpaper, skirting boards black with grime, an empty light socket dangling from a ceiling covered in polystyrene tiles. There's a doorway on the left and then another at the end of the corridor. A flight of stairs leads up to an attic room.

Sebastian shoves Isobel along the corridor. The carpet underfoot is sticky and sucks at his boots. The air is barely warmer than outside, and his breath mists before his eyes. Isobel is shivering, her arms wrapped about herself. Her white uniform is the brightest thing in the miserable light.

The first doorway opens into a small kitchen. Lank curtains cover the window, stuck to the glass with filth. Utensils litter the sink and draining board, festering and teeming with life, flies and ants and wriggling maggots. The stench is appalling and Isobel gags. Black and white chequered lino on the floor, smeared with grease and food, everything congealed into a rank wet mass. There are no doors on the cupboards and no drawer-fronts on the units. The place is ransack and ruin. The putrid foodstuffs and wriggling life makes Sebastian feel like he's in the belly of a living creature, the festering shit-riddled insides of some great slopping monster. A cream-coloured fridge rusting against the far wall produces a low level hum, not electrical, something else. Sebastian wonders if it is somehow full of flies.

They go deeper along the hallway, to the doorway at the end. The room, occupying the back of the flat, is equally nasty. At one time it would have been the main living space. The patterned wallpaper is all but invisible beneath grime and incoherent graffiti tags both sprayed and etched into the walls. Sebastian can make out maybe one word in ten – inane obscenities directed at who knows what. Rotting planks have been haphazardly hammered over the window, thin strips of watery light lance between the boards, catching dust in narrow beams and casting subtle shadows over a carpet so thick with filth Sebastian's boots actually sink through it.

A ragged hole has been sledgehammered in the wall to the left. Discarded masonry and crumbling lumps of plaster are strewn about the floor.

Sebastian gestures for Isobel to step through the hole into the flat next door. As she moves, he glances through a gap between the boards blocking the window, looking down into the high street below. The snow is criss-crossed with footsteps. Shoppers shuffle along, braving the weather in coats, scarfs and hats.

Sebastian follows Isobel through the hole into the flat next door. The room beyond is almost exactly the same as the one they just left, except for two major details: dirty floorboards instead of filthy carpet, and half a dozen occupants. Sat on the floor around the room, propped up against the wall or slumped over on their sides, wraiths and retches, mostly bundled in threadbare clothing, all but one unconscious. A woman, impossible to tell her age, sits with her chin on her chest, the front of her coat decorated with a foul river of vomit. A guy is slumped with his head tipped back, his mouth filled with black crumbling teeth, eyes rolled back in his head showing the whites, and a face so haggard you might think he was dead, if not for the faint wisps of his breath, clouding and dispersing. A girl shivers in nothing but knickers and vest. She hugs her knees, her twig-like arms livid with welts and scratches, bright and seeping puncture marks at the top of her shrunken thighs. She looks up at Sebastian and Isobel with vacant eyes.

The sight of the girl hits him like a hammer. What happened to the dreams she had as a child? While he fights to save his life, she's working on destroying hers. How far is she complicit in her fate, how much of a victim? Perhaps I should ask Isobel the same question, Sebastian wonders.

Or even myself.

He shoves Isobel onwards, out into the hallway. This flat is identical to the first, but all in reverse, the stairs up to an attic room on the left instead of the right, the kitchen on the right instead of the left. There is another hole, in the hallway wall this time, hammered through to the third flat along. Sebastian has no idea how many of these flats have been knocked through, or how many people are in this rabbit warren, and he doesn't really know what he's looking for either, just somewhere that feels right.

He climbs through the hole after Isobel into the third flat. Piles of rubble on the floor threaten to upset his balance as he steps through. The décor is becoming repetitive, the stench familiar. But the noise however, is different. From the big room at the end of the corridor come mumbled voices, low moans, and the occasional gasp. There are more occupants in this flat, but Sebastian cannot tell how many.

Isobel looks at him, and he tries to dispel the uncertainty flooding through him. The fear he hoped to instil is waning. It is obvious he doesn't really have a plan.

"Get moving," Sebastian whispers. He gestures with the gun down the hallway.

Isobel holds his gaze a moment longer, then turns and moves silently towards the room at the end. She pauses at the threshold.

"Dear Christ," Isobel whispers.

An older man wearing a filthy black suit, stained and worn shiny at elbows and knees, is heating a spoon over a primer stove, a needle clamped between his teeth and all but lost in the tangles of his massive, matted beard. A woman, barely twenty years old, is naked beneath an old duffle coat. She straddles an unconscious man, her narrow hips grinding pathetically against him, weak hands struggling to keep the coat closed against the cold. Her eyes are glazed and her lips split and bleeding, cold sores or herpes rupturing at the corners of her mouth. The man between her legs is a pale smear of flesh on the filthy floorboards, his eyes rolled back in his head and a thin line of drool winding down his cheek to pool on the floor. His arms, stretched out above his head, are cross-hatched with old scars around the wrists. His ribcage seems to pulse against his skin as his rapid shallow breath whistles in and out through his dry, grey lips. A fresh pile of shit steams in the far corner. The reek of human decline is pungent. Sebastian's free hand covers his nose.

The man in the suit looks up.

Sebastian points the pistol at him. He is muttering to himself, the words forced out from behind the needle clamped between his teeth, coming fast but unintelligible, his big beard twitching. His black sunken eyes register no emotion as he looks down the long and silenced barrel of the gun.

Isobel is transfixed by the woman with her duffle coat, the sheer hopelessness of her pleasure in this squalid liaison written large across her ruined face. She seems oblivious to everything around her, lost to the heroin fugue and perhaps the distant pleasure of the man beneath her.

The man in the suit drops his eyes, his attention returning to his cooking.

Sebastian nudges Isobel. They move across the room and step through the wall into the fourth flat along.

The big room at the back of the fourth flat is deserted. One of the panes in the big window overlooking the high street down below is broken. Glass glints wickedly on the black carpet. Snow blows in through the window, carried on a cold breeze that is fresh and invigorating after the fetid stench next door.

They move into the hallway. The flight of stairs leading up to the attic room ascends not into darkness but daylight. Sebastian motions Isobel to climb. The banister is rickety and the stairs creak. At the top an open door leads into a large attic space. A small bay window juts out from the sloping ceiling, the glass dirty but unbroken, letting in stone grey light. Mildewed beams rise and meet overhead. Filthy floorboards groan underfoot and in the corner under the eaves lies a double mattress, stained yellow with old sweat. Little puffs of dust explode up from their shoes as Sebastian pushes Isobel into the room. This place will do, and the creaking stairs will announce the arrival of any visitors.

"Sit down."

Isobel doesn't move. She stands in the centre of the room, arms crossed, shivering in the cold. She looks at Sebastian through the curtains of her hair, dark circles under her eyes, a picture of anguish and upset. She looks about ready to burst into tears. Sebastian shoves her over to the mattress.

"Sit!"

This time she does as instructed, perching herself on the edge, knees drawn up to her chest like the young girl in her underwear a couple of flats along.

Sebastian takes a moment to gather his thoughts. Most soldiers are never trained in interrogation techniques and he has no idea how best to proceed, other than pointing the gun at her and demanding she answers his questions. But what if she refuses to answer them? He doesn't want to hurt her. He probably couldn't bring himself to do it even if he wanted to. But she doesn't know that. It's the only card he has to play.

Suddenly, Sebastian is overcome by a sudden, powerful urge to laugh. This time yesterday he was expecting to make a routine delivery and earn a chunk of money. Now he's in a junky hellhole with a hostage and three dead men on his conscience. He's been knocked out, raped, and if he can't find the cargo he was supposed to deliver, a bounty will be placed on his head and he'll be dead. He can hardly comprehend the speed with which his life has been turned upside down. Standing here, pointing a silenced pistol at this wretched, shivering woman at his feet, Sebastian is overcome by the feeling that none of this is real, that he's somehow fallen into a dream.

"Can I wake up, please?"

He didn't mean to say it out loud. Isobel looks up at him. With his lips twitching as he fights the urge to laugh, he suddenly looks insane.

"I don't know anything."

"The hell you don't."

"I don't."

"Why did you knock me out?"

"I had to. I had no choice."

Sebastian crouches down so that he is eye level with Isobel. He puts the barrel of the gun against her forehead. With the silencer attached, it seems enormous so close to her face. Sebastian shudders to think of the shattering power of it, the mess it would make of her if he were to pull the trigger. He struggles to stop his hand from shaking.

"Explain," he says.

"There's nothing to say. I did what I did because I had no choice."

"Who gave you no choice?"

"I don't know."

"How can you not fucking know?"

"A guy. Just a voice on the phone. I don't know who he is."

"Have you ever met him?"

"No."

"Seen him? Know what he looks like? Know where he lives?"

"No. Nothing."

"You fucking with me?" He shoves her head backwards with the gun, pushing her back on the mattress, kneeling above her.

Isobel shrieks, then stammers, "I'm telling the truth. I don't know anything about him. He calls me and tells me where to go, what to do. That's it. That's all."

"Why don't you tell him to go fuck himself?"

"Because..." She pauses, wide frightened eyes staring straight up into his. "Because he terrifies me."

Sebastian backs off, getting up off the mattress and going over to the far side of the room, giving Isobel some space. He glances out of the window. When he turns back she seems a little more composed.

"Who was the woman at the hotel?"

She looks back at him blankly.

"After you knocked me out, I woke up in a hotel room. A woman there who... disappeared?"

Isobel is shaking her head before he finishes speaking.

"I don't know. I don't know what happens after. I never saw who came to take you away from the river. I've no idea what happened to you. You're the first one to come looking. You're the first to live through the night."

"There have been others?"

"Yes," she says quietly.

"How many?"

"I don't know. Some. They usually turn up in the river a few weeks later."

This comes as a shock. Sebastian had been operating under the assumption that for whatever reason, this was all about the cargo. But Isobel's revelation implies some other motive, something beyond the theft of his employer's merchandise, whatever it is.

"What happened to the car I was driving?"

"I drove it away."

"Where?"

"Some house, some street. I was told to drop it off and walk away."

"What about the bag on the back seat?"

"What bag? I never saw a bag."

"A holdall. Large. Heavy. You never picked it up?"

"No."

"Are you fucking lying to me?" Sebastian walks back over to her, raising the gun. Theatrics.

"I'm not lying." Her voice barely above a whisper, eyes downcast and staring at the floorboards.

"I believe you."

And he does. Her story tallies with Daniel's from last night: instructions from an anonymous voice, and the threat of violence if they're not carried out. It seems unlikely, but Daniel was clearly no hardened criminal and if two bullets in his legs didn't loosen his tongue, then there was nothing more to tell. Isobel may be manipulative, but he has no reason to doubt the essence of her story.

"The people who own the bag are going to kill me if I don't get it back for them."

"Who are they?"

Sebastian sighs, sitting down on the floor.

"Just like you I serve anonymous masters. I was supposed to hand it over last night. That's why I said I had to be somewhere."

"But instead I knocked you out."

"And I woke up in some hotel room."

"What happened?"

He hesitates before answering, not wanting to admit he was raped, not sure that allowing her to ask questions is a good idea.

"There was a woman. She helped me and then left. After that two guys came in. I killed them."

Isobel is looking at him intently, a question in her eyes. Sebastian wonders how she came to be involved in all of this. But he mustn't let his thoughts idle. Isobel has at least given him another lead to chase. But what does he do with her now? He should let he go, but he still needs her help, and although he believes her story, or lack of one, he cannot be sure that she won't somehow betray him again. Warrington once said that the mark of a good soldier is the ability to make decisions under pressure, to be mindful of all the variables in any given moment and to act strategically.

"Do you know his name?"

"Who?"

"The guy on the phone, the one you're afraid of."

Isobel shakes her head.

"I just think of him as Mr Punch."

Isobel stares into his eyes. She tucks her hair behind her ear. She turns her face to the side; then she turns back to Sebastian. Her action is slow and deliberate, loaded with meaning.

For a moment her behaviour seems surreal to Sebastian and he looks at her uncomprehendingly. But then a fist clenches in his guts as realisation dawns.

He raises the gun.

Tears spill from Isobel's eyes.

"Help me!" she says, but silently, her mouth forming the words without sound. She turns her head to the side again. The earpiece is discreet but clearly visible.

She's been wired this whole time.

The realisation hits Sebastian like a hammer. Someone has been listening, watching, like the webcam back at the hotel.

Sebastian's eyes bore into Isobel's. Far from being some kind of enemy, her silent pleading is so naked and desperate, he can't think of her now as anything but a victim.

Isobel's eyes flick downward, once, twice. What is she trying to say?

Whoever Mr Punch is, he is here in this room. He's heard everything. He must have anticipated the move on Isobel. Sebastian has just been played.

Once again she's suckered me. You idiot! Sebastian curses himself. That's why she's been so cooperative. She's under orders.

Isobel flicks her eyes downwards again. Sebastian notices the black button on her tunic. Is that what she's indicating?

But then a sudden, inexplicable shout rings out in the silence, coming from somewhere down below.

Sebastian and Isobel go rigid.

Listen.

There is a creak, from the stairs just beyond the doorway. Someone has found them. Someone is coming.

Sebastian puts a finger to his lips.

He points the gun at Isobel and mouths the words:

Don't. Fucking. Move.

She's stitched him up again, good and proper this time. Should I have seen this coming? he wonders. It doesn't matter now. The fight is here and he'll either live through it or die.

Back up against the wall. Gun extended to the open doorway. Patient.

There is another creak from the stairs, closer to the door.

Isobel waits nervously at the opposite side of the room, by the window. Whoever comes through the door will see her first.

It suddenly occurs to Sebastian that with Isobel standing there, Mr Punch can probably see him with his back pressed against the wall, waiting by the door.

Is Mr Punch in real-time contact with those coming up the stairs? If so they already know where he is. Too late to worry about it now. But he needs to get Isobel free of the surveillance as soon as possible. Look at her standing by the window, her white nurse's tunic, with the obvious black button. It's got to be that.

Another creak from the stairs. Whoever he is, he's right at the top now, just around the corner. Without making a sound Sebastian drops low.

The doorway is at the top of the stairs. You can look around the corner before you've reached the top step, giving you a worm's eye view.

Silence.

The gun in Sebastian's hand is shaking.

Then: a shaggy blond head pokes around the corner and is gone. Too quick for Sebastian to react, too fast for whoever it was to see much of anything – the actions of a nervous man, a sign of inexperience.

The blood is hammering through Sebastian's veins. He wills himself to be calm, to control his breathing, to stay focused.

The shaggy blond head reappears, low down, close to the floor. Sebastian reacts cat-quick and drops the silenced barrel into that mass of hair. The head goes rigid, then slowly turns, looking up at Sebastian.

Young blue eyes set in an undistinguished face, early twenties, unshaved. He does not look like the sort of man who'd willingly work for a criminal organisation.

"How many?" Sebastian whispers.

"Lots," he whispers back. His blue eyes cross as he tries to look at the silenced barrel pressed against his forehead.

"Where?"

"All over. Searching."

"How many behind you?"

He shakes his head. He doesn't know.

Lots.

No chance to get away without violence. Indecision makes Sebastian hesitate. Is the young man a victim like Isobel? Afraid? Manipulated?

Warrington's voice echoes through his mind: *A good soldier must act!*

Sebastian pulls the trigger.

The silencer takes the sting out of the gunshot. The boy's blond curls explode across the floorboards, lurid crimson.

Isobel shrieks.

Sebastian stands up. He takes a quick peak through the doorway and down the stairs. There is nobody there. He grabs the boy by the shoulders and hauls him into the room, leaving the stairs unblocked.

"Oh Christ." Isobel is bent over, trying not to heave.

In the boy's dead hand is a high-calibre revolver.

"We need to move." Sebastian's voice trembles, his hands shake, his pulse is slamming in his temples, the blood rushing through his veins. Adrenalin is focusing his perception. His breathing is too fast. *Control. Stay in control.*

Isobel is shaking her head. Sebastian suddenly sees an opportunity. He grabs her by the front of her uniform and yanks her close, ripping off the button as he does so. He flings it across the room into the wall and in the same action belts her forcefully up the side of her head with the flat of his hand, knocking the earpiece free. He shoves her back against the wall and moves in close, deliberately stepping on the device, hearing it crunch beneath his boot.

Isobel is trembling, one hand pressed against the side of her head. She's hurt, but there is relief in her eyes.

Time to get out.

Isobel has given him another lead to pursue, another hope along the road, but only if they make it out of this warren alive.

Lots.

"Whatever happens, stay close to me."

Isobel nods. She hugs herself, shivering, close to shock. Her eyes stray to the boy, his blond hair, blood and brains on the floorboards by the door.

Sebastian edges back along the wall and peeks around the doorframe, aiming the pistol down the stairwell, keeping his body mostly in the attic room and hidden, presenting as small a target as possible.

Everything below is completely silent. He flashbacks through the journey they took through the warren: four flats, each one the mirror image of the one preceding it. At the bottom of the these stairs the hallway runs along to the main door, beyond which there should be some means of getting down to the ground and out to the street.

Whether or not Kenosha's car is still there is another matter.

Isobel creeps up behind him.

Sebastian is searching for the slightest movement, the slightest fluctuation in light or shadow, anything that might give away the enemy.

Nothing.

He takes a deep breath, holds for a count of three, then starts down the stairs with Isobel fast on his heels.

10

Treading lightly, Sebastian descends. Everything is silent and still. The door to the outside at the end of the hallway is tantalizingly close. Isobel is right behind him.

The steps begin to creak.

Sebastian hesitates for just a moment, his breath caught in his throat. But they are past the point of no return

At the bottom of the stairs, Sebastian points the gun down the hallway towards the room at the back. Isobel moves behind him.

"Back up, towards the door," Sebastian whispers.

They retreat along the hallway, their footsteps silent on the muck-layered carpet.

The door to the outside is closed. Isobel reaches out to grab the handle, but there are noises from the other side: whispered voices, the soft impact of shoes on the metal gantry. The door creaks as someone leans their weight against it.

Sebastian grabs Isobel, dragging her away as the handle turns and the door swings slowly open. With the gun pointing past Isobel's shoulder, his finger tight against the trigger, Sebastian hustles them back along the hallway, past the bottom of the stairs, towards the kitchen and the big room at the back of the flat.

The door creaks on its rusty hinges and bumps gently into the wall. Light streams into the hallway. A fleeting shadow moves across the opening.

A pale, scared face peeks around the corner.

Sebastian fires once and the gun bucks in his hand. Despite the silencer the shot seems loud. But the face is gone and the bullet slams into the wall. There is a sudden black hole in the plaster at the centre of a fractured web; a slowly dispersing mushroom of dust drifts across the daylight flooding through the open door.

Something about the bullet hole brings reality crashing into Sebastian in a way the dead blond boy didn't. Gripped suddenly by a fist of panic he turns and grabs Isobel by the collar of her uniform and propels her down the hallway and into the kitchen, ducking through the door just as returning gunfire opens up from behind.

Bullets slam into the walls and into the stairs and whiz past the kitchen door as the assailant blind-fires down the hallway. Concussive blasts rip through the air, the tight confines of the flat containing and amplifying the noise, loud enough for Sebastian to feel it in his chest as well as deafening his ears.

Isobel crouches down in the far corner of the kitchen, hands over her head, screaming. Sebastian is taking cover just inside the doorway, hoping that the walls at his back are load bearing and brick instead of lathe and plaster.

And then silence.

It takes Sebastian a few seconds to realise, his ears ringing in the aftermath, but the gunshots have stopped. The air is thick with plaster dust. Each lungful of oxygen feels like it's scratching his airways. The ache in his ribs is back already.

He leans out into the hallway, sighting down towards the open front door. The first guy bursts in and Sebastian takes him out – double shots, *thump-thump* – blood misting as he drops, and there's another one close behind already shooting. Sebastian ducks back inside the kitchen as the doorframe explodes.

Sebastian is working hard to control his breathing, and to control the jitters in his hands. Whoever these guys are they're not taking any chances.

The gunfire stops. Without knowing how, Sebastian can sense the shooter right by the doorway, on the opposite side of the wall, practically back to back, just a brick's width apart.

He's waiting for me to poke my head out. Sebastian knows this because that's what he would do. How long will he wait before impatience gets the better of him? How long until more of them turn up?

The kitchen doorway is full of dust, and if not for the ringing in his ears Sebastian would be able to hear the nervous breathing of the guy on the other side of the wall.

Then the assailant's gun hand pokes around the doorway. He blind-fires a single shot, sending Isobel ducking for cover, before Sebastian puts a round through his hand.

Screams.

The gun is dropped and Sebastian moves into the doorway and shoots the man once in the face. He falls, the centre of his face punched in by the bullet.

Hideous. The stuff of nightmares.

The man is wearing some kind of shop uniform, as if he got involved in the gunfight on his way to work.

Sebastian turns back to Isobel. She's crouched in the opposite corner, shaking but unhurt.

Three down.

Instinct tells him to forget about the front door and move back the way they came through the flats instead. He hoists Isobel to her feet. Despite her shivering, her eyes are focused.

"We're not dead yet. Stay close."

He pats his pocket, checking for the pump. But he doesn't want to use it yet. This could get a lot worse before it gets better.

Sebastian steps out into the hallway. Two dead men here and one above. That makes six in total, and for a moment Sebastian feels vindicated. *Fucking Warrington. I wish you could see me now.*

Moving with purpose he enters the room at the back of the flat. Beyond the window the snow is still falling. Sebastian crosses the room towards the hole in the wall.

A man bursts through the hole right on top of him. He's too sudden and too close for Sebastian to have time to shoot. The collision knocks the gun from his hand and he's propelled backwards as the man comes in through the hole. Sebastian looses his footing and drops to one knee. The man, realising he has the upper hand, backs off and raises his gun, just millimetres from Sebastian's face.

Isobel barrels into the guy, knocking him off balance. The shot goes wide. He turns on her, about to fire again, but Sebastian is quick, instinct giving his movements a fluidity he couldn't possibly equal if he had time to think about it.

The man, caught unexpectedly, moves to adapt his aim but he's too slow and Sebastian, rising up to full height, jabs him in the eyes with his fingertips, and as the man stumbles backwards Sebastian draws the second gun from the waistband of his jeans and shoots him point blank.

The man drops like a stone.

Sebastian turns back to check on Isobel. She has picked up his dropped gun. She releases the clip to check its load, slams it back into the grip and chambers a round.

Sebastian puts his back to the wall on one side of the hole. Isobel takes up the same position on the opposite side.

The man Sebastian just shot is sprawled on his back, a red stain spreading across his chest. The gunshot may not be fatal. Sebastian doesn't know enough about wounds to make a guess. There is a wet whistling noise as the man hitches in little ragged breaths. It reminds Sebastian of his own ragged and rapid breathing. He looks over at Isobel. She watches, transfixed, as the man struggles to live.

Sebastian glances through the hole in the wall. The bearded guy and the couple fucking are all still in the room. Beard is up on his feet now, a giant of a man, his filthy suit stretched taught over a barrel chest, cuffs halfway up his forearms. He's stomping around the room with a blank expression on his face. The woman is still grinding away against the guy between her legs. He appears a little more animated now, his spidery fingers pinching the tight flesh of her narrow thighs. The woman's eyes are shut, her split lips stretched around the *oh* of her pleasure, completely oblivious.

Why haven't they run? Maybe they're so fucked up they haven't even noticed the gunfight. Sebastian steps through the hole and Isobel follows. Beard stops moving. The vacant expression in his small black eyes suddenly vanishes as he spies Isobel. Inexplicably, he bows low, almost mockingly formal is if in parody of a period drama.

"Top of the morning to you." His once deep voice is ragged and watery; thick frozen lips mangle the vowels and the great twists of beard muffle the volume. But still, his intervention is so unexpected that after a moment of shocked silence a smile breaks across Isobel's face.

A gunshot rings out from the hallway and splinters the boards over the window. Sebastian and Isobel drop low and scurry out of the line of fire as another shot rifles through the door, this time striking the wall closer to the fucking couple. Taking cover against the wall, a few feet from the doorway to the hall, Isobel and Sebastian press in close together.

Strategically, they're finished. They can't go forwards. Rushing up the hallway would be suicide. The only option is to retreat or wait for the assailants to break cover. But if they wait, they could be flanked. One assailant only needs to go outside and come back in through the flat they just left, and they'll be hit from two sides.

Beard is still standing in the middle of the room, a look of fury distorting his face, heavy brows coming together. A guy of his size, mashed on whatever he's plunging into his veins, is a danger and an unknown variable. Sebastian can feel the situation unravelling fast.

"Stay calm," he whispers, to himself as well as Isobel.

In the ringing silence following the gunshots Sebastian can make out whispered voices in heated conversation. The voices are too low, or his ears too deafened by the gunfire, to hear the words, or even distinguish one from another. Sebastian drops low, creeps to the end of the wall by the hallway door, and takes a quick peek.

Three at least, one in the kitchen doorway, one on the stairs to the attic and one in a vulnerable position in the hallway itself, close to the hole in the wall that leads into the next flat.

Sebastian takes a second to control his breathing, holding the image of them frozen in his head. He breaks cover, moving fast across the doorway, *thump-thump*, *thump-thump*, two shots at the vulnerable guy, who drops, two at the guy on the stairs, who's already ducking for cover. Both those shots slam into the wall, leaving two little puffs of plaster dust hovering in the air.

Sebastian is across the doorway, hunkered in the narrow corner of the room directly behind the staircase as the two remaining gunmen open fire in return. Isobel holds fast on her side of the doorway.

Beard is hit, once, twice, three times, his body rocking back but not going down, bellowing pain and fury at those shooting into the room.

A pause in the gunfire and a moment later the gunmen rush the room, bursting through the doorway, taking Sebastian and Isobel by surprise.

Sebastian drops low as they open up, bullets thudding into the wall where his head and chest would have been. He shoots back straight away. Isobel does the same from the other side of the room. One man is hit from two sides, his body contorting before dropping to the floor.

Beard grabs the other man, his huge hands whirling the guy around and flinging him against the wall. The man is yelling and firing crazily and Beard's barrel chest bursts open but he keeps coming, the drugs in his system somehow keep him moving. He's dead already but he doesn't know it. The guy's gun is empty now, just a dry-firing click as the hammer rises and falls. Beard takes the man by the collar of his overalls and with the last of his strength hurls him at the splintered boards over the window. The man crashes through with a shriek and drops out of sight.

Snow billows in on the breeze and Beard sinks to his knees, dead. Distant screams rise from below as shoppers down in the high street react to the fallen man.

The woman in her duffle coat is dead and slumped, bleeding on the man she was fucking, who is now struggling to pull himself from under her body, the chaos and death finally penetrating his fugue.

Sebastian pulls Isobel from the room and out into the hallway, gun up and searching for targets, but his hand is shaking something fierce and he can't remember how many bullets he's fired. His breathing has lost its rhythm, hitching through his lungs in ragged little gasps.

The dead man in the hallway is painfully young, still in his teens, wearing an ill-fitting suit that perhaps his mother said he would grow in to, maybe a first-year college student on work experience.

Sebastian yanks at the main door at the end of the hallway but it's locked or stuck and they can't get out. No choice but to go through the hole into the next flat.

They stumble through into flat number two. This one Sebastian can easily remember; there were half a dozen people in the room at the end of the hall.

Their footsteps sound muffled on the dusty hallway floorboards, their ears still ringing from the gunshots. The stairs just in front ascend into darkness. There could be anyone waiting up there. Sebastian darts his head into the kitchen as they make their way along the hallway to the front door. They're staying bunched up and close together now, moving fast and struggling to resist the temptation just to bolt for the open in a last, desperate effort to get clear.

Panic will get you killed.

Warrington's voice is in Sebastian's head as he pulls open the main door. Light floods in. But this time there is no metal gantry and no steps down to the yard, just a fifteen-foot drop with a couple of smashed televisions and what looks like a ceiling fan waiting below. The jump wouldn't be so bad if there was a flat surface to land on.

Cursing, Sebastian pulls the door closed. Isobel, right behind, is about to ask, but Sebastian shakes his head.

"No stairs. We can't make the jump." The words are hard to control through his wheezing. He is feeling the strain now – battle fatigue and creeping nerves. After the initial rush comes the doubts: are we actually going to make it out? But he can't allow his thoughts to wander. Doubts will get them killed too.

"We'll go out the way we came in. It's the next flat along." His voice is nothing but a dry whisper.

They start down the hallway, cautiously, past the kitchen to the room at the end, and the hole in the wall to the next and last flat.

The room is empty, the junkies that were here before have scattered. The boarded window leaks light, narrow beams capturing little plumes of dust spiralling up from their careful footsteps. Sebastian has a two-handed grip on his gun, raised high and sighted. His nerves are wound tight and the muscles in his arms and shoulders are vibrating with tension. He is painfully aware of how the gun barrel is waving subtly in the air, knowing that the longer this takes the less effective he's becoming. Isobel is in equally bad shape, her aim just as unsteady. She looks about ready to collapse, all colour drained from her face.

They press themselves against the wall, to the side of the hole. The rubble underfoot is precarious. The flat on the other side is where they came in. The way out is tantalizingly close. The sounds coming from down in the high street are quickly escalating. The fight, and the man who fell from the window, will be drawing lots of attention. Time is running out for them to get away clean.

Sebastian grabs the asthma pump and takes a deep hit. The familiar action alone and the sense of comfort and safety that comes with it is enough to take the edge off his immediate anxiety. He lets the breath go slowly, a long, deep exhalation. The scratch in his lungs subsides just a little.

Isobel, pressed in tightly behind, is looking at him with a blank expression. Sebastian can feel her body trembling. He leans out and takes a glance through the hole into the flat next door.

The girl wearing just a vest and knickers is kneeling in the centre of the room, shivering with her thin arms crossed against her breasts. The man standing behind her is wearing a charcoal grey suit with subtle pin striping. He looks like a city professional, with clipped fingernails and a neat haircut – successful, wise, sympathetic. He wears delicate rimless glasses and looks as if he belongs behind a desk in a bank. The gun he is pointing at the back of the girl's head is chrome plated and embossed with a skull and crossbones, the type of gun a gangbanger in some LA suburb would literally kill for.

Again, Sebastian wonders how these people came to work as henchmen for a criminal outfit. The bank manager is clearly terrified. His hand is shaking so much he's pushing the gun into the girl's lank hair to keep it steady. The girl, head down, is muttering under her breath. She is so painfully thin it's a wonder she's alive.

"Sebastian," the guy calls out, his voice high-pitched and trembling with fear. "Come out or I'll shoot."

Motivated more by fear than anything else, and without consciously thinking about it, Isobel leans into Sebastian's ear and whispers, "He got that from a film."

Stunned by her intervention, Sebastian looks back at her, and then he snorts with laughter as all the tension of the previous minutes suddenly collapses inside him. It takes him a few seconds to get control of himself before he calls out: "What do you want?"

"I need you to come out Sebastian. I… I can't let you get of here."

This is starting to feel like a stand-off, but Sebastian doesn't have the time to mess around. The banker might have reinforcements on the way. That could be the plan, stall for time until others arrive. Whether true or not, the authorities are definitely on the way.

The girl kneeling before the banker is only small. He's left the top part of himself fully exposed.

"Why not let us walk out and we can all go home?"

"I can't, I can't let you leave. Come out or I'll shoot the girl."

"Will you really?"

"Yes."

"Do you know what happens when you shoot a girl in the head, point blank like that? Do you know how much of a mess her brains'll make on the carpet in there? You'll get her blood on your posh suit."

He laughs nervously and shouts, "I'll fucking do it Sebastian. I really will."

Isobel is looking at him intently, her arms crossed over her breasts, the gun clutched in her fist and pointing at the ceiling. She is shivering with shock or from the cold. Her pale face is drawn and haggard and her eyes are huge and frightened. There is a striking similarity between her and the girl kneeling on the other side of the wall. But at the same time, Isobel seems calm, focused and in the moment. She is waiting for him to do something.

The banker is still babbling away, but Sebastian tunes him out and takes a breath. He darts out and squeezes off a single shot, hitting the banker in the chest. The man staggers back away from the girl and Sebastian fires again, *thump-thump*, hitting him in the chest and the face. He collapses down, gun still held tightly in his fist, body twitching.

Sebastian steps through the hole and pulls the girl to her feet. He presses her against the wall, keeping her out of the way. Isobel follows him through and they take up position on either side of the doorway leading into the hall.

They wait, and everything is silent and still. That rich and putrid smell seeps through the air from the kitchen.

He moves out into the hallway towards the kitchen, foul and rotting but clear of assailants. He edges further on along the hall, and gently opens the door at the far end. Stone grey light floods in.

Outside, everything is deathly still and quiet; snow whirls lazily through the air. The gantry is clear and he can't see anyone waiting in the yard below.

Sebastian glances back along the hallway. The girl in her vest and knickers is stood in the doorway of the big room, looking back at him with serene eyes. She raises a hand and waves. Isobel waves back.

Sebastian steps out into the cold morning, moving swiftly along the gantry and down the stairs into the yard. He can sense Isobel right on his heels. The temptation to throw caution to the wind and just sprint for the car is huge, and takes a conscious effort to keep in check.

They back up against the yard fence.

Listen.

Nothing.

Sebastian nudges the gate open and takes a quick look. No movement, but plenty of hiding places in the street beyond.

He steps out through the gate into the street. No one shoots. He crosses to the car, digging for the key in his pocket, the gun still held and ready, his senses firing, totally alert, heart hammering and lungs constricted.

The car beeps open and he yanks the door handle and gets in. Isobel gets in the passenger side.

Sebastian is expecting bullets to suddenly riddle the side of the car. But nothing moves except the falling snow. He starts the car and pulls away gently, the wheels spinning for a second before finding purchase.

He cannot believe they are still alive.

11

As the morning unwinds towards afternoon, the snow becomes heavier, drifting down from low-slung clouds. The weather causes chaos on the roads. Busy at the best of times, they are now clogged with long lines of stalled traffic, bumper to bumper, exhausts belching steam into the cold air. Bluebell Hill is impassable, a jack-knifed lorry backing up traffic all the way down Maidstone Road and under the viaduct. Carefully moving cars struggle along Dock Road, gradually stacking up too. Everyone is desperate to get home before night falls.

Sebastian, frustrated by slow-moving traffic and treacherous conditions, wants to stamp the gas and accelerate, all his instincts screaming to put as much distance between them and the carnage back at the flats as possible.

He swings around the roundabout and heads down towards the dockyard. Although his knowledge of the town isn't great, he does know that the Medway tunnel and the motorway are in this direction, giving them the ability to run if needs be. If the traffic allows.

He checks the mirrors every few seconds, wondering about a tail. An armoured truck filled with mercenaries brandishing automatic weapons wouldn't surprise him at this point.

Sitting next to him, Isobel is still shivering, her face turned to the window and her body curled up on the seat. She is still holding the gun tightly in her hands.

Up ahead is another roundabout. To the left is the Odeon cinema, Dickens World, and the Dockside Outlet Centre. To the right is the university, and straight over is the exit into the Medway Tunnel and St Mary's Island. Despite what his instincts might say, Sebastian knows he cannot run. To do so will only draw out his death. His employers will find him, of that he has no doubt. He must stay in town and fight this thing out to the end. Isobel has given him his next move. It may not produce anything useful, but he must follow it up. He has nothing else.

Sebastian turns left. He guides the car into the car park of the shopping centre and pulls into a space, tucked away at the back. He turns off the ignition. The windshield wipers cease their arcs, returning to the bottom of the screen. Snow settles on the windscreen, gradually obscuring the view. The engine ticks as it cools.

Sebastian is in bad shape. He wheezes painfully and he suddenly feels dog-tired. His hands are shaking.

Isobel stirs in her seat, turning her head to meet Sebastian's eyes. They stare at each other in silence for a few moments. Then Isobel turns away.

"Can I have that, please?" Sebastian indicates the gun in her hands.

Isobel stairs at the pistol as if seeing it for the first time. She hands it over, and Sebastian tucks it into his jacket pocket. Then he leans over and grabs a fistful of Isobel's hair, exposing her ear. He roughly turns her head to check the other one. Then he starts patting at her clothes, his shaking hands dragging across her nurses uniform, feeling for a wire.

Isobel fights back. She strikes out at his face, fists clenched, socking him straight in the eye. Sebastian is instantly quelled, stunned by her decisiveness.

Isobel glares at him

"You finished? There's nothing else."

"You fucking set me up. Twice."

"It wasn't me."

"Of course not."

"You still don't get it, do you? I'm a nurse. A *nurse*! And look at what I've done to you. Is that because I'm a maniac? Or evil? Of course not. It's because I'm a coward and I'm afraid of what he'll do to me if I disobey."

"I'm not buying it. You can't just turn ordinary people into killers."

Isobel barks a short laugh.

"You don't know anything."

"Who is he, Isobel?"

"I don't know." Isobel sighs. "He's been in my life so long, I don't know which way is up anymore." She turns her face away to the window.

"Come on," Sebastian says, opening his door and climbing out. He crunches through the snow around to Isobel's door and helps her out. Her legs are unsteady and he puts an arm around her waist, closing the door with his foot. He beeps the car locked and together they walk through the snow towards the shopping centre, Isobel shivering in his arms. They are both shell-shocked and Sebastian is paranoid about the few who glance in their direction, imagining them all to be in contact with the authorities, his employers or the man who wants him dead.

The Dockside shopping centre is split over two levels inside a large old building, retrofitted with steel walkways and staircases. At the back is a large discount homeware store; at the front, a big entrance space given over to various promotional activities. A bunch of different shops and cafes fill the space in between. Despite the preservation of the occasional decorative concession hailing from the building's distant glory days, the interior is devoid of any charm. The large, echoing spaces would seem chilly at the height of summer.

A few dedicated shoppers browse and move on, while bored sales assistants pace up and down between the aisles, occasionally moving products around on the shelves.

Isobel is freezing. She walks through the shopping centre hugging herself, attracting the curious eyes of anyone who spots her.

"Wait here." Sebastian disappears inside a shop filled with outdoor clothing, boots, hats and base layers. Isobel sits down on a nearby bench to wait.

Sebastian returns and wraps a large ski jacket around her shoulders. It's too big, and coloured deep green. Isobel smiles up at him, grateful. Sebastian pulls a matching green beanie hat down on her head.

A bit further in and they find an Australian-themed café with tables and a counter along the far wall. Sebastian gets Isobel seated as far from the door as possible then orders two large double shot coffees. As he hands over the money he notes that his hands are still shaking, but despite the severity of the last hour he is once again calm and lucid.

I was made for this, he thinks. The army should never have put me behind a desk.

He takes his change and goes back to Isobel. A few moments later, a waitress arrives and delivers the drinks.

Isobel pulls off the beanie hat and wraps her trembling fingers around the mug. She is lent over the table, her long hair hanging in her face. She looks tired. Sebastian feels a modicum of sympathy.

"Who are you?" Isobel suddenly asks, eyes wide.

"I told you my name."

"Yeah, you did. But that's not what I meant. Who *are* you, Sebastian?"

"I'm just a guy, nothing special. I was supposed to deliver a bag and then you got in my car. I'm not a criminal."

"You're very good at shooting people."

"I was in the army. I told you that."

"You said you've never been in combat."

"I haven't."

"Then why are you so good at shooting people?"

Sebastian stares into his coffee cup, unsure how to respond.

"I had some training in the army, and some things you get used to. Most people, they hear a gunshot and they freeze or panic. I don't. I was taught to think and act under fire, and I guess it never leaves you." He is about to say more, but then stops. Isobel knows that he is holding something back.

"And what?"

"I don't think those guys this morning were killers."

"They seemed like it to me."

"I mean they weren't, I don't know, henchmen or thugs. They were like you. Just ordinary people. One was wearing a fucking shop uniform for Christ sake."

"So what're you telling me? That I'm not alone in this?"

"I don't think you are. Those guys were sent by someone who has power over them. They certainly weren't trained." Sebastian sighs. "I mean, you're a nurse, right? But this voice says go out and beat this guy in the head, and you do it."

Isobel can see what he's driving at. It does make sense. Mr Punch is completely anonymous as far as she's concerned. Entrapping her years ago, he has blackmailed, threatened and coerced her into doing things that she would never have thought she was capable of. It's perfectly possible that he may control others. Others willing to kill for him. After all, what she does is only one step away from murder itself.

Sebastian is keeping a wary eye on the people walking past, and Isobel takes the opportunity to study him. She has no idea what's going on behind his eyes. All she knows is that he is both extremely determined, but also weak. Despite all he's done, his asthma is ever present. She can hear him wheezing. How long before he runs out of breath? But he is dangerous. Perhaps not to her, but she cannot know that for sure. Not so long ago he had his face pressed between her legs while she beat him about the head with the butt of a gun. Now she's supposed to just sit here and assume they've become allies in this fight against Mr Punch? His motivations are self-serving. He wants his bag back, otherwise his employers are going to kill him. He doesn't give a fuck about me, she thinks. Once he's got the bag, that'll be it. He'll vanish and I'll be left facing the consequences on my own.

"Are you alright?"

Isobel nods, unable to meet his eyes. She stares out over his shoulder, watching the occasional shopper walking past.

"Were you expecting me to come looking for you?"

She takes a gulp of coffee before answering.

"Yes. He called me this morning and said you'd be coming."

"Do you have any idea who he is?"

"None. He gives nothing away."

"What did he say when he called you."

"The barest minimum. Something went wrong last night, and your next move would be to find me. He told me to do everything you said."

"And now?"

"What do you mean?"

"What do you plan to do now?"

Isobel shrugs. "I can hardly think straight. All I can see is that blond guy's brains on the floorboards. I don't know what I'm doing here with you. You might be more dangerous than Mr Punch."

"I'm not dangerous."

"Tell that to the guys back there."

"That was self-defence. I'm not homicidal. I just want an easy life."

"Don't we all?"

An old couple bustles into the café, their thick coats, hats and scarves covered with snow. They seem to make a big deal of unburdening themselves of their outdoor clothes, draping everything over chairs and huffing and puffing as if they'd walked twenty miles through the arctic. The old boy, his white fluffy beard oddly appropriate for the weather, accosts the youth behind the counter. His wife, sitting down in the chair, looks across at Sebastian and Isobel.

"Terrible weather."

"It is," Sebastian answers back, turning to Isobel immediately after, not wanting to get stuck in a conversation, but finding her presence oddly comforting nonetheless, knowing that the world is continuing on its merry way, despite faceless maniacs and missing bags and murderous meat puppets.

The old guy with the beard wanders back over, tucking his wallet into his trousers. Taking a seat opposite his wife, they begin chatting loudly. Presently, the same waitress brings them a tray piled high with coffee and cake.

Isobel watches them, wishing she knew something of their contentment.

"You know he won't stop."

"What do you mean?"

"Mr Punch. You're marked, Sebastian. For whatever reason, it doesn't matter. He wants you dead and he won't stop."

"I don't think it's as simple as that." Sebastian flashbacks to the hotel. Who was that other woman? She's the big unknown here. Why was she raping him, and who was watching via the webcam? Sebastian assumes that it was Mr Punch, but why, and for what? To blackmail him and use him the way he uses Isobel? How can that make sense when, according to Isobel, all the people she's knocked unconscious turn up dead in the river?

"How did you get mixed up in this?"

Isobel looks at him over the rim of her mug.

"It's a long story." She doesn't want to talk about it.

"Of course it is."

Isobel sips her coffee.

"What happened? Why does he have so much power over you?"

Isobel turns away and looks out at the rows of shops, discount stores and branded signs. A few people are browsing, fewer still actually buying. Her thoughts turn to long ago. She's never spoken of what happened back when she was a teenager. No one but Mr Punch knows the truth. That's where his power comes from, because nobody knows what she did. Can she bring herself to speak of it now? Can she open up to this stranger who she attacked and left for dead? Would that not be the height of perversity, to confess to a man who is also one of her victims? But then if she can't tell Sebastian, someone already inside her turbulent life, then she can't tell anyone. Talking may also diminish the power Mr Punch has over her, because there would be another soul in the world who knew the details of her secret. With

Sebastian, there's nothing to lose. He already knows everything else.

"When I was sixteen I had an affair with a much older guy. I won't bore you with the details. I was young and he had a lot to lose. We used to meet in the woods up in Darland. All we did was fuck, but I was stupid and believed he would leave his wife for me."

Isobel suddenly barks a desperate laugh.

"I was so fucking dumb." She looks over at the old couple, but her eyes are unfocused. She takes another sip of coffee, gathering her thoughts.

"I guess he'd been spying on us for a while."

12

It was by chance that he was on his way home from work that day. He had developed the habit of sometimes forgetting his lunch, leaving it on the kitchen worktop as he rushed out of the door in the morning. Forgetting his lunch was a ruse; he had an eidetic memory and never forgot anything. This apparent lapse was one of a number of minor quirks he had adopted as camouflage, initially to put his father at ease. Pretending to be late was another. He'd go into the bathroom, slide the bolt on the door, and run the taps in the sink. He would stand in the corner of the room, waiting for his father to knock on the door. Usually it would take around fifteen minutes. When the knock came and his father dutifully informed him of the time, he would turn off the taps, listen to his father's receding footsteps as he disappeared down the stairs, and then bolt from the room and rush out of the house. On these days he would deliberately forget his lunch. The ruse also helped when he arrived at work. He was never actually late, but close enough for the others to think he could be, and this made him seem fallible. It helped the others think he was just like them.

His lunch break began at eleven forty-five. One hour away from the forklift and the palettes and crates. Usually he would sit in the canteen with the others, eating his lunch, perched on a chair at the corner of the table. He would intentionally slouch, smile when a joke was told, frown when the subject was politics, blush a little when the subject was sex. He was excellent at feigning the appropriate emotional response. The others considered him an interesting and enigmatic individual, with a sharp, penetrating intelligence far beyond what was required for success in the warehouse. Although he never socialised, he was well liked, even respected. A few people wondered about his life outside of work. They asked after girlfriends, his weekend, whether he'd watched the football. His responses were deliberately contradictory and almost always funny; misdirection came easily, and none of the others ever had a real handle on his personal circumstances. It wasn't long before he was voted union representative.

He didn't mind the menial work. He experienced neither pleasure nor discomfort operating the forklift and moving things around. For most of the time, he wasn't even there. He had developed a technique of putting his mind to sleep. For the hours spent in the warehouse he was effectively a robot, running through the various processes without any conscious thought. He was the fastest, most efficient worker the company had ever employed, and he never made a mistake. Not one.

On the days when he deliberately forgot his lunch he would leave the warehouse at eleven forty-five and sprint home again through the woods. A tiny part of his mind registered an objection to this. It was inefficient. But the charade was necessary. People made mistakes. They forgot things. They experienced emotional responses to conversations around the table at lunch. People expected him to be the same. They would have been disturbed to realise he was something different.

Over the years these little affectations had coalesced, forming a patina of ordinariness that enabled him to navigate the world without arousing suspicion. He was exceptionally good at fitting in.

On this day in 1996 he was twenty-seven years old. It had been fifty-two days since the last time he'd forgotten his lunch. At eleven forty-five he ducked under one of the shutters after informing his supervisor he was stepping out for lunch. It was a hot day, and he was dressed in just a T-shirt and jeans. He could wear a T-shirt in the winter too, he could regulate his body temperature precisely regardless of the weather, but he'd learnt in the past that doing so aroused interest. Most people experienced being cold and hot, so now he dressed accordingly.

He set off across the loading dock at a dead sprint. The others who saw him go always assumed he would slow down soon enough, but he didn't. He could sprint continuously until he reached his destination, wherever it was. He never ran out of breath.

The woods were extremely quiet, no wind agitating the leaves, no birds singing, everything still and humid. He remembered playing war games here when he was a child, back when he experienced the thrill of tracking Infiltrators across land he considered his. He took such risks back then, and he discovered how powerful a well-placed lie could be, especially when coupled with general assumptions. Adults found it impossible to believe he could have done those things.

He followed his usual route, the hard-packed dirt of the narrow path snaking through the trees, his rapid and precise footsteps kicking up little puffs of dust. He ran almost entirely without sound, on the balls of his feet, like a dedicated athlete who'd spent a lifetime in training. Only he never had to practice. His abilities had grown and developed simply as he'd aged; they were always there. Even back when he was a little boy, he was stronger, faster, more focused and more intelligent than everyone around him. He was also silent, able to pass through just about any environment without making a sound. Again this isn't something he practised, or even something he consciously tried to achieve. He just had a knack of finding the path of least resistance, so light and rapid on his feet he left barely a ripple in a puddle.

But then he heard a sound.

He stopped instantly, so abrupt anyone watching would have registered something strange; in cartoons it might be funny, but in reality it was unnerving. He stood, utterly still, his acute ears listening for the unmistakable sound, so foreign to the environment he was immediately able to register it, of a woman approaching orgasm.

He backtracked along the path. He let his ears guide him, moving slowly, eyes tuned for the slightest movement between the trees. As he drew closer, the noises got louder. He had seen a few couples fucking in these woods over the years – always the same clipped and gasping vocal expressions, everyone too self-conscious to let rip and bellow their passions at the trees.

He could see them now, through a small gap between some bushes. As a teenager, he had fucked a couple of girls in exactly the same spot. Very carefully, very slowly, he moved through the trees. He was aiming for one in particular, one that he could climb easily, for a much better view. One that had so many branches he would be well hidden by the leaves.

He climbed, high enough for his outline to be broken by the foliage.

The guy was on top, his pale arse bobbing vigorously. All he could see of the girl was her tanned arms and legs, fingers scratching, ankles crossed in the small of the guy's back. And her face. Her young, innocent little face. The girl rolled the guy over, straddling her lover. He was treated to a marvellous view of her arse as she bucked up and down. The girl rode the guy hard. But now he couldn't see her face.

When they were done, she rolled off to the side, both of them now lying on their backs, staring up at the trees. He kept absolutely still, confined for the time being.

Conversation came drifting up and he listened intently, curious about the nature of their relationship. There was an opportunity here, somewhere. All secrets are exploitable, and the relationship between these two was obviously clandestine. The age difference between them testified to this, if nothing else. But he needed to be cautious. Such situations are governed by their own rules, and he must make his plays with care. But if he remained vigilant and patient, something would present itself. It may come to nothing, a simple diverting opportunity, occupying his time for a few days or weeks. But perhaps it could lead to something he could use to further his other, more entrepreneurial ideas. He already had a handful of people under his influence, people who, for one reason or another, were obliged to obey his instructions. Of course, none of them had any idea who he was. He had learnt a long time ago that anonymity came with its own special power.

The girl was walking away. The guy likewise, moving in the opposite direction to the girl, crashing through the woods as if fighting for his passage.

He gave them five minutes to get clear before climbing down, the wheels in his head turning over what to do next. For sure he'd be back there tomorrow, ready and waiting for when, or if, they met again. He'd bring his Polaroid, and leave himself in a position to move quickly. The main thing was deciding who to follow, the guy or the girl? Which of them offered the greatest potential? The guy would probably have more to lose, thus maximising the leverage.

He ran through the woods, heading home for his lunch. He'd have to eat quickly in order to be back at work in time. And he'd need an excuse for tomorrow. Perhaps he could call in sick. He'd never done that before. No one would doubt the lie.

* * *

"Our affair ended badly. He was married, twice my age. We saw each other for a few months before he started getting cold feet. The last time we met in the woods, the bastard fucked me before dumping me. I was sixteen. Hurt. Angry."

Isobel glances at Sebastian. Then she lowers her eyes.

"I called him some terrible things. He slapped me. That just made me angrier. I pushed him back. He wasn't a big guy, and he stumbled and fell. Hit his head on a rock."

Isobel takes in a big breath. Talking about this after so many years is much easier than she imagined it would be, but nevertheless there's a weight in her guts.

"I didn't stop to check he was alright. I didn't think he was hurt, not really. I just left him there. Nobody knew about our affair and I thought that would be the end of it. But when I saw the news I got scared. For years I thought I'd killed him. That he'd died when I pushed him over. I carried that guilt. That fear. But now I'm not so sure. Now I think *he* killed him."

* * *

He emerged silently from the bushes, wearing camouflaged fatigues and face paint, the camera on a strap slung over one shoulder. He walked into the secluded clearing and stood over the man.

The girl had flounced away just a few seconds ago, spitting curses as she went. He could still hear her blundering through the woods. He wasn't worried about her coming back. He knew that she wouldn't.

The man was coming around. His limbs twitched, eyelids fluttered. He murmured a name:

"*Izzy. Isobel.*"

He bent down and quickly rolled the man over onto his front. He picked up the rock that had knocked the man out when he fell.

The guy came back to his senses. His eyes opened fully.

"Isobel?" he muttered.

He slammed the rock down into the back of the man's head. The man went limp. Brains oozed out of the split in the back of his skull.

He put the rock back, precisely where it came from, and rolled the man over again.

He stood, watching, as the man died at his feet.

He registered no discernable emotion at this act. All he saw was a multitude of possible scenarios unspooling from the man's death. In time, his leverage over the girl will be absolute.

After a minute, the man's limbs stopped twitching.

He faded back into the woods, moving with his usual speed and grace, leaving no trace of his presence behind.

* * *

"Exactly one year later, I received a photograph. Just one. To the very day. It was sealed in an envelope. No stamps. No address. He must have put it through the letterbox in the middle of the night. Just my name was printed on the front. I was still living with my Mum. My Dad had vanished when I was a little girl. The photo showed us fucking in the woods. Then the telephone calls started. He told me I was a murderer. He told me he'd saw me kill him. That he had pictures of me pushing him over and standing there, watching as he died. I was to earn his silence, otherwise he'd go to the police."

Isobel takes a sip of coffee, her eyes distant. Sebastian waits for her to continue.

"He waited a whole year before coming to me. He let the news cover the story, let the investigation play out. The police suspected someone else was involved. His wife had suspicions he was having an affair. I felt so guilty but I couldn't bring myself to go to the police. I was so scared. His wife was on the television, this wild, distraught looking woman who seemed so formidable to me. She was so angry that this had happened to her husband. So I kept quiet and prayed that it would all go away. And it did. Eventually."

"But then he contacted you?"

"He must have been watching me for a whole year to see what I would do. And then when it was over, when he was sure I wasn't going to own up to it, he made himself known to me. That level of patience terrified me." Isobel breathes in deeply. "It still does. At first it was just courier stuff. Take something from A to B. A bit like what you're doing now. Then it was getting rid of things, weapons mostly, guns. And then he started using me to entrap people like you. He didn't just tell me to go and hurt someone. He built me up to it, bit by bit. Each time he would send me a photograph, something incriminating, something I'd done for him that he could use against me. Over time it got so he owned me. He exploited my cowardice. Now I'm in so deep I can't get out."

"And you have no idea who he is?"

Isobel shakes her head.

"I've no idea. I just think of him as Mr Punch. He could be anyone. Anyone I've met, someone at work, an ex. Anyone."

Sebastian is silent for a long time. The spectre of Mr Punch grows in his mind. What kind of man would do such a thing? It is amazing Isobel is still alive. But it explains the loneliness he can sense in her. It must be difficult to lead a double life, one in the real world with colleagues and friends, and one in some distorted nightmare as a stooge for a faceless psycho on the far end of the phone. Only one of those lives will be real, the other just a charade. Guess it doesn't take a genius to work out which is which.

The coat he bought for her is way too big. Isobel wraps it tightly around herself.

"Where did you take the car?" Sebastian asks.

"What?"

"Where did you take my car last night?"

Isobel looks at Sebastian as if not understanding the question.

"You said Mr Punch told you to take my car before the others arrived. You left me on the pier and drove off in my car. Where did you take it?"

"Just a house."

"Can you show me where it is?"

"Yeah, I think so. I guess so."

"Are you sure? I don't want to drive around in the snow, wasting time, while you struggle with your directions."

Isobel gives him a look and then turns away.

Sebastian doesn't have a choice about trusting her. Finding the car is his last play, without it he's got nothing.

He's anxious to be away, but he doesn't hurry them along. What they've just been through would be tough for anyone to deal with.

They sit in silence, drinking their drinks. Then:

"I want you to kill me."

"What?" Sebastian is shocked.

"Not literally. But I want you to say you have. I want you to pretend."

Sebastian looks at her, uncomprehending.

"Mr Punch is never going to stop. You're on a collision course. Either you kill him or he kills you. That's the only way this can end. I want you to tell him you've killed me. If he thinks I'm dead, I can disappear. That's the deal. I show you where I took the car, and you tell Mr Punch that you killed me."

Isobel hasn't monitored her voice and Sebastian glances at the old couple at the next table. They're oblivious, or pretending to be so.

"Alright."

"That's it? Just alright?"

"What else am I going to say? I'm not a psycho. I want out of this as much as you do. You help me get the bag and if I have to I'll tell Mr Punch I put a bullet in you."

"Then let's do this." Isobel swallows the last of her coffee and gets to her feet.

Part 2

13

"I can't do anything else. I'm sorry." Talissa gets off the bed and goes to the door.

The naked man, hog-tied, shell-shocked and raped, looks up at her with a mixture of confusion, gratitude and fear.

Talissa has no idea who he is, where he comes from or even what his name is. All she knows is that he is about to die. The two assassins waiting outside the door will be as anxious as she is for this night to be over.

Freeing the man's ankles and loosening his hands is all she can do. Maybe it will be enough. Despite his confusion and fear, there is resilience in his eyes. Perhaps he will survive where so many others have not. Either way, she has played her part like always, degraded herself with a stranger, and now she must leave.

Talissa takes one last look at the man on the bed. He is breathing fiercely through the gag in his mouth, working furiously to squirm his way free of the belts around his wrists.

The two so-called assassins are waiting in the corridor. When she steps through the door they look up at her, then across to each other. Their moment has arrived, but Talissa knows they would rather be somewhere else. One guy, the younger of the two, swallows dramatically. Both look apprehensive.

"You don't like this part either, do you?"

The older guy looks down at his shoes, then up again at Talissa, a degree of wariness in his eyes. Several times they've all been through this routine, but Talissa has never spoken to them before.

"Why don't you let him go?" She nods back towards the door of the room, wondering if the man on the bed has got himself free.

The youngest barks a desperate laugh.

"Are you kidding?"

"Rather him than us," adds the older one.

"How do you sleep at night?"

"How do you?"

Talissa walks away along the corridor, her footsteps hushed by the carpet. Behind her the two men move through the door. There is a yell, a bang, the muffled sounds of a struggle. Her steps do not falter. She rounds the corner into another corridor and comes to the door marked EXIT. She descends the staircase and hurries into the lobby.

The kid at the reception desk looks up as she crosses through reception. Talissa pushes through the main door and out into the night.

Snow is falling and everything seems calm, while inside she is screaming. At least the man she just raped is putting up a fight.

The white BMW is parked on the far side of the car park. She's never seen the men who occupy it, but she knows they are there in case something goes wrong.

Talissa climbs into her own car and pulls the door shut. How many men have I put in danger tonight? She is complicit in the possible murder of one man, but by trying to save him she's risked the lives of four more.

At least they have a choice, whereas the guy on the bed has none.

But she knows that isn't the case. Those caught in the web can struggle all they want, but nobody gets free.

Nobody has a choice. Not really. Not even those with guns.

The engine starts and she pulls carefully out of the car park, wondering who is dead and who is alive.

She cruises through the white streets, deserted at this ridiculous hour of the night, down through town towards the Medway Tunnel. Snow falls fast and silent, the roads slippery and treacherous. Driving demands her full attention. Her silver Ford motors along the dual carriageways, through the tunnel and left at Frindsbury Hill towards the Hoo Peninsula. Talissa shifts up into the lowest gear the little car can manage on the incline, hoping the wheels find purchase.

The Hoo Peninsula is mostly rolling scrubland, snow covered and grey in the darkness, unfolding towards the winking lights of the power station down by the river. She hangs a left. Almost home.

It is just a few paces from the car to Talissa's front door, but she slips in the snow and goes down, landing on her arse.

She flops back in the snow, staring up into the darkness and letting the gentle flakes settle on her face. Everything is whisper quiet. She stays there for a few minutes, until the coldness creeps through her clothes to chill her bones.

How nice it would be to fall into that sky, to get lost among the clouds. Free to drift, to float. At peace. More and more Talissa has been thinking of peace, of time without pressures, without the indomitable spectre of Ichabod looming over her every waking breath. Soon. Soon.

Once inside she shuts the door, slides the three bolts and then turns the key. Home sweet home.

She goes upstairs and despite the hour runs a bath, pulling off her clothes while the tub fills. Debasement clings to her like dirt and sweat and she cannot get into bed without scrubbing the victim from her skin. She lights some candles in the small en suite and climbs into the hot water, laying back and closing her eyes.

When will this nightmare come to an end?

Talissa can see the guy tied to the bed. The confusion and fear in his eyes breaks her heart.

But I've been a part of this for so long, it's a miracle I still have a heart to break. How easy it would be to feel nothing. Dead, from the inside out. But that isn't me, she thinks. All I have left is compassion. The only thing he hasn't taken from me. I'll die before he gets that too. It won't be long now. And I just don't care.

Talissa's mind unwinds through the long years of her relationship with Ichabod. The hopes she had when he first entered her life, the dreams. How could I have got it so wrong? Why didn't I see what he was?

Talissa fell in love before she learned to hate. If it had happened the other way around, perhaps she would have escaped altogether. But fate saw fit to place her by his side, and very quickly he bound her wrists and forced her to beg at his feet.

At first she made excuses for him. He was misguided, upset, under pressure. She blamed herself for not making him happy. It took a long time to accept that the man she'd fell in love with was nothing more than a lie.

Ichabod had manipulated her from the very beginning.

Talissa sinks to the bottom of the bath, the hot water closing above her head, the harsh realities of her world disappearing, if only for a few moments. Everything is so quiet. I would like to stay here, she thinks, stay here until my breath runs out, and then stay a while longer.

But then he would win. And she can't let that happen.

She breaks the surface and gasps for air. Her vision clouds to black. She must have been under for longer than she thought. When her equilibrium returns to normal she hoists herself from the bath.

Back in her bedroom, wrapped in a towel, Talissa rubs moisturiser into her legs as water drips from her hair onto the bed. In the early days she went to such lengths to take care of herself, to look good for him.

She is no less fastidious about her routines now, but she no longer cares what she looks like, especially in his eyes.

Talissa trims and files her fingernails, then rubs the towel through her hair. She sits at her dressing table, lights a tall, thin candle and stares at her reflection in the mirror. Under the warm light of the amber flame she looks ten years younger, except for her eyes. Such darkness; she has trouble holding her own gaze.

She picks up a silver-handled brush, a gift from her mother when she was sixteen, more than half her life ago, and begins brushing her hair. Despite everything that's happened to her, everything Ichabod has subjected her to, she still maintains her one hundred strokes before bed. It is a calming ritual, as if she can brush away the guilt and the humiliation along with the knots. The repetitive action quietens her mind, leaving her free to sleep in peace.

But it wasn't always so. In the early days, after she found herself bound to Ichabod, when his true nature began to assert itself, when she was still searching for reasons that would excuse his behaviour, she would go to bed in torment. She was plagued by insomnia for months at a time. Barely awake, but never able to sleep, she moved through life in a daze, as if drugged.

It was her mother's death that brought her round, a shock so sudden it was like one of Ichabod's brutal slaps. Her miserable life snapped back into focus. It was then that she returned to her rituals, finding in the familiar, repetitive acts a comfort and solace that enabled her to sleep at last.

Over the years it became an obsession. The one hundred strokes before bed, and scrubbing the violence from her skin, were the only things she could control. It was how she learned to cope.

At stroke seventy-eight she hears muffled noises coming from the back garden beneath her bedroom window.

Despite the freezing weather, she always keeps her windows open. The cold stops her getting comfortable. It stops her feeling cosy. She doesn't ever want to forget the men she's sent to their deaths, or the way she's debased herself for Ichabod. It doesn't matter that in the beginning she loved him and made excuses for him, it doesn't matter now that she hates him and fears him in equal measure, all that matters are her actions. One hundred strokes allow her to sleep, but the cold stops her from ever forgetting.

At stroke eighty the kitchen door rattles in its frame. The door is bolted, and Talissa hears an angry curse from the back garden.

It didn't take him long to get here.

14

Ichabod boosts himself over the back gate and lands silently in Talissa's garden. He walks up the path along the side of the house and pauses at the corner, caught by the view. Snow, ethereal, serene, is erasing the garden and the field beyond. The sight is beautiful and for a moment he forgets the rage that has fuelled his sudden trip across town in the dead hours of the night. The insidious notion of betrayal that sliced up his heart, conjuring visions of pain and blood, Talissa's blood, is suddenly engulfed by an upswell of melancholy.

I wish I could obliterate everything with such ease. He shakes his head. But if I could, I'd destroy the whole fucking world.

"I wouldn't be able to stop myself." The wind whips the words from his lips and hurls them out into the night. A grin splits his face in two. The melancholy that had gripped his heart is crushed beneath a fleeting sense of chaos, total abandonment to impulse and instinct, like a beast in bloodlust rampaging through a herd of prey.

I wish I was a crocodile.

He snaps back to the moment, blinking snow from his eyes. Suddenly he is cold. His T-shirt is wet and freezing and he begins to shiver. Chattering teeth. He wraps his muscle-bound arms around his body and shuffles along the back of Talissa's house, kicking plant pots, sending them skittering through the snow, cursing out loud. He grabs the handle on the back door but it fails to turn.

Denied, he turns and bellows his frustration into the night. He kicks out at the garden table on the patio, sending a chair end over end. But then his footing slips from under him and he smacks down in the snow, knocking the wind from his lungs.

You impulsive boy!

His father's stern face leers over him in the darkness, looking down through half-moon glasses, contempt like tears leaking from his eyes.

"Fuck you. Fuck you all," Ichabod whispers into the night.

Hello my simpleton son! My idiot and heir!

Ichabod was at home when the call came through. It was Joshua, one of the backup guys stationed in the white BMW.

"Something's gone wrong. Sebastian's walking away."

It took Ichabod a moment to understand what he'd just been told. Nobody had ever gotten away. Such things simply didn't happen.

"What did you say?"

Joshua gulped; Ichabod heard him down the phone.

"He's walking away. He must have killed the two in the room."

How? He was tied up, trussed up. Ichabod had just watched Talissa rape him.

Oh the thrill of that power!

His debauched little hussy. His restrained victim. He'd brought them together and conjured something beautiful from their union. Naked in his apartment, using the vibrator on his anus, watching through his laptop while Talissa thrust away in the motel with Sebastian unconscious and slack between her legs.

And then Sebastian woke up. He struggled. *The look of confusion on his face!* Ichabod's long arc of semen splashed across his chest. He laughed. On screen, Talissa climaxed too. Such synchronicity.

We are so in tune. Joined at the genitals. My little Tally.

But ultimately, Sebastian had to die. It was punishment for failing to deliver his previous cargo. Car jacking was not an excuse.

He had decided.

But execution was so cold, and not much fun. Why not use Talissa, his obedient little love slave, to give the man a parting gift?

But now Joshua is asking:

"What should we do?"

"Kill him. Whatever happens, just make sure he's dead." Ichabod cancelled the call. Talissa must have let him go. It's the only explanation. The hurt was so deep he felt it in his bones. On the back of betrayal came rage and he bolted from his apartment intent on revenge.

Catching sight of himself in the elevator mirror he realised he was still naked and clutching the vibrator. Hilarity split his sides, but his laughs became anguished cries. He went back along the corridor to his apartment and got dressed. Before he left again he looked at his face in the bathroom mirror and wiped away his tears.

Toughen up, my simpleton son! Or your bitch will lynch you with her apron strings!

Ichabod picks himself up from the snow and grabs one of the plant pots, intending to pitch it through the backdoor window. But Talissa is standing on the other side, looking out at him. Her breath fogs up the glass, dissolving the details of her face. Ichabod drops the pot and steps forwards. There is a click in the silence as Talissa unlocks the door.

* * *

Will this night ever end?

Talissa steps aside as Ichabod brushes past her. She reaches out to brush the snow from his back but he knocks her hand away. He seems to fill the small kitchen to bursting point, a massive animal in the darkness. Talissa closes the backdoor and leans against it.

"Why are you here?"

He doesn't answer and Talissa shrinks before him, her skin crawling. She can feel the heat coming off him and can hear his wild breathing, like a beast in the forest.

And then he seems to deflate and with a weary sigh he drops into a chair at the kitchen table. The clock on the cooker casts a green light across his face and he looks up at her with chaos raging in his eyes.

"Don't you love me anymore?" His voice is small, like a wounded child.

Talissa groans on the inside. How many times must I pretend that things are just great? It amazes her that Ichabod has no conception of how crazy he is. Sometimes she wants to scream in his face and laugh and cry and just walk away or stab him in the heart with a kitchen knife. But she knows that any of these things will only result in her own torment, perhaps death, and although she sometimes indulges the fantasy, she hasn't yet tipped over the edge.

"Yes, I love you still." She sighs and sits down at the table, expecting long hours of massaging his ego and rubbing away the stain of his depression.

"THEN WHY DID YOU FUCKING BETRAY ME!"

Ichabod rears up and rips the table from the floor sending it crashing into the cooker. Talissa screams as he hurls her from the chair towards the back door. She strikes her head against the glass hard enough for it to crack; he is so strong, so fast, his face is right up in hers and she can smell the sour stench of his breath.

"You untied him after you turned off the laptop, right? And then you left while he got his shit together. And when my two little puppets went through the door, he killed them, and then strolled right out of the building. Just a minute after you did. Right? You FUCKING BITCH!"

The ringing of his mobile cuts through the rage. Ichabod backs away a step, draws out the chirping phone and looks to see who is calling. By the light from the screen Talissa can see the anguish and pain in his face.

I've really hurt him. Whatever this fucked thing is between us, for him it is real. Talissa has a momentary flash of hope. Perhaps she can do far more than just hurt him.

Ichabod flicks open the phone.

"Who is this?"

"Sebastian."

Ichabod stares straight ahead at Talissa, who is hovering by the back door, one hand wrapped around the handle, poised for flight. Ichabod's aggression suddenly deflates and a fleeting cloud of confusion blows across his face. Whoever is on the phone has knocked him completely off guard.

"Are you there?" asks the voice on the phone. Talissa can just hear it in the silence.

"You were supposed to make your delivery," Ichabod says.

"I was attacked."

"Robbed again? Seems like it's becoming a habit, Sebastian."

"This was different."

"Do you still have the cargo?" Ichabod sets the table back on four legs and sits down. Despite the darkness, Talissa can see a wicked grin slashed across his face.

"No."

"Who does?"

"I've no idea. I didn't get a chance to ask the three men I killed."

"Three? How resourceful of you Sebastian. You surprise me."

"Yeah well. I surprised myself."

"So what do you propose to do now?"

"I don't know."

"That's twice you've let us down."

"I'm aware of that."

"It makes your position an interesting one."

"How so?"

"You're a dead man walking."

"What if I get it back?"

"The cargo? How do you propose to do that?"

"I have a lead."

"A lead?" Ichabod laughs. "You sound like a television detective."

"I'm serious."

"I'm sure you are."

Ichabod rubs his chin with his free hand and sits forward, elbows resting on the table.

"Okay," he says eventually. "You've got twenty-four hours to recover the cargo. The clock is ticking as of now. If I haven't heard from you this time tomorrow, the contract goes out on your life and you'll be dead by Monday morning. Are we clear?"

"Yes."

"And Sebastian?"

"Yeah?"

"Don't use this time to run. You may have called me from a pay phone, but I can find you faster than you'd believe. Deliver my cargo and you keep your life." Ichabod snaps the phone shut and chucks it on the table. He rubs his eyes with the heels of his hands and sits back in his chair.

Cautiously, Talissa moves away from the backdoor. She sits down, looking at Ichabod from across the table. He appears to have completely forgotten about the violence he was about to unleash. He stares at the table top, lost in thought, his handsome face like something from a nightmare, his eyes sunken and lost in shadow.

He runs a hand through his black hair and picks up his mobile again and speed dials a number. In the silence of the darkened kitchen, Talissa can hear the ringing at the other end.

The call is connected.

"It's me."

"I know."

"Something went wrong."

"Explain."

"He's still alive."

"How?"

Ichabod glances at Talissa. She drops her eyes to the table.

"I don't know. But he just called me. He's killed three of our guys."

"He just called you?"

"Yeah. Get this, the fucking moron hasn't realised it was us."

"What do you mean?"

"He called to say he's lost the cargo. I gave him twenty-four hours to retrieve it."

The voice on the phone is silent for a moment. Ichabod waits and Talissa, not looking but listening, suddenly realises that he is waiting for instructions.

"He'll go after Isobel."

"He said he had a lead."

"I'll put her back in play, and put some guys on alert. We'll wait for Sebastian to make contact."

"Sounds like a plan."

"Have you retrieved the cargo?"

"Not yet."

"Not yet? What have you been doing, Ichabod?"

"I had something to take care of."

"The cargo is what you have to take care of. Go get it now."

"Alright."

"And Ichabod, this is the last time I indulge your little games. Do you understand?"

"Yes."

"Next time, we simply kill the guy. No fucking about. It's costing us too much."

"What about the hotel? Sounds like a mess."

"Your mess."

"I'll go there before getting the cargo."

"Just make sure they're all dead. And no fucking about, Ichabod. No games. This is starting to get out of hand."

The connection is cut. Ichabod puts the phone down on the table.

Talissa looks at him, like a frightened rabbit she keeps as still as possible, waiting for whatever comes next.

He is statue still, staring at her. He looks like a corpse, Talissa thinks.

Ichabod rises, scraping the legs of his chair across the ceramic tiled floor. Talissa keeps her eyes averted, not wanting to provoke him. He pulls open the back door and Talissa turns to watch him go, breathing a sigh of relief, but he is still standing there, still watching her. Snow blows in through the open door. The night outside is completely silent.

"We're not done yet," Ichabod says quietly. He walks out into the night, leaving the kitchen door wide open.

Talissa, shivering in her dressing gown, slams it shut. And locks it.

* * *

The police. They scurry about in front of the hotel, moving in and out of the lobby, carrying cases full of equipment, no doubt dusting for prints in the room, taking fibres, trying to identify the bodies.

That idiot boy on the front desk is probably spilling his guts. Something will have to be done about him. Ichabod spits in the snow. Something about that little clerk makes him feel dirty.

The whirling blue lights cast a surreal ambience over the car park. Watching from the far side of the bushes, it reminds Ichabod of a Scandinavian detective series he'd been watching on the television. Those sombre cops in their thick jumpers, what would they make of his army of meat puppets?

"They wouldn't stand a chance against us," he says out loud.

Not far away, a team of police are crawling over the white BMW, its doors still wide open, a line of footsteps in the snow leading from the doors to the bushes where the two men bullied their way through.

"And neither do you," Ichabod says to the officers at the car, louder this time, enjoying a brief thrill at the prospect of being heard.

But the police are oblivious, too focused on their investigations, and his words are swallowed by the darkness.

Ichabod grins.

He moves away from the bushes, keeping himself low, heading off in the direction of the tracks, visualising the chase in his mind. Joshua said Sebastian strolled out the front door of the hotel. He and Daniel would have chased him hard, as hard as they could anyway. The lives of their families depended on it. They had both been caught in the web long enough to know the consequences of failure.

There are more police up ahead, following the same tracks in the snow, investigating the path of the chase.

Ichabod knows the industrial estate intimately. Most of these factories and warehouses have been here since he was a boy, and this whole area backs onto the woods, his playground, his territory. He can anticipate the course the chase would have taken. Sebastian said he killed three. That means one was left alive. Joshua or Daniel? Either one would have talked. Could this be Sebastian's lead? No, definitely not. Neither of them knew anything. None of the meat puppets do.

He is right: Sebastian's lead must be Isobel.

But where would Sebastian have made a stand? Where would he have interrogated the one he didn't kill? Based on the direction of the tracks, Ichabod can make an educated guess.

He sets off, heading into the darkness, moving fast and easily through the snow. He keeps to the shadows, making little noise. All those years playing in the woods have instilled a modicum of stealth in his actions.

More rolling police lights flash through the darkness. Multiple cars sit in the car park of a warehouse up ahead. Ichabod skirts around the activity, moving towards the back of the warehouse, closer to the loading bay. He needs to know which one survived.

But his concerns are unfounded. Concealed in the shadows, he watches as a gurney is wheeled into a coroner's van. Joshua, the postman, lies rigid with his eyes still open.

A little way out from the back of the factory, out in plain sight on the loading bay, is Daniel. Just as dead, face down in the snow. The legs of his jeans are black with blood. A long black trail of blood shows the path of his crawl, leading back behind the warehouse.

Ichabod can see the course of events easily enough. Joshua shot and killed in the narrow gulley behind the warehouse, Daniel interrogated, shot in the legs to loosen his tongue. After Sebastian left, he tried to crawl, but he bled out in the snow before he was clear of the loading bay.

Sebastian must have hit an artery.

Was that deliberate? Is he that serious? Ichabod grins in the dark, hoping he is.

"Ah Sebastian, I didn't give you enough credit. You're going to be fun."

* * *

His hands are cold after being out in the snow. He stabs at the A/C button and turns the temperature all the way up. He grips the steering wheel tightly, driving cautiously, sitting forward on the edge of the seat and peering through the windscreen with a diligence that would seem almost comical to an impartial observer. But Ichabod is far away from the treacherous roads, thinking about how Sebastian took out four of the meat puppets. Ichabod doesn't care about the lives of those men, but as far as he's concerned he owned them nonetheless. They were his property, and after observing the scene back at the industrial estate he feels violated, as if something precious had been stolen.

Fucking Sebastian. The excitement he felt at the prospect of the games ahead is fading already, as another thought swells up from his turbulent heart: Talissa let him go.

Is there a connection between Sebastian's phone call and Tally's betrayal? Are they in league together? Do they have a plan? Is he going to take her from me? *Just let him fucking try it!* I'll scrape the flesh from your bones Sebastian, and feed it to you piece by little fucking piece.

Ichabod's hands tighten on the steering wheel as rage engulfs him. His body goes rigid, tendons and muscles screaming, and he vomits a harsh and bitter tirade of threats and insults, rising in pitch until a sustained, anguished cry rattles the windows and leaves his throat raw.

His focus on the road has gone entirely and the car glides through the snow into the wrong lane and bumps up the curb. Ichabod snaps back into the moment, panics, floors the accelerator and stabs the brake; the wheels spin before the engine stalls and the car glides in a smooth arc and comes to rest back on the correct side of the road.

Ichabod flops over the steering wheel, takes a deep breath and closes his eyes.

In the darkness he sees Talissa and Sebastian rutting on a mattress stained yellow with sweat, while his own dead body hangs from the neck in a corner of the room; his swollen tongue lolls on his cheek and both Sebastian and Tally turn to look at him and they smile and laugh.

My simpleton son. Don't feed your optimism to the devil. He shits out paranoia if you do.

Get a grip, otherwise this whole thing is going to run away down the rabbit hole. And if it does, he'll be pissed. And we don't want that. Oh no. Sebastian is just a dumb cunt who got lucky because Tally went all gooey and took pity. That's it. She's just testing her boundaries like a nice little slave and he's running off the back of some military training and a thin slice of fortune.

Your imagination will get you into trouble.

Ichabod opens his eyes.

"Sometimes my imagination gets me into trouble."

The silence is absolute and Ichabod's spoken words ring hollow in the absence of a confirming response.

"From time to time. But only with him, and he loves me so it doesn't matter."

Ichabod gets the car moving again. Focused on the road and concentrating on his mission, he tries to forget Talissa's betrayal, turning his thoughts instead to the excitement of having Sebastian chasing his own tail. Such a cunning play. Such devious games.

Ichabod hangs a right into a broad street lined on either side with large Edwardian houses, generally well kept, with driveways and front lawns. The snow makes the street look like a Christmas card; Ichabod ponders the view and suddenly feels warm and nostalgic at the thought of Christmas, as memories of presents and rich food flood through his heart.

The houses here all look alike and with the snow obscuring the detail he is unsure of which house he is looking for. But then he spots the car, old and knackered with a thin layer of snow covering its bonnet and roof. It sits on the driveway, out of place in this street of generic middle-management saloons and hatchbacks.

Ichabod pulls up in front of the drive and gets out. He goes to the car and brushes snow from the back window and peers in. On the backseat is the large holdall

Sebastian brought up from Dover. Ichabod tries the door, but it is locked. The old car is parked on the driveway of an ordinary-looking house. Ichabod strolls up to the front door and searches beneath the matt. Finding the key he returns and unlocks the door. It takes him but a moment to transfer the holdall to the boot of his BMW. The heavy bag makes a loud thump when it hits the boot and the car bounces on its springs. Ichabod regards the holdall for a moment. The temptation to tear it open and look inside is almost too much to bear and he decisively slams the boot.

Need to nip that particular urge in the bud. The holdall is padlocked shut. Only one man has the key and he'll be angry if I fuck around with it. Upsetting that miserable cunt's not worth the trouble.

Ichabod returns the key under the matt. He gets back in his car and drives away.

15

Snow is drifting; the wind sculpts elegant slopes and ridges against walls and parked cars. Traffic on the roads is slow moving and Sebastian is impatient, acutely aware of the minutes slipping by as they inch along, bumper to bumper.

After what seems like hours, they finally make it off the main roads into a maze of residential streets. There is far less traffic here, but the roads are far more hazardous. Sebastian drives cautiously.

This is a good part of town. The houses are large Edwardian places, front gardens converted to driveways for the most part.

Nestled halfway along the road, parked on the driveway at the front of a house that looks just like all the others, is the old car Sebastian was driving last night. Its black paintwork looks glossy in the cold light. The roof, windscreen and bonnet buried in snow.

Sebastian gently brings Kenosha's Mercedes to a standstill. He glances at Isobel, but she's looking through the window at the house.

Sebastian gets out and walks up the driveway. He's the only person on the street and there is no sound except the crunch of his boots in the snow. He feels so conspicuous he might as well have 'criminal' emblazoned on the back of his jacket.

Sebastian peers in through the side window of the car. Nothing. He moves to the back for a better look, brushing snow off the rear window.

The bag isn't there. Disappointment burns through his stomach. He hadn't realised how intense his hopes were.

Isobel is waiting in the Mercedes, watching Sebastian through the window. Her face is deathly pale, carved with tension. She watches as he lashes out with his foot, kicking the wheel of the battered old car. He hangs his head and stands motionless for a long moment.

When he turns and trudges through the snow back to the Mercedes, Isobel knows he doesn't have what it takes. He'll never triumph over Mr Punch. She presses the button to roll down the window.

"It's not there?" she says.

"No."

"What now then?"

"We have to go in the house."

"Break in?"

"Maybe. Depends if anyone's home."

"If they are, I doubt they'll let you in."

"With a gun in their face they won't have a choice."

They hold each other's gaze for a long moment. Then Isobel rolls the window back up and gets out of the car.

Sebastian starts back up the driveway. Isobel follows.

"I'm not sure this is such a good idea."

"Me either, but there's no other play. Even if the bag isn't in there, the car's on their driveway. They must know something."

The front door is painted glossy black, adorned with an elaborate brass knocker carved in the shape of a fish. Something about this doesn't feel right. Sebastian can't explain it, but he's tense, filled with a sense of expectation. All his instincts are suddenly pinging away and he slides one of the guns from his coat and flicks off the safety.

"What is it?" Isobel whispers.

Sebastian doesn't knock on the door. Instead, he gives it a gentle push. The latch gives way with a click and the door swings open. The hallway beyond is dark. From somewhere deep in the house is the faint burble of the television. Polished floorboards run away from the front door towards the staircase. Sebastian steps into the house, with Isobel close behind.

"Shut the door."

Isobel does so. There are no windows in the hallway, just bright narrow strips at the bases of the doors. Sebastian opens the first one. A large living room, with tall windows looking out on the driveway, an ornate fireplace, bookshelves in the alcoves and an elaborately patterned rug on the polished wooden floor. Aside from the furnishings, the room is empty.

Another door leads into a large kitchen, solid wood cabinets and granite worktops, a full-size Range Master and a Bellfast sink. An old clock ticks loudly from the wall and a tap is dripping with a rhythmic *pock-pock-pock*.

The hallway seems to go on forever, the house deceptively larger than it looks from the front. Isobel is rigid with tension, her breathing fast, but Sebastian doesn't bother to tell her to be calm. He's not much better himself.

The television is getting louder. There is a door at the back of the staircase. Sebastian gently pulls it open, hoping to find nothing but a storage cupboard. But stairs lead down into light and noise. A cellar, converted to an entertainment room by the sound of it. What to do now? Go down or finish searching this level? There are two more doors off the hallway, one across from the cellar stairs and one at the far end. For a long moment Sebastian is conflicted, undecided. Then he carefully eases the cellar door closed again. He needs to know the ground floor is clear first.

The door across from the cellar leads into a shower room, tiled and bright despite the dull light coming through the frosted window. There are blue towels on a heated rail. Sliding glass doors enclose the shower.

Sebastian moves on to the last door at the end of the hallway. A narrow strip of light glows at the bottom. A shadow slides along the light; there is movement on the other side of the door.

Sebastian tightens his grip on the gun. He motions Isobel to one side of the door. She backs up, out of the line of fire should someone start shooting. Sebastian reaches for the door handle.

There is a muffled thump from upstairs, something falling maybe, hitting carpet. Sebastian pauses with his hand on the door handle. Isobel is looking up at the ceiling. Sebastian can feel the situation spiralling, running away from his control – movement from behind the door, movement from above, sounds from down below. What have they walked into?

Sebastian pulls open the door and moves fast into the room, crouched low, focused, gun steady, checking all four corners, senses tuned for movement of any kind.

There is nothing in the room save for a long dining table of some highly polished dark wood, and a large ginger cat strolling across the gleaming surface. It turns as he bursts through the door, its nonchalant walk pauses for a heartbeat as its yellow eyes look into his. Then it carries on strolling along, before gracefully jumping onto the rug and disappearing through open French doors into a large conservatory.

Sebastian remembers to breathe.

He moves deeper into the room, around the table, towards the French doors. The conservatory beyond is tiled and open. The cat is perched on the windowsill looking out at the snow. The garden is a smooth blanket of white.

"Jesus," whispers Isobel. "That was tense."

Sebastian turns to look at her.

A small boy of about ten, wearing Spiderman pyjamas, is staring at them from the top of the cellar stairs. An Xbox cordless controller dangles from one hand. The door to the cellar is open again, but there is no sound now. The boy has paused his game.

The boy looks Sebastian and Isobel up and down.

They stare back. Then the spell breaks.

"Mum!"

The boy turns and sprints for the stairs, absolute panic in his ear-splitting scream. A thump from above, as of something being dropped, followed by hurried footfalls crossing the room. The boy is already bounding up the stairs.

Isobel is closer to the door and already moving, across the dining room and into the hall. Sebastian catches up with her at the base of the stairs, moving past, gun raised and sighted up the narrow flight.

From somewhere above the agitated boy is struggling to tell his mother. Any moment now she'll pick up the phone and dial 999.

Sebastian scoots up the stairs quickly, with Isobel right behind him. Many doors lead off the landing, but Sebastian already knows where to go. He can hear the boy urgently talking to his mother.

The bedroom at the end of the landing spans the entire width of the house. A large bay window looks out onto the back garden. The boy is sat on the bed, his mother kneeling before him, her hands on his shoulders. She is urging him to be calm, to speak clearly, to tell her what's wrong.

She is wearing just her underwear. There's a towel and a hairdryer on the floor. Her white skin gleams with moisturiser and there is a faint lemony tang to the air. It takes her all of two seconds to sense Sebastian's presence in the doorway. She turns slowly, eyes widening.

"Don't move."

Sebastian steps into the room. The boy is up off the bed in an instant, shooting past him towards the door.

Isobel grabs him, picking him up and hurling him onto the bed with such economy and authority that Sebastian is, for just a moment, astonished.

"Control him. Or I will," Isobel says to the mother.

The mother pulls her son to her breast, and backs away towards the far side of the bed.

"Don't move," Sebastian says again.

"Take whatever you want." Her voice is barely a whisper. She has one hand protectively around the back of her son's head, his small body held tightly against her own.

Sebastian glimpses a dark path, straying far from his moral compass.

He lowers the gun and takes a deep breath.

"We're not here to hurt you, or your son. We just need some answers." Sebastian looks towards Isobel. "Right?"

Isobel's face is blank. She is probably more in shock than the boy, but the mother doesn't know that. All she sees is a man with a gun, and a woman one step away from complete nervous exhaustion. Isobel looks like a junky run ragged chasing down a score. Sebastian doubts he looks much better. The last few hours have taken their toll.

The mother is looking from Sebastian to Isobel and back again, her big white eyes almost popping from her face.

"What's your name?"

She doesn't answer. Not defiant, just in shock.

"Your name," Sebastian repeats. He raises the gun, just a little, for emphasis. Clearly this is going to be hard work.

The mother flinches.

"Mary," she whispers.

"And your son. What's his name?"

"Albert."

Sebastian hesitates. Who calls their son Albert nowadays?

"Okay, Mary, I'm going to ask you some questions. Do you understand?"

Mary nods yes.

"The car in your driveway. Who owns it?"

"My husband."

"What's his name?"

"Why are you…"

"Answer the fucking question," Isobel interrupts quietly. The strain in her voice is unmistakable and she sounds dangerously on edge.

"Daniel," Mary whispers.

"And were is Daniel now?"

"Next door. He popped round to get some teabags. We've run out and getting down to the shops in all this snow will be a nightmare." Mary is whispering almost to herself.

Any moment now husband Daniel is going to come back.

"Sit down on the floor." Sebastian gestures towards the furthest corner of the room with the gun. Mary remains motionless, starring at him dumbly.

"NOW!" Isobel roars.

Mary jumps and almost drops her son, then hurriedly sits on the floor in the corner.

"If you let on to your husband that we're here, I'll shoot your son in the kneecaps. Do you understand?"

Mary nods her head up and down vigorously, her wide eyes glistening with tears. She clutches her boy to her chest.

Sebastian looks through the windows at the gently falling snow, across rows of back gardens to the houses beyond. Is anyone over there watching? Can they see in? Are they calling the police? Nothing he can do about that now. Nothing left but to wait for Daniel and hope that he has something of value to say. This whole thing is already feeling like a fools errand; waiting around in this house is tactical suicide. Few exit routes, with any number of people potentially seeing them come in, police or worse possibly on the way, and a completely unknown quantity in the guise of Daniel about to come through the front door. But there is nothing else.

Sebastian suddenly wonders if the bag could be here in the house. He's been so on edge, anticipating guns and violence at any moment that he hasn't been thinking straight. The fucking cargo could be stashed under the bed right here, or down in the cellar. He's just about to ask Mary when the front door bangs shut downstairs.

Mary takes a sudden, sharp intake of breath. Sebastian puts a finger to his lips.

A voice from downstairs calls out:

"Gosh it's cold out there."

Sebastian looks towards Isobel. She just stares back with her turbulent eyes.

"Next door only has Tetley, no Earl Grey I'm afraid."

The voice is faint now. Most likely Daniel has gone into the kitchen. How long before he decides to come upstairs and find out why his wife hasn't responded?

Again Sebastian is stumped by the situation. Should I go down and confront him, he wonders, leaving Isobel up here with Mary? But would Mary take a risk and fight back if I weren't here? She doesn't seem the type, but then all parents are desperate and unpredictable when their children are in danger.

Tactics, the one thing that separates a soldier from an officer. Warrington's voice whispers in Sebastian's mind.

The shooting he can handle. A small amount of training and instinct takes over. Plus if you get it wrong you probably won't live long enough to regret it. But when there's time to think it starts getting difficult. And with a woman and child as hostages... Fuck, I don't know. I'm so far out of my depth it's not even funny.

Somewhere below a television starts burbling and Daniel's voice rings out over the top.

"Kettle's on. Are you coming down?"

Sebastian pulls the second gun from his jeans and holds it out to Isobel. She looks at it blankly for a moment, then shakes her head.

"I have to go down there. I need you to take this and keep them covered. Just for a couple of minutes," Sebastian whispers.

Mary is watching the exchange, watching Isobel's hesitation. Her son is sat in her lap, still held tightly to her chest. He might be asleep, or deep in shock.

Isobel takes the gun.

"Safety's off." Sebastian is looking at Mary when he says this. Hoping the message rings home.

"Stay over there, Mary. Stay quiet, and keep your son quiet, and I promise you everything will be okay." To Isobel he says, "Don't take your eyes off them. I'll be back in a minute."

The landing now seems dark after the brightness of the bedroom. He treads lightly, gun raised, his ears straining for sounds from below. In his mind he runs back through the layout of the house: the living room, the kitchen, the shower room, the dining room, the cellar. The stairs creak under his weight as he goes down.

He scans the hallway. The television is loud, coming from the living room just across from the foot of the stairs. Sebastian ducks his head in. But the room is empty.

The next door along is the kitchen. Sebastian slides up to the doorway.

Daniel is in the kitchen, holding a mug in one hand, a teabag in the other. He is wearing dark trousers and a white shirt open at the neck. He is tall, muscular and handsome. Certainly not the kind of man Sebastian was expecting. The kettle on the granite worktop comes to the boil and clicks off.

"Daniel," Sebastian says quietly.

Daniel turns around. It takes a moment for him to register what he's seeing and then he drops the mug. It shatters on the tiled floor and Daniel nearly jumps out of his skin.

"Take it easy."

Daniel has gone deathly white and his eyes appear huge. Shock is a natural reaction to a gun-wielding intruder in your home, especially one who knows your name.

"This way." Sebastian beckons him forwards.

"What do you want?"

"Walk towards me Daniel."

"Take anything. Just don't hurt us."

"Right now I need you to walk towards me. Don't make me ask you again. Hands on your head while you're at it."

He moves slowly, raising his hands, still clutching the teabag. Sebastian backs out of the kitchen, keeping the gun steady and staying out of his reach. Daniel keeps coming. Sebastian backs down the hallway towards the front door.

"Now up the stairs. Slowly."

Daniel turns and starts to climb. Sebastian, now behind him, follows him up.

"The room at the back."

Daniel sees Isobel pointing a gun at his wife and son and pauses in the doorway. Sebastian gives him a hard shove into the room. He's so big it barely moves him, but it seems to get the point across and Daniel shuffles over to the bed.

Now they have the whole family at gunpoint.

"Kneel." Sebastian motions downwards with the gun.

"Don't hurt my family."

"Don't give me a reason to." Sebastian takes a deep breath, and feels calmer. Having Daniel beside his wife and son will make him think twice about any attack. With his family right here, he'll be putting them in harms way if tries anything.

"The car in your driveway. Last night there was a bag on the back seat. Where is it now?"

Daniel shakes his head.

"The bag, Daniel. Don't make me ask you again."

"I don't know anything about a bag." Fear is etching deep lines across his face.

"You lying to me Daniel?"

"No."

"You'd risk your life, the lives of your family for the contents of that bag?"

"I swear, I don't know anything about a bag."

Isobel is getting anxious. The hand holding her gun is growing dangerously unsteady, still pointing in the general direction of Mary and the boy. Sebastian tries another question:

"Do you own the car?"

"Yes. I don't use it much, but it's mine."

"If it's your car, how come I picked it up from a car park in Brixton last night? How come it was brought back here in the early hours of this morning?"

Daniel swallows and shakes his head.

"Jesus, answer him you dumb cunt!" Isobel pushes the barrel of her gun hard against the side of Daniel's head, her face a mixture of rage and fear and desperation.

Mary shrieks and begins to rise and Isobel turns the gun on her, reflexively pulling back on the trigger.

There is a dry click, followed by a moment of stunned silence. Isobel's mouth drops open in horror.

Daniel tries getting to his feet, but Sebastian is on him in an instant; one swift strike to the side of his head with the barrel of the gun sends him sprawling to the floor.

Mary is now on her feet and struggling over the bed, her son clutched in her arms. Isobel is still pointing the gun at the empty space where she was crouched just a moment before.

Sebastian takes the gun from Isobel. The clip is empty. He used all of the bullets back at the junky rabbit warren. He tucks the gun back into his jeans as Isobel turns startled, tear-filled eyes to him.

"Go wait downstairs."

She blinks, swallows hard, then turns and walks out of the room.

Mary is down on her knees beside Daniel. She stares at the blood gushing from his eyebrow and soaking his shirt. But it's an injury that looks worse than it is. There is such confusion in her eyes. Her son, clutched in her arms, is sucking his thumb.

"I'm not fucking around. I really will hurt all of you if you don't tell me what I need to know."

Both Daniel and Mary turn their eyes up to Sebastian, and he stands over them, aiming the loaded pistol at them.

"This one is loaded. Next time around, Mary, you'll be dead." He tries to make his voice flat and hard, the voice of a man capable of executing a family. But the breath wheezing in and out of his lungs undermines the effect. Nevertheless, the threat is enough to start Daniel talking.

"Awhile ago we had some problems. Financial problems. Share prices in this company I was involved with dropped sharply and..."

"I don't care, Daniel."

He stops, swallows, starts again.

"I was drunk, you know. Really drunk. And I got talking to this guy at the motorway services.

"Get to the point."

"I told him about the company failing. I'm not really sure what I told him. But it basically ended with him saying he'd rent the car off me."

"Rent?"

"Yeah. It was my brother's old car, and I bought it off him, thought I'd use it for pottering around town or something. I was going to sell it but this guy said about renting it every now and then. I don't really remember. But I must have given him my number because a few days later I got a call, from a withheld number. The guy said he wanted to use the car for a couple of days. Said to leave the key outside, and he'd put five grand through the letterbox. The car went in the middle of the night and when we came down in the morning there was the money. The car reappeared two days later and the key was posted through the letterbox. Who took it and what they did with it I haven't a clue."

"When did this happen?"

"It's been going on for about two years. The car goes maybe once every month, less than that."

Despite how improbable the story sounds, Sebastian can't help but believe it. Using the car makes sense. Obtaining one in such a basic and simplistic way is an obvious, easy thing to achieve. Who wouldn't say no to renting out a car they hardly use, especially when they were struggling for cash?

"You said the motorway services?"

"Yeah."

"What were you doing drunk at a fucking motorway services?"

Daniel looks down at his hands. He doesn't answer.

Something about this isn't sitting right with Sebastian.

The modus operandi is what he would expect now from Mr Punch. But that would mean...

All of a sudden the pieces slot together.

Sebastian tries not to shudder too violently in front of Daniel and his family.

"And the guy you spoke to?"

"I was drunk. I don't really remember."

"What was his name?"

"Uh, it was odd sounding, I don't know."

"Think, Daniel. Or I'll shoot your wife."

Daniel wipes blood from his eye with the heel of his hand.

"It was Ichabod."

"Ichabod?"

"Yeah."

"You fucking with me, Daniel?"

"No, I swear."

"What kind of name is Ichabod?"

"Washington Irvine used it for the hero of *Sleepy Hollow*."

"What?"

"The Headless Horseman."

Daniel begins to cry.

Time to leave. Sebastian backs out of the room. Downstairs he finds Isobel waiting by the front door. She is wide-eyed and sweating, greasy hair hanging in her face, and the smell of vomit wafts along the hallway from the kitchen.

Sebastian opens the front door and they hurry back out into the snow. The cold wraps its icy fingers around them.

16

Sebastian puts a few streets between them and the house before pulling over and turning off the engine. He looks out at the street beyond the windscreen, watching the snow.

"I've been played," he says.

Isobel, curled up in the passenger seat, looks over at him.

"You think that guy was lying to you?"

"No, I think he was telling the truth. That's the problem." Sebastian's hands clench tightly around the steering wheel, squeezing with all his strength.

"Fuck it!" He lashes out and punches the dashboard.

Isobel, shocked, recoils in her seat.

"I've been set up from the beginning."

"I don't understand."

"The man who hired me to deliver the bag also sent you. He jacked his own cargo. He already has the fucking bag. He gave me twenty-four hours to get it back just to stop me from running." Sebastian turns to Isobel. "You and I have the same employer."

"I don't get paid," Isobel says quietly. "How do you know?"

"Think about it. My employer supplied the car. I picked it up in Brixton, drove it to Dover, picked up the cargo and came here. You were told to dump the car after attacking me, but you dumped it right back where it came from."

"I guess that makes sense."

Sebastian sighs heavily. Rage and confusion makes him want to scream. But at the same time, a sudden lightness creeps into him. The cargo doesn't matter. There is no ticking clock. There is nothing but his employer and the imperative for survival.

I could run, he thinks. I could take Kenosha's car and drive out of here and never look back. But how far will be far enough? From what Isobel has said, this is no ordinary maniac. What resources does he have at his disposal? How far can he reach?

"Will he ever stop, do you think?"

"He won't give up. If you run you'll be running for the rest of your life."

"Or I can kill him."

"You can try. If you can find out who he is."

"I know who he is. Daniel told me his name."

"And you think he told Daniel the truth? Believe me, it won't be that simple."

"Maybe not, but I'm still alive." The realisation of this hits Sebastian. Nobody expected him to survive. They've underestimated me, he thinks. I'm better than all their guys because they're not trained, they're just ordinary Joes. The little empire this guy has built is sinister and the anonymity has merits, but it's not designed for war. And that's what I've been waging against them. How many more men can this Mr Punch have? What will he do when he runs out?

"I can beat him," Sebastian says to himself.

He pulls out his phone and taps in a number. Isobel is staring at him. Inside, his guts are twisting. The phone rings just once before it is answered.

"Ah, Sebastian. Feeling brave enough to call me from your own phone. How're you getting on? Found the bag yet? Tick-tock, tick-tock."

"Fuck you, you crazy bastard."

"Well, that's the spirit."

"I know you set me up. I know you've already got your fucking cargo."

"I wondered if you'd figure it out. You really would make a good television detective."

"I want to meet you."

"Of course you do. I'm rather partial to the motorway services on the edge of town. Why don't you meet me there?"

"No matter how many guys you bring, I'll kill them all."

"I believe you. You've proved that already. That's why I'll be there in person. I think it's time we ended this, don't you Sebastian?"

"Yeah, one way or another."

The line goes dead. Sebastian chucks his phone up on the dashboard.

* * *

Ichabod slips his phone back in his pocket. For a long moment he stares at Mary and her son. They played their part well. He wasn't sure whether they would give him away. He was confident Mary would play along, under the belief that by doing so she would be saving her real husband. But the boy was different. Ichabod really had no idea how the boy would react to this stranger pretending to be his Dad. In the end, the shock of it all seems to have rendered him mute. Good.

When Sebastian and Isobel left, Ichabod had gone downstairs to the living room and watched through the window as they drove away. Blood from his eyebrow where Sebastian had hit him was drying on the side of his face, staining his shirt. He didn't care. The ruse had worked.

He'd gone back upstairs to where Mary and her son were still cowering in the bedroom. He'd sat on the bed and watched them until Sebastian had called. He felt strangely calm as he told Sebastian to meet him at the motorway services. Despite the risks, he'd felt reassured. For a while things had gone sideways, but now he had a measure of control. He was back in charge of the game. Almost.

"You played your part well. You had me believing I was really your husband."

Mary's weak smile is full of desperation.

"If I had my way, I'd play your husband for a while longer. I'm sure there are lots of fun husband and wife games we could enjoy together." Ichabod slides over to Mary. She is still holding her son.

Ichabod looks pointedly at her breasts, at her thighs.

"That really is some attractive lingerie you're wearing. Daniel was a lucky man."

Mary's eyes fill with tears.

"Oh, I'm sorry. Did I say 'was'? You see, Daniel died last night. When I said you could save him, I lied. The man who was just here shot him in both legs and left him to bleed to death behind a factory."

Ichabod grabs Mary's chin. She tries to slide away from him, but he forces his lips upon hers, sliding his tongue into her mouth.

"I would've liked to be your husband for a couple of hours. But I'm not allowed today."

Ichabod stands up. He pulls a small pistol from his pocket and shoots Mary and her son.

He surveys the mess, looking for some revelation in the pattern of blood on the sheets.

Finding nothing, he leaves the house.

* * *

"You know it's not Mr Punch." Isobel, sat in the passenger seat, is staring out of the window.

"What do you mean?"

"There's no way he would ever turn up. It just doesn't fit his style. You're being set up."

Sebastian is silent for a time.

"Maybe. But at least I'll get to end it."

"No, you won't. If you survive it won't be over because he won't have been there."

"What about you?"

"This is where you kill me. I'm not doing this any more."

"Why run now, after all these years being too scared to do it?"

"I just pulled the trigger on an innocent woman. Imagine if the gun was loaded. I can't do this anymore, Sebastian. And you're my ticket out. You killed me. Dumped my body at the side of a road in some country lane before heading to the motorway services. That's what you say if you ever get the chance."

"You know he won't believe me."

"I know. But I'm hoping you'll be able to give me a head start. Just a few hours to get clear."

"I can do that."

"Thank you."

"Why I should, I don't know. The only reason this has happened is because of you."

"Hardly. You agreed to work for him. You only have yourself to blame."

Sebastian is silent for a time. Isobel is right, but he doesn't want to admit it. You go to work for an obviously criminal organisation, even if your job is only to deliver a bag, and you step through the curtain into a world where the usual rules don't apply. Nobody made that choice for him. The responsibility is his.

Isobel is rummaging in the glove box for a scrap of paper and a pen. She jots a phone number down and hands it to Sebastian.

"This is a friend of mine. He'll be the only one who knows how to reach me. If by some miracle you win, let him know so I can come home."

Sebastian takes the scrap of paper.

"Who is he?"

"His name is Andrew. He's a friend."

For a long moment they hold each other's gaze. Then Isobel opens the door.

"Good luck." Sympathy and no small degree of pity fill her voice. She's pretty certain he'll be dead before dawn.

"You too."

Isobel swings the door shut. Sebastian watches her through the windscreen as she walks away through the snow. He wonders if he'll ever see her again.

Sebastian chucks the scrap of paper with Andrew's phone number on the passenger seat. He puts the empty gun in the glove compartment and checks the clip on the other one. Half empty. He sighs. He tucks the gun into the pocket of his jacket. He's going into an unknown situation with a single, half-empty weapon. Suddenly, running doesn't seem like such a bad option.

He pulls out his asthma pump and takes a deep hit. His lungs are hurting constantly now, an ache felt in his ribs, pushing up into his collarbones and round his back to his kidneys. He's had plenty of lung infections before, even pneumonia one particularly bad winter when he was a teenager. He knows the aches associated with it. If he lives through the rest of the day he'll be laid up in bed tomorrow.

Sebastian gets the car started and drives off towards the motorway services.

* * *

Ichabod comes out of the house and gently shuts the front door behind him. He strolls down the driveway and trudges through the snow, down the street to where he parked his car. He gets in behind the wheel and thumps the door shut. Taking his mobile from his pocket he speed dials a number. The phone is answered on the third ring.

"What now?"

"It's me."

"I know. Where are you?"

"Just leaving the house where your little filly dumped the car."

Mr Punch sighs.

"Don't whinge," says Ichabod. "You'll never guess who I've just been talking to."

"I don't care."

"Ah, but you will."

"Who, Ichabod?"

"Sebastian and Isobel. Really, I don't know why you've kept her on ice all these years. She's not looking too good at the moment. But then maybe all the blood and death has tipped her over the edge."

"What were you doing at the house?"

"Playing husband."

"I told you, action at the house is too close. There's a direct link to us. It's a weakness, Ichabod. It makes us vulnerable.

Ichabod's face splits into an enormous grin.

"Yeah. Great isn't it?"

"Great? Are you out of your fucking mind?"

"C'mon, when was the last time things got this exciting?"

"We're close to going out."

"Don't be so dramatic. Nothing wrong with a challenge every once in a while. This guy's just shaking us up, keeping us on our toes."

"Toes? Ichabod, did you know that in the last twenty-four hours we have lost so many men, people are more afraid of dying than they are of us? Did you know that? The influence we've built up over the years is being eroded by some dumbass who won't die. We're running out of people we can force into the streets to take this guy on, because everyone else we've sent after him has turned up dead."

"Everyone'll fall back in line when we win."

"Achieving that seems to be a little difficult at the moment. Did you talk to him?"

"Yeah."

"Then why didn't you just fucking shoot him and be done with it?"

"Because like you said, the house is too close. Besides, what fun would that be?"

"So what did you do?"

"I sent him to the motorway services."

Mr Punch considers this for a few seconds.

"Okay, good. I'll drum up everyone we've got left. We'll throw everything we've got at him."

"There's something else. I think he has help in town."

"What sort of help?"

"The car he's driving. It's too ostentatious to be stolen. I think he borrowed it."

"That'll be Kenosha, the friend he mentioned to Isobel last night. Did you get the plate?"

"Yeah." Ichabod tells him the plate number.

"Let me check this out. What are you going to do?"

"I'm going back to see Tally. I need to know why she let him go in the first place."

"No more fucking about, Ichabod. This has gone too far, well beyond games. We are threatened by this now, do you understand?"

"I know."

"We need to finish this completely. Sebastian, and this Kenosha."

"What about Isobel?"

"If she survives the motorways services, which is doubtful, then I'll deal with her myself."

"You sure? You've been cultivating her for a long time."

Mr Punch is silent. Ichabod wonders how deep the connection is. To have controlled her from afar for so long is quite extraordinary.

"I'll do it for you, if it comes to it," Ichabod offers.

"No. She's my problem."

Mr Punch breaks the connection.

Ichabod chucks the phone onto the passenger seat and starts the car.

17

It is no warmer inside the telephone box than it is out on the street. Isobel punches in his number and waits, the handset pressed to her ear. She watches the traffic inching past as the phone rings.

"Hello?"

A child's voice. For a moment Isobel is stumped.

"Hi. Is your Dad there?"

"Yeah, hang on."

Isobel listens as the child shouts for his Dad. There are other sounds too, the sound of a woman singing, the banging of pots and pans, the laughter track of some television sitcom and the distant laughter of another child.

This is not the sterile family environment that he always described.

"Yeah, hello?"

"Hey."

"Isobel?" Andrew's voice is surprised. Then, quietly, "I thought you were working today?"

"I…"

"Hold on." The phone is suddenly muffled and Isobel can hear faint voices talking on the other end. Andrew's wife, maybe?

"Look Isobel, it's a bit awkward at the moment."

The background noise is no longer there. He's moved to a different room, a quieter part of the house.

"I know, I'm sorry. But I need your help."

"Aren't you at work?"

"I was. I'm popping back there on my way home. I need you to meet me."

"Why? What's going on?"

"I can't explain now. Just meet me at my place, please."

"Are you alright?"

"No."

Silence for a moment, and then Andrew says, "I'm not sure I can make it right now, Isobel."

"Please Andrew. I wouldn't be asking if this wasn't really important. I know it's difficult because you're at home with your family, I know. But this is really serious."

"Where are you?"

"I'm at a payphone."

"A payphone? What's going on?"

"I can't tell you now. I'm going to walk. No point trying to catch a cab because the roads are fucked. I'm going to the hospital to get some stuff and then home. I'll be there in about an hour. Please just go round to my place and sit outside in the car and wait for me to get there. If…"

"Isobel?"

"If what we've done together has meant anything, then please, Andrew, just do this for me."

Andrew sighs down the phone. "Alright, alright. I'll be there in an hour."

"Thank you. See you soon." Isobel hangs up. She steps out of the phone box back onto the street. The light is fading fast and bright yellow headlights punctuate the line of cars snaking by. She trudges through the snow, her breath misting in front of her eyes, the cold sucking at her shoes, which are completely inappropriate for the weather. The boots she walked to work in are still in her locker at the hospital, along with her door keys, her phone and her purse. She has buttoned the coat Sebastian bought her all the way up; her hands are thrust deep in the pockets and wrapped around her narrow body, pulling the coat even tighter. She is chilled to the bone, her poor feet numbed and wet, her long hair plastered to her scalp and hanging limply in her face. It feels like she's been cold and wet ever since Mr Punch sent her out into the rain the night before.

A gang of kids go hurtling past, launching snowballs at each other and at the stationary cars stuck in traffic. Angry drivers lean from windows to shout reprimands. The kids curse back, hurling insults as easily as snowballs. Other drivers scoop snow from the roofs of their cars and return fire. One narrowly misses Isobel and the driver shouts an apology. Isobel doesn't look up, doesn't acknowledge the world around her. She is afraid the wrong person might recognise her.

At the junction where Fort Pitt Hill meets New Road, a car has come sliding down out into the traffic, pranging at least three other cars. The poor lady driver, dressed in a duffle coat, gloves and scarf, is trying to fend off a group of angry motorists, her car cutting into the line of traffic inching along New Road and backing it up, possibly for miles.

Beyond Luton Arches, at the bottom of Chatham Hill, the walking gets harder. The incline of the hill and Isobel's useless shoes conspire to send her slipping to the ground more than once. But she presses on.

Isobel wonders what Andrew will say when he sees the state she's in. She wonders what she will say to him when he asks her what's going on. How will she explain the need for a lift to Ashford International? Less than twenty-four hours ago she was fucking him, now she's going to ask him to help her flee the country. He'll want to know why. But the less he knows the safer he'll be.

All she can hope for is that Sebastian somehow manages to triumph. But she knows that isn't going to happen. He may find his employer and take him out, but Isobel doesn't believe for a second that this guy is the same man that she calls Mr Punch. She isn't sure how she knows this, but she's never been so sure of anything before. The notion is inconceivable. Sebastian may kill his employer. But he'll never find Mr Punch.

All Isobel can hope for is that she'll be able to slip away unnoticed and untraceable, to find a new life somewhere in a different county.

Not much of a plan, barely even considered, but it should give her enough time and space to refocus and figure out where to go.

Perhaps Holland. Lay low in Amsterdam, become a call girl working at an agency under an assumed name. Paid in cash. No bank accounts, no credit cards, nothing involving her real name. That sounds possible.

Halfway up Chatham Hill and her shoes betray her and she slips, falling heavily, banging her knees and hip. A guy hanging outside Dominos Pizza laughs uproariously, making no move whatsoever to help her.

Isobel struggles back to her feet, cursing the guy silently. But she avoids looking over at him. She doesn't want to be slowed down or drawn into anything. As she regains her feet, more kids go hurtling by on sledges, almost knocking her over again.

The snow continues to fall steadily and she trudges past a car with its windows painted black. Deep thumping bass issues from some extravagant sound system, reverberating in her skull and sending her thoughts haywire.

Gradually the bass dwindles, as step after step she puts distance between herself and the ridiculous car, until the racket is lost in the ambient noise, the incessant rumble of cars filing slowly by, the crunch of her feet in the mounting snow, the shrieks from nearby kids. Isobel plods on, one foot after another, cresting the top of the hill, moving past the church on the left and the pub on the right, past the grammar school to the junction of Ash Tree Lane.

She waits at the lights, then crosses the A2 and turns left, leaving the chaos of the main road behind, descending into the quiet of the residential streets. Here the snow is relatively unmarked, what footprints there are gradually erased by new snow. The lampposts are already aglow, casting their jaundiced light over the tall and elegant façade of the houses. The noise from the main road dwindles at her back, until the only sounds are her shoes crunching in the snow.

Apprehension begins to flutter in her stomach. The chaos of cars and people lent a certain amount of comfort, but here, getting deeper into the labyrinth of narrow roads, descending into stillness and quiet, by degrees the prospect of some kind of ambush grows.

Isobel looks into the darkened windows of the cars in the street, wondering if anyone is lurking in the shadows, primed to spring as she shuffles by.

But gradually the traffic begins to increase, and the world seems to come alive again. The hospital, at the centre of a web of narrow residential streets, is full of life and noise.

* * *

What if they're waiting at my flat? What if I've brought Andrew out to his death? Isobel arrives at the front door of her building. The old house, converted into a number of flats, is silent. No lights burn in the windows. Her neighbours are probably out at work.

She managed to get into her locker at the hospital and grab her stuff without incident. She walked out of the main doors without anyone glancing in her direction, just another weary face in the constant ebb and flow of people bustling in and out.

On the walk from the hospital to her flat the streets became quieter again, and apprehension gripped her heart. It was all too easy. Something was bound to go wrong.

A hand claps Isobel on the shoulder and she shrieks, spinning around and loosing her footing in the snow, tumbling down. She scrabbles away, kicking herself backwards with her heels, looking up through her wet hair at the looming shape above.

"Jesus. What the hell's going on?" Andrew, palms out, is looking down on Isobel, stunned by her reaction. Isobel is breathing hard and trembling, looking up at him, a mixture of emotions warring for dominance over her face – anger, relief and fear.

"Don't fucking do that!"

"Do what?" Andrew steps forward and hauls Isobel to her feet. Holding her by the forearms he looks into her face and is shocked at what he sees.

"What's going on, Isobel?"

She turns from him without a word, opening the front door of her building and climbing the stairs. Andrew follows her inside.

Isobel creeps along the landing to her flat.

"Isobel?"

"Sshh!"

Andrew following close behind, is at a loss.

"What are you doing?"

"Be quiet!"

Isobel inspects the lock on the door, looking to see if there are scratch marks, anything that might indicate someone has broken in. They could still be in there, waiting.

She puts her ear to the door and listens for almost a minute.

Andrew, stood in the hallway with his hands in his pockets, watches Isobel with a mix of amusement and concern.

Isobel slips her key in the lock and turns it slowly, as quietly as she can. She pushes the door open. The flat is silent. She steps in and Andrew follows behind. He closes the door after them.

Isobel creeps through her flat, expecting at any moment to be jumped by a gang of Mr Punch's desperate foot soldiers. But the place is empty, and for the first time in what seems like hours she allows herself a moment to relax, sinking to her bed.

Andrew fills the kettle in the kitchen, but Isobel calls out:

"Don't bother. We're not staying."

"We're not?" Andrew walks through into the bedroom to find Isobel pulling a suitcase from under the bed.

"Where are you going?"

"Europe."

"Why?"

Isobel yanks open drawers and dumps underwear into the suitcase. She grabs an armful of clothes from the wardrobe, dresses, jeans and jumpers, and stuffs them in too.

"You're starting to scare me now."

Isobel laughs.

"Scared? You have no fucking idea, Andrew." She pushes past him into the bathroom, scooping toiletries from the cabinet.

As she walks back into the bedroom Andrew grabs her by the shoulders, his powerful hands holding her fast.

"Talk to me." There is a commanding authority in his voice, a sense of power and capability. For a moment all she wants to do is fling her arms around him and fuck him senseless, wanting pleasure, release. But just as quick the desperation and fear reassert themselves, that sense of the clock ticking, that at any moment someone might come crashing through the door, guns spitting death, killing Andrew.

"In the car," she says. "I'll tell you in the car. But right now we need to get out of here as quickly as possible."

Andrew lets her go, sensing that the fastest way to the answers will be to let her play this out in her own way.

Isobel pulls the bottom drawer of her bedside cabinet all the way out and practically flings it across the room in her haste to get to what's hidden beneath it. She pulls out a small roll of twenty pound notes, no more than a few hundred in total, her passport and a small jewellery box. She grabs a rucksack from her wardrobe and puts the money and passport inside. The jewellery box she stuffs in the suitcase and attempts to squash the lid down. Andrew helps her, bringing all his weight to bear, and Isobel zips it shut.

She shrugs off the coat and quickly changes out of her uniform into jeans and a jumper.

"Lets go." Isobel pulls the coat back on, hefting the rucksack and marching back through the flat. Andrew follows with the suitcase. They descend quickly, but at the front door Isobel stops.

"Where are you parked?"

"Just over the road."

Isobel opens the front door a fraction and takes a peek. The road is silent, snow falling gently.

Nothing for it but to try their luck.

"Be quick."

She darts through the door and out into the street, over to Andrew's Audi. Isobel sinks into the passenger seat as Andrew chucks her suitcase in the boot and gets in behind the wheel. The car roars to life and Andrew pulls carefully away from the curb, wheels spinning, windscreen wipers flicking snow back and forth.

18

Ichabod is frustrated. He is stuck on the bridge over the Medway, trying to get across into Strood. It is the quickest route to Talissa's house over on the Hoo Peninsula, quicker than the tunnel anyway. But what should take no more than fifteen minutes is proving to be an hour-long expedition.

Ichabod watches the river slide past the castle wall. He counts and re-counts the decrepit-looking boats bobbing at anchor, as the snow spirals lazily through the air. His fingertips drum on the steering wheel, an erratic tattoo with no natural rhythm.

I should have taken the fucking tunnel.

The car in the lane next to him is a shitty-looking Ford, driven by a kid with a flat Burberry cap on his head and elephantine ears sticking out underneath. Chunky gold rings wrap the fingers on both his hands. Tinny-sounding bass vibrates from the cheap speakers in the rear of the car, resonating through Ichabod's BMW, setting his teeth on edge.

He hears the snap and swish of his seatbelt unclipping and retracting. He sees the door swinging open, feels the cold on his face as he storms over to the Ford. His fist rams through the window, the kid dragged out into the road. His terrified, idiot face collapsing as Ichabod stamps on his head. The glorious burst as his heavy-duty boots hammer home. Red mess on the white snow.

Oh please let me do it.

You'll cause a scene, and he'll be angry, my simpleton son, my idiot and heir.

The car directly in front rolls forward, engine revving and wheels spinning. It travels no more than two feet, and then stops again, brought up short by the next car in the jam. Its brake lights flare brightly in the miserable dusk.

"What's the fucking point?" Ichabod screams. "You can't fucking go anywhere!"

He takes a long, deep breath, and then very carefully takes his foot off the brake and rolls forward to fill the minuscule gap.

Such bullshit.

Everyone inching forwards, slow, slowly, slower. Be still, he thinks. Be calm. Murder is an isolated pleasure to be enjoyed by one's self. It should not be a public spectacle. That road leads to ruin.

The interior of the car is shrinking. The *swish-thump* of the windscreen wipers beats out the seconds one by one. Every moment of inactivity is a knife across his nerves. Ichabod's fingers tighten around the steering wheel. His knuckles turn white. He shuts his eyes, searching for some turbulent fantasy where he holds sway over the motorists stuck in the traffic, able to control the very thoughts in their heads. But nothing sticks. There are too many distractions – the rumble of stationary car engines, the crappy bass thumping from the kid's Ford, winding him tighter and tighter. *Swish-thump, swish-thump, swish-thump.*

Ichabod is about to scream when his mobile starts ringing.

"What?"

"Where are you?"

"Stuck in *fucking* traffic."

"Never mind."

"I'm telling you someone is about to fucking get it." Ichabod looks over to the Ford. The kid has a magazine spread across the steering wheel.

"Ichabod, calm down. We've got enough problems as it is."

Ichabod remains silent.

"I have some information on this Kenosha... Ichabod?"

"I'm listening."

"He lives in the new-build apartments off Hope Way, and he works as a gigolo."

"How does he know Sebastian?"

"Don't know. I'm going to text you his address."

"And telephone number."

"You're not going to book the guy for the night. Why do you need his number?"

"So I can call the cunt and find out if he's in. Or so I can ring his mobile and find out where he is if he's out. Christ's sake, when was the last time you did one of these?"

"Don't fuck about, Ichabod. No games. Go there, cut his throat and then go home. You understand?"

"Yes, I fucking understand. Christ in a cartoon you miserable cunt, fuck you."

Ichabod cancels the call and hurls his phone at the windscreen. It strikes with a solid smack and drops to the dashboard, bouncing to the floor. He runs a hand through his black hair and pushes his palms into his eyes. Dear God, Tally, where are you when I need you? Soothe me, calm me, make the traffic disappear. Ichabod keeps his eyes tightly shut, conjuring Talissa's image, naked, sat at the kitchen table smoking a cigarette. She looks at Ichabod, meeting his eyes. Talissa exhales smoke and smiles.

My simpleton son.

Ichabod's eyes snap open. He takes a deep breath. The car in front is slowly pulling away. Ichabod waits a moment to see when it will stop, but it doesn't. At last. He sighs, putting the car in gear.

On the far side of the bridge, Ichabod has to squeeze the BMW through a gap at the side of the road, around the arse end of a jack-knifed truck. A couple of police cars sit silent, blue lights revolving steadily, splashing colour across the buildings by the side of the road. Snow caught in the revolving lights, like a visual effect, appears beautiful and tranquil amid the roaring chaos of the traffic and holds Ichabod's attention as he edges past the lorry, waved on by the police.

It's like the end of the world, he thinks, as he turns right and cuts up onto Frindsbury Hill, still heading for Talissa's place, despite Mr Punch's instructions.

An idea suddenly rifles across his mind. His face is abruptly cleaved through the middle by a wide grin. He turns to the side window and bares his teeth at the few pedestrians trudging along through the snow.

What games.

As if on cue, his phone beeps from the floor where it fell. That'll be the text with Kenosha's telephone number.

19

Talissa was almost thirty when cancer killed her mother. She was a lifelong smoker and the hacking cough was so familiar, an affectation as common as the cigarette itself. Two weeks after the diagnosis she was dead.

Ichabod was a rock, supportive and patient. During the funeral he held her hand. At the wake he was charming, sensitive and eloquent. Talissa's few relatives believed she had caught herself a prince.

On the day her mother's estate completed probate and she received a modest inheritance, Ichabod beat her unconscious with a hob-nailed boot.

She came round to find herself tied to the bed. A man wearing a leather hood was raping her. Ichabod lay by her side, leaning over her face, looking into her eyes.

"See me," he said. "Remember my face."

After the man in the leather hood had finished, Ichabod beat her unconscious again.

When she woke a second time she was still on the bed, but no longer tied down. Ichabod was sat in a chair across the room.

"Why?" she asked.

"Now your heart really does belong to me," he said.

It took Talissa a while to realise what he meant. As she suffered, and burrowed inside herself looking for somewhere safe to hide, she recalled confessing to Ichabod a story from her teenage years.

It was early in their courtship when Talissa told him about her stepfather Carl. She was afraid of him, when her mother first brought him back to the house. Over the next ten years, she came to accept Carl as her dad. But as she grew into her teens, as she grew towards womanhood, Carl's fatherly affections became inappropriate.

He tried to rape her when she was fifteen.

Forced on her back, with Carl's hand squirming between her legs, Talissa found herself paralysed, unable to fight back.

Ichabod was enthralled, moving from shocked concern to surprise as Talissa described how her mother saved her, attacking Carl with a vacuum cleaner. She divorced him afterwards, of course, but never pressed charges.

"Ever since then," Talissa confessed, "Carl has haunted my dreams. Whenever I hear of something evil in the world, it is his face I see. I couldn't imagine meeting a more twisted individual."

Later that night, as Ichabod led her to bed, she admitted being afraid of men. Sometimes that fear was a little bit exciting.

Ichabod promised to treat her heart gently.

"As if it were my own," he said, seemingly, with genuine sincerity.

But lying on the bed, in shock at such casual and yet horrific violation, as she watched Ichabod watching her, Talissa understood why: Ichabod wanted to usurp Carl has her personification of evil.

* * *

Talissa is in the kitchen making dinner when Ichabod walks through the front door. Her heart sinks.

"Talissa!" Ichabod yells. "Where are you?"

Talissa walks through into the hallway. "I really wish you would stop just walking into my house without asking."

"Shut up. You're going to do something tonight."

"No, I'm not. You're going to leave, and that's all."

Ichabod stares at Talissa. She stares back for as long as she dares. Eventually, her eyes drop to the floor then flick over to the television, and then back up to Ichabod.

"Go make me a cup of tea."

Talissa returns to the kitchen, switching the gas on under the kettle. She takes a mug from the cupboard and slams it down on the worktop. While the kettle boils Talissa returns to making her dinner, even though her appetite vanished the moment Ichabod crossed the threshold. She picks up the large chopping knife and slowly draws the blade through the courgette. The point of the knife clinks sharply against the marble chopping block.

Ichabod stands in the living room, looking at the television with his mobile pressed to his ear.

"Hello?" says the voice when the call connects.

Ichabod grins.

"Uh, yeah, is that Kenosha?"

"Yes. Who's this?"

"You don't know me. I got you number through a mutual acquaintance."

"And who might that be?"

"I'd rather not say. The less you know about me the better, but lets just say she recommended you most highly."

"Right." Kenosha's voice is tinged with humour. "So what can I do for you?"

"Ah, not for me. For my wife."

"Your wife?"

"Yeah. She, well, she always wanted to… you know, with two guys. I don't know if you do that, but…" Ichabod allows his sentence to trail off, struggling not to laugh.

"Is your wife there?"

"Ah no, not at the minute. She's been held up in traffic, you know this weather."

"Well, get your wife to call me back, that way I know she exists. Do that and then we'll talk some more."

The line goes dead.

In the kitchen the kettle is whistling away. Ichabod strolls through just as Talissa turns off the gas.

"Just talked to the guy you're gonna fuck tonight."

"I am not."

"He's a professional. You'll love it. You need to call him and invite him over."

"I don't think so."

"I want you to beg him over the phone. If you don't I'll scar you for life." He says it so casually it could almost be in jest, but Talissa knows the threat is real, sharp and visceral.

"Why?"

"Because I'm tired of your smart mouth, and this will be a nicer way of teaching you a lesson. I love you so much I want to spare you some serious pain."

Talissa hands over the mug of tea.

"I don't want to do this anymore."

"Do what?" Ichabod takes a sip.

Talissa turns away. There's no point in talking. She knows his mood. He would allow her to protest, to make her case, and he would respond in kind. Calmly.

Tonally it would sound like a conversation other people have, everyday chat about days at work, while she pottered in the kitchen preparing dinner, talking about how the boss is a pain in the arse and the intern can't spell. But Ichabod twists the rules of the world into something grotesque, and Talissa, a prisoner for so long, can only just remember what the world looked like before it was bent so out of shape.

Calm it would be, but as she contemplates arguing she knows the conversation would be all about power, about control, and pain, and perversion. She would cry, as she has done so many times, and he would take her into his arms and hold her tight. He would whisper, *I love you*, then press her hand against the kettle until she screamed.

Talissa knows exactly what would happen if she argued. So she stays silent, and submits.

20

The journey to the motorway services is slow and hazardous. Everyone is desperate to make it home before the night sets in, the darkness creeping, bringing a much deeper chill.

The heater in Kenosha's Mercedes is turned all the way up. The air blasts at the windscreen, trying to keep it from misting as Sebastian crawls forwards, bumper to bumper in the traffic. A number of people have abandoned their cars; left at angles at the side of the roads, they only serve to back up the traffic even more. But Sebastian doesn't mind the journey. It gives him time to think.

There's a big part of him that wants to keep on going, down to Canterbury, down to Dover. But what's the point? Isobel is right. He'll never be allowed to walk away. If he runs, he'll spend the rest of his life looking over his shoulder. It is such a simple choice, to either run and hide or stay and fight. It is a choice that cuts to the heart of what kind of a man you are.

As a boy, Grandpa encouraged him to stand and fight. Boys with asthma cannot run. When your back's to the wall, what other choice do you have? In the army, Sebastian gave it everything he had. But his lungs weren't good enough for active service, and a desk job was a kind of defeat he wasn't willing to accept. For years, the desire for combat was like an itch he couldn't scratch. He needed to prove himself, to know for certain that when it came to it, he would not run and hide.

Now he knows. It doesn't matter whether he still wears a uniform. He *is* a soldier. It's in his blood, his bones. He *does* have what it takes.

His phone starts ringing. It's Kenosha. Sebastian puts the call on speaker.

"What's up?"

"I need my car back."

"Sorry mate, I'm on my way somewhere."

"Fuck, Sebastian, I've got to work tonight."

"Tonight? I thought you said I could borrow the car."

"Not indefinitely."

"When do you need it?"

"I'm supposed to be there at eight."

"I doubt I'll be back."

"I'm not asking, Sebastian. It's my car."

"Kenosha, I don't think you quite understand what's happened to me today."

"There are people after you, I know. And you're trying to sort it out, I know that too. But I have to work. I'm not part of your problem."

"Work. Yeah, having some girl suck on your dick and then paying you for the privilege."

"Three times my usual rate because of the snow. So I need my car."

"Not gonna happen."

"That means you've stolen it. From a friend."

"I appreciate your predicament, but this isn't going to be over by eight."

"Are you really stealing my car? I'll call the police."

"This is about my life, remember. These people aren't giving me a fucking detention, they want to kill me. Do you understand?"

"I'm dialling the police on my other phone."

"Go ahead. They'll be looking for me already."

"Why, what've you done?"

"Shot lots of people."

"Oh yeah, like last night?"

"Kenosha, I've got two guns. You saw them last night when you picked me up. What did you think, that I was lying?"

"How should I know? Your fucked-up criminal mates probably left you out there for a laugh. Some dumbass gangland initiation ceremony."

"This isn't funny."

"Shut up Capone. I need my car back."

"Get a taxi."

"A taxi? I have a reputation, Sebastian. I can't charge a grand if I arrive in a taxi. You have to look like you're worth it."

"Tell her James Bond borrowed the Aston Martin."

"I'm not fucking about. Bring my car back."

"I can't. I'm miles away and heading in the other direction. I've got a meeting to keep, a man to shoot and my life to save."

"What happened to the bag? I thought you were going after some luggage, and you didn't even know what was in it."

"Things have changed. I'm not so sure the bag is an issue now, if it ever was."

"That's vague."

"The less you know the better."

"Great, now get back here with my car."

"Sorry. Can't."

Without another word Kenosha hangs up. Sebastian isn't worried. He'll live through the night and make it up to Kenosha in the morning, or he'll be dead. Either way it isn't going to be a long-term problem.

Sat in traffic with nothing to do, watching the snow and the night settle over the streets, Sebastian flashbacks to Grandpa in the back garden, rolling a snowball back and forth. Sebastian was watching from the kitchen door, bundled up in mittens, bobble hat and duffle coat, watching as the snowball grew bigger and bigger. He was maybe six years old, and in the absence of a father his Grandpa was the man at the centre of his world. He seemed like a giant of a man, indomitable, even though he was nearly sixty. Sebastian wanted to go outside and roll the snowball too, but he wasn't allowed. He didn't have any wellingtons and Ma said his feet would get wet in his usual shoes. And besides, the cold played havoc with his little lungs.

A thud on the passenger window jolts him from his memories and he looks out at a couple of school kids strolling by, the view marred by a large clump of snow stuck to the glass. A girl with long blond hair scoops up two handfuls of snow and compresses it between her slender pink hands before hurling it at the next car along. Her friend laughs and calls out, as the driver winds down the window to yell. The teenagers quickly move from hilarity to aggression and the motorist rolls the window back up. The kids carry on down the pavement, trudging through the snow but moving faster than the traffic.

Sebastian closes his eyes. In the darkness he sees two faces. The first is Daniel, the man he interrogated behind the factory; the second is the blond guy he executed in the flats earlier that morning.

Surviving this far makes him feel vindicated. They should never have pulled him out of active service. But he also knows both those guys were victims more than thugs, just ordinary people forced into extraordinary circumstances. Just like everyone who had died since all this began.

An enormous sense of guilt hammers him in the stomach and he hitches in a breath. Fuck. He strikes out at the steering wheel, once, twice. He had done so well to stay in control for so long, but now everything comes rushing at him at once. His body starts shaking, he struggles to draw breath, tears sting his eyes. The fucking traffic. If he weren't stuck he wouldn't have so much time for thoughts.

Sebastian grips the steering wheel with both hands and squeezes with everything he has, his eyes closed, forcing himself to get back in control. He opens his eyes and takes in a deep breath. A sharp pain stabs through his ribs, making him gasp. Jesus, this day is taking its toll.

The traffic in front has opened up a little, and when he gets himself back under control, Sebastian rolls the car forwards, just a few feet, to fill the gap.

He flashbacks to when he was a kid, maybe twelve, when Ma brought home a stray cat. It was a tiny but ferocious tabby with a mischievous streak a mile wide, one of those cats whose wild ancestry was plainly visible behind its eyes. Sebastian named it Sherwood, after the forest he sometimes dreamt about.

One morning, some time over Christmas when Ma was out shopping, Sherwood managed to capture a magpie, getting it inside the house and stalking it around the living room. The bird, which was bigger than the cat, took refuge on top of a little brass lamp in the living room. It sat up there with its black eyes staring down at Sherwood below and shitting on the carpet.

Sebastian tossed the cat out of the room and shut the door. Ma always kept a blanket down by the settee in the winter; she got cold in the evenings and wrapped it around herself when she was ironing or watching television. Sebastian threw it over the magpie. After that it was easy to catch. He carried it out to the garden and down to the shed, where he shoved it in an old cardboard shoebox and firmly put the lid on. Poking a few holes with a screwdriver so it could breathe. He kept it for a couple of days, wondering what to do with it.

A few streets over, in some council care accommodation there lived a woman called Ruperta, but all the local kids called her Mental Maureen. She was learning disabled, and every weekend the kids would watch her groaning her way down to the shops, shuffling along with a wicker basket slung over her shoulder. Kids can be rotten and most of them made her life a misery, Sebastian included.

There were some garages at the bottom of her overgrown back garden, and he would sit up there throwing stones at her back door. She would think somebody was knocking and come and answer it, looking out at her garden, sometimes for minutes at a time, before going back inside.

Sebastian would be hunkered down on the garage roof, laughing behind his hands. A minute or two after Ruperta went back inside he would throw another stone and she'd come back, going through the same routine.

Sebastian noticed that the window by her back door was always open, regardless of the weather. He'd spent a long time with his friends discussing what would be the perfect thing to shove through it to seriously weird her out. That Christmas, he decided it should be the magpie. It would freak her out like nothing else.

He went round to all his friends, one after the other, to see if any of them could come out. But none of them could, so he decided to do it by himself. Bundled up against the cold, he took the magpie in its box and clambered up over the garage, dropping silently into the weeds and long grass of Mental Maureen's garden.

Moving stealthily, not unlike Sherwood the cat, he crept up to the back door and peeked in through the glass. She wasn't there, so he took the magpie from the box, cupping his hands around its wings. It sat docile in his hands and he held it up and looked into its eyes. He couldn't see much in there. They were so completely black. He poked the bird through the open window and it took off around the kitchen, eventually settling on top of a cupboard. Sebastian crept back up the garden and hid on the garage roof, waiting for the fireworks.

He sat there in the cold for an hour. Nothing happened. He was hoping for screams and running and some hilarious groaning as she came hooting through the back door in terror. But it wasn't to be. Thoroughly disappointed, he went home.

Hours later, Ma came back. She was as white as a sheet and extremely upset. Sebastian made her a cup of tea. Ma said she'd been at the hospital with Ruperta. It turns out that the magpie did have the desired effect, except Mental Maureen went bursting out of her front door instead of the back, straight into the street.

Sebastian's Ma ran her over. It was one of those unlikely coincidences you sometimes read about in the papers.

Mental Maureen was alive, but she'd never live by herself again, probably never walk again. It took Sebastian's Ma the better part of a year to return to herself, and she was a nervous wreck behind the wheel of a car for the rest of her life.

No one ever knew that Sebastian put the magpie through Ruperta's kitchen window.

But he's carried the guilt ever since.

And now he carries even more.

Sebastian wishes he hadn't killed them.

If only there was another way.

* * *

The slip road to the motorway services runs up and over the embankment, and for a moment Sebastian doesn't think Kenosha's Mercedes will make it up, but the tires find purchase and with the engine revving into the red he wheel spins his way up to the car park.

He gets out and slams the door shut. The world is silent. The car park is ringed by streetlights. Snow swirls, churned by the wind, caught in the jaundiced light. Down on the ground, the same wind is busy scooping the drifts into elegant arcs. Across the way there is an alternate route out of the car park, leading away from the motorway back into town. It probably would have been faster to come in that way.

Sebastian studies the motorway services building, a long and narrow bridge-like structure spanning the entire width of the motorway. There are glass windows all along one side, blazing with light in the encroaching darkness, and two main entrances, one on either side of the motorway, but no way out in the middle unless he smashed through the windows and dropped maybe forty feet down to the motorway below.

Sebastian trudges through the snow across the car park, the collar of his jacket pulled up around his neck, the pain in his chest flaring with every deep inhalation. He feels for the gun beneath his coat. After the lull stuck in traffic, the cold air has sharpened his senses. He climbs the stairs up to the main entrance and yanks open the door. He steps in out of the cold.

The place is soulless in a way seemingly specific to motorway services, full of cheap and empty gestures to style and class, undermined by the various retail outlets catering to the lowest common denominator. There is a restaurant in the near corner, wipe-clean plastic menus spilling from a stand at the door. Thin partition walls, the lower half panelled, the top made of glass, separate the restaurant from the rest of the services. Inside, tables are surrounded by moulded plastic chairs based on American dimensions, for a population settling into its obesity crisis, and there are large plastic booths with fake-leather bench seats. Next door is the Magic Bean coffee shop with its gleaming silver apparatus, selling the usual mix of latte, mocha, espresso, cappuccino, all at London prices, though the drink still comes in a paper cup with a plastic lid. Further along, Burger King offers the expected menu at grossly inflated prices. In the far corner is WHSmith, its shelves stacked with only the latest chart CDs and books and magazines. On the opposite side, between the main entrance and the floor-to-ceiling windows, there is a tiny arcade, or what Sebastian would have called an arcade when he was a kid playing *Double Dragon* and *Donkey Kong*. But the Lucky Coin Emporium, as the gaudy signage names it, is entirely full of bleeping, flashing fruit machines, their incomprehensible displays organised by some esoteric design that only those of a gambling disposition ever manage to fully understand.

Lots of tables and chairs are arranged haphazardly in the large open space in front of the outlets. Only the restaurant has its own dedicated seating.

Aside from the arcade, the outlets run all the way along one side of the building. Opposite, the row of windows looks down on the motorway. A sporadic stream of traffic trundles underneath, cutting tracks through the snow, piles of black sludge alternating with long strips of pristine white.

It is colder now, now that night has come early and sucked away the daylight.

The snow is falling harder.

* * *

Sebastian waits. He sits close to the exit nearest the car, a position that allows him to see all the way across the long narrow space to the WHSmith on the far side. It's been almost an hour now, and he's getting impatient.

He keeps getting looks from Andrea, the woman behind the counter at the Magic Bean coffee shop. When he strolled up and ordered a latte she was more than willing to talk to him; it was a slow day at the services and the weather was the hot topic of conversation. Sebastian saw an opening and asked about a man called Ichabod, whether she knew who he was, how often he was there. Andrea didn't know anything. But now she keeps staring over at him. He can't decide if she's interested in a date or spooked by his presence. Either way doesn't matter, so long as she doesn't call the police.

In the meantime, he has nothing to do but wait, drink coffee and press his face up against the window to watch the falling snow.

He has already walked up and down, checking the place out. He explored the restaurant and ducked his head into the Lucky Coin Emporium. He watched the kid loafing behind the counter at Burger King and didn't see any signs of life behind his eyes. An officious-looking manager at WHSmith, tall and narrow with grey hair, was zooming around the place, giving two bored employees a hard time about maintaining standards. He was messing with the placement of books on the rack, repositioning magazines on the shelves. Sebastian returned then to his seat by the door. Now he sips his coffee from the paper cup. He waits.

There are a handful of other customers, dotted about here and there. One guy, dressed in a smart suit, is eating a Whopper and slurping loudly at his bucket of Coke. A woman wearing an expensive fur coat is sat by one of the windows, watching the snow spiral down. Every now and then she glances at her watch and fidgets in her seat.

Sebastian goes back to Andrea at the Magic Bean and orders another latte. She goes about the task without much enthusiasm, pulling the leavers and knobs on the gleaming metal apparatus, as if navigating some submarine in a boys' own adventure. When she hands him the drink she opens her mouth to say something, and then closes it abruptly. She's maybe forty, voluptuous if you were feeling charitable. Her large breasts stretch the word "Bean" across the front of her shirt.

"What?" Sebastian asks, accepting the coffee and handing over the extortionate payment.

Andrea's eyes are looking intently into his and she clearly has something she wants to say. But she turns to the till, shaking her head and stabbing at the screen to ring up the bill. She drops the coins and slams the draw shut.

"Shouldn't you be getting on home?"

"Sorry?"

"Keep hanging around here and the snow will cut you off for sure."

"I'll be alright."

"They were saying on the radio the snow could last all week. I'd get home if I were you."

"Thanks, but I'm waiting for someone."

Andrea blinks, as if surprised. Sebastian can't imagine what's going through her head. Does she think he's waiting for her? In the silence that spins out between them, he becomes aware of a buzzing sound from one of the fluorescent lights overhead.

"I'm meeting a friend."

"Okay. Don't say I didn't warn you." Her expression is difficult to read. Then she starts cleaning the coffee machine. Sebastian returns to his seat near the door, unsure about what exactly just happened.

He glances at the window and sees his reflection staring back at him. He presses his face close to the glass and looks out at the night.

The light spilling through the windows illuminates the motorway a short distance. Snowflakes go whipping past, driven into swirls and vortexes by the wind. Down below, the cars crawl by, a succession of headlights coming slowly closer only to vanish below the line of the window.

But then a different light catches Sebastian's eye; a car is approaching the slip road with its indicator blinking orange. It cruises up the incline, some kind of four-wheel drive, rugged and practical.

Sebastian checks his watch: just after six thirty. Could this be Ichabod? From this distance it's impossible to make out the occupant.

He turns his gaze to the doors. The gun is heavy in his jacket pocket.

21

Kenosha stands naked before the mirror in his bedroom, scrutinising his body and making a mental inventory of all the things he must do in preparation for tonight's client: shave, moisturise, trim and file tocnails and fingernails, tweeze nasal hair, pluck eyebrows. He runs his hands over his chest, waxed just the other day, so that's okay. He lifts his cock and strokes his scrotum. He adds 'shave scrotum and trim pubes' to the list. His lean body is evenly tanned, muscles tight in his chest and abdomen, but not over the top – he's no body builder, no athlete. In his opinion he strikes just the right balance between fit and natural. He turns his back to the mirror and looks over his shoulder, trying to see his arse. Nothing worse than a rogue zit, that can cost you a hundred quid straight away. It will be bad enough not having his car. Fucking Sebastian, who needs enemies when you've got friends?

Kenosha is struck by a sudden thought. He goes to the window and looks out, cupping his hands around his face to blot out the light in his bedroom. The snow is falling thick and fast. Suddenly wondering if he'll be able to get a taxi, he calls a cab company after hunting through his wallet to find a card with a number. After haggling he manages to secure a cab to take him out to the Hoo Peninsula, but at a truly extortionate price.

Fucking Sebastian.

Kenosha checks the clock, ninety minutes until the cab arrives. Should be enough time to get ready. He goes into the lounge where a porn movie humps along on his giant flat screen television, midway through an orgy scene.

Some guys suffer from premature ejaculation, but for Kenosha the problem was the precise opposite. It usually took him an age to reach orgasm. In the eyes of a few women he'd been with, this was a virtue, not a problem. But mostly timing was everything, and every once in a while he serviced a client who demanded he came on cue. Although Kenosha could suppress his orgasm almost indefinitely, reaching that peak in the first place required such a delicate balance of stimuli that early on in his career he started masturbating before meeting a client, tugging himself almost to the point of release, and then stopping, stoking his sexual fire until it blazed so brightly it was in danger of burning itself out. Once there, he would allow the moment to pass, remaining unsatisfied. Provided he kept himself aroused he could climb back up quite easily, but always in control, ensuring that the lady in question would get her money's worth, while at the same time, if his client was the type who wanted to watch him come, he could do so when called upon.

Also, she might have a face like a cow's arse, or a body like a beach ball. In which case, stroking himself beforehand was his only hope of reaching orgasm.

Kenosha is sprawled on his sofa, cock standing tall and wrapped in his vigorous fist, eyes glued to the television, watching the spunk-covered girls taking yet more men, the gasps and slaps and *oh yes!*

Such things we do for a living, he thinks idly, as the pressure in his cock steadily builds and the moment comes rushing up from his balls. And then, right at the critical moment, he releases his grip as if casting away a suddenly burning object, his body arches, his head and shoulders press back into the sofa and a loud gasp escapes his open mouth. But he doesn't come.

A few moments later he feels faintly ridiculous, as always. Masturbating, at least for men, is somewhat absurd in Kenosha's eyes. Beforehand the need to do it grows so huge it can eclipse the world, but after he just feels a bit stupid and secretly glad that no one was there to see it. Perhaps it is the narrowing of awareness, the way that absolutely nothing but the mounting pressure exists, and then afterwards, whether he's resisted because of work or exploded all over the place for himself, the world comes rushing back in and what was so desperate just a few moments before now seems faintly ridiculous and of little importance.

Also, Kenosha firmly believes it is impossible for a man to masturbate with dignity. In his experience, women are able to pull it off, so to speak. Slender fingers and arching backs and thrusting hips, aesthetically women can look good when they masturbate. But there is nothing elegant about a guy frantically tugging on his cock, whether laying down, standing up or anything in between. He hates it when the client wants to watch him come. It doesn't happen often, for which he is grateful, but every now and then he'll take a woman to orgasm without reaching it himself, and then she'll say she wants to watch him while he wanks. It's fine if she gets involved, if she kisses him or sucks on his balls or masturbates herself, then they are joined and the sex is mutual. But when they just lay back and watch, that's the hardest for him. He feels like such a moron.

Hoping that tonight won't be like that, he gets up from the sofa and heads for the shower. He is in and out in a matter of minutes, his routine so familiar. Standing on the bath matt as steam from the shower billows out through the bathroom door to fog up the window in his bedroom, Kenosha carefully inspects his face in the mirror. Using tweezers he plucks some wayward hairs from his nose, then sets about shaving and moisturising his face.

Sebastian would laugh his arse off if he could see me doing all this, he thinks, but then I get laid for a living and he's out there in the snow playing soldiers with criminals.

Whose got the better deal?

Kenosha stares into the mirror, meeting his own brown eyes and realising for the first time that there is a look of concern etched deeply into his face. Ever since Sebastian rang last night, Kenosha has being trying to make light of the situation, unwilling to play up to Sebastian's melodrama, believing his friend to be exaggerating the severity of the situation.

But Kenosha knows Sebastian isn't really that kind of guy. He knows him well enough to recognise when something is wrong, and for Sebastian to be as anxious as he was last night, then something very serious and extremely dangerous must be happening.

Kenosha rubs both hands over his face, trying to rub away that look of concern.

"It's not my problem," he says to himself. "Seb is a big guy; whatever it is, he can handle it."

Back in his bedroom, Kenosha flicks through his clothes in the wardrobe and settles on a grey Paul Smith suit. The cut is clean and elegant. The suit makes him look expensive, which may just offset his arrival by taxi.

Once dressed, his final order of business is to double check the contents of his kit bag. Inside are an assortment of vibrators and dildos, handcuffs, a black satin blindfold, an assortment of coloured buttplugs and a string of beads, a small whip which he's never used, a can of whipped cream, and a large supply of assorted condoms in a variety of colours and flavours. Lastly, he checks what is, in his opinion, the most important part of any sex worker's tool kit: baby wipes.

He has half a dozen packets.

With his body and kit in order, he is ready for work. He goes back into the lounge. The taxi will arrive any minute.

22

Right from the beginning Andrew knew there was something damaged about Isobel. He could see it behind her eyes, and when they started fucking he could taste it on her skin.

His leather-gloved hands grip the steering wheel confidently. The Audi plunges through the snow with ease, rushing headlong into the blizzard. There are no guarantees that any trains will be departing from Ashford International in weather like this, but Isobel insists on going.

She is slumped low in her seat, staring out through the windscreen at the falling snow, her arms wrapped across her chest, hugging herself.

"What's happened Isobel? Who're we running from?"

Isobel stares through the windscreen, oblivious to Andrew's question. He reaches out and takes her hand and she jumps in her seat, turning suddenly, eyes huge and afraid. Andrew risks a quick look across at her. He squeezes her hand.

"You're safe," he says. "Who're are we running from?"

The sudden tension in Isobel's body dissolves and she turns her face back to the night.

"The less you know the safer you'll be."

"I don't need protecting, Isobel."

"I've given your number to a friend. I don't know if he'll call you, but he might."

"Who? What friend?"

"Just so you know."

"For God's sake, Isobel, talk to me. What's going on? Whatever it is, you can tell me."

"No, I can't. It's impossible to explain. It's too old and too far in the past and too much a part of me for you to understand. All that matters is that I need to leave, and what's happened between us stays a secret."

Andrew sighs. "Where will you go?"

"The first train out of the country."

"But where? Europe's a big place."

"It doesn't matter. But I'll probably head to Holland. You can get by there speaking English."

"What will you do?'

"Don't know."

"I'll miss you."

Isobel looks over at him.

"I'll miss you too." There is genuine warmth in her words. "You'll be the only thing I'll miss."

"How long will you stay?"

"A long time."

"I'll come and visit."

"I'd like that."

They drive for a time in silence.

* * *

Ashford International looms out of the darkness in a blaze of light, the terminal lit from all sides with white floodlights. Andrew cruises through the car park looking for a space as close to the entrance as possible. He pulls in and kills the engine.

For a moment they sit in silence, the falling snow cocoons the car and there is a part of Isobel that would like to stay in that enclosed space forever.

Andrew pops his seat belt and leans across the car, one hand gently turning Isobel's face to meet his. Passion ignites as their lips touch and they gasp and grab at each other, undoing buttons and buckles until Isobel, kneeling above him, kicks off her jeans and spreads her legs, pulling her knickers to the side and she slides down the length of his cock with a gasp.

Afterwards, Isobel falls forwards, arms reaching all the way around the seat, the tension in her body draining away. Andrew, lost in the hollow of Isobel's neck, her hair tumbling on all sides, smells old perfume and stale sweat. He kisses her under the chin, and she angles her head downwards, her mouth finding his, one last love-filled and lingering kiss.

"Come with me," Isobel whispers, her hands now cupping Andrew's face. "Let's start over together. There's nothing keeping you here."

"I'd love to."

"Then lets go."

"I can't. My passport's at home."

Isobel sighs, kisses his eyes, his neck.

"Then meet me. I'll go now and you come back with your passport. I'll meet you in Paris and we'll go on to Holland together."

"That sounds like a dream."

"It sounds like a plan."

"But I can't just leave."

"Why?"

"You know why."

"There's nothing here worth staying for."

"What about my kids, my job, my house, my wife?"

"So what? Leave it. None of it matters. You can get another job. We'll move on from Holland and go to Italy, find that house on the beach, in the sun. I can be your wife. We'll make some more kids."

Andrew kisses her instead of answering, his hands cup her buttocks and he pushes his wilting cock deeper into her. For a few moments the ruse works, as Isobel sighs and kisses him back. But then she pulls away.

"What are you afraid of?"

"Two things: one, you're lying to me and all of this is some elaborate story, which leaves a lot to be said for your emotional balance and state of mind; or two, you're telling the truth and there is something here that has got you so scared you're willing to move countries to avoid it. Either way, it doesn't bode well, Isobel. Under normal circumstances moving abroad with you would be a very attractive idea. But right now, like this – I'm sorry, I just can't do it."

Someone outside trudges past the car, slips in the snow and goes down. A flailing arm catches the front wing and there is a thud, causing Isobel to jump, her head snapping round to look out of the windscreen. All she can see are vague shapes through the steamed up glass, like apparitions gliding through mist. She turns back to Andrew.

"I can't explain, so I guess I can't convince you." She raises herself up and Andrew slips out of her. Now the passion is spent her movements in the tight interior of the car are undignified and here, at the end of the affair, she feels self-conscious as she readjusts her clothes.

Outside the coldness hits them like something solid and they hurry through the car park leaving footprints in the snow.

Inside the terminal a handful of people are bundled up against the weather, waiting for trains. A coffee shop attracts Andrew's eye and he moves away, intent on getting them something hot to drink. Isobel goes off to buy her ticket.

After the ticket office, she ducks into one of the many outlets and buys a cheap pay-as-you-go phone. Isobel dumps her old mobile in a trash bin on her way back to Andrew.

He sits at a newly cleaned table with a cappuccino in front of him; Isobel sits down opposite and he slides a hot chocolate over to her. She sips gratefully.

"Guess you better get used to this."

"What?"

"Sitting about in coffee shops. Different culture on the Continent."

Isobel appreciates his attempt at lightness and offers him a weak smile. She brings the mug to her lips.

The large soulless terminal whispers around them, the low buzz of conversation punctuated by the soft echo of footsteps. A family blunder by trailing suitcases on wheels, one squeaking rhythmically, shrill and irritating. The dark-skinned man serving the coffee is muttering in an African language and across the way a group of white Europeans talk animatedly in Dutch or Danish, Isobel cannot tell the difference.

Her ticket is one way. She'll write her landlord a letter saying she is defaulting on her rent. All the stuff she has left behind he can keep, sell or give to charity. Either way he won't kick up too much of a fuss, everything from her television to the underwear she left behind will fetch a price somewhere. Her landlord will make out, and she'll be away.

"Do you remember the first time we met?" Andrew asks.

"Yeah, it wasn't that long ago."

"It feels like a long time."

"That's because we've given in to each other."

Andrew doesn't know what she means by this. His expression prompts her to elaborate.

"From the first time, we let ourselves go completely. When you share yourself like that, you form a bond, I guess."

Andrew looks at her, still not sure what she's talking about.

"Fuck, I don't know," Isobel says. "I guess a lot has happened since we started fucking."

Andrew turns away, casting his eyes around the terminal, looking at nothing specific, feeling nothing specific. "It's been a strange day," he says, almost to himself.

Isobel bursts out laughing, harsh, almost hysterical. Andrew looks back at her, wondering about the way her beauty has shrivelled up, leaving in its wake this haggard, deranged-looking woman, her pale features eroded by anguish, leaving only haunted, black-ringed eyes.

"What's happened Isobel? What's going on?" he tries one last time. But Isobel only looks away, her tired eyes suddenly distant. A few moments of silence before he asks, "Who did you give my number to?"

"A friend."

"Who? Why?"

"In case he needs to find me."

"Why would he?"

"I don't know."

Andrew sits back in his chair, exasperated.

A booming voice announces the train is now boarding, repeating the message in a variety of languages.

Isobel stands and Andrew asks, "When will I hear from you?"

"When I get settled."

"Promise me you won't disappear from the face of the earth."

"Promise. You can come and visit. It'll be nice to see you for a weekend."

"I'd like that."

Andrew takes her in his arms and holds her tight. When he lets her go, Isobel walks off towards the departure gates without another word, clutching her suitcase tightly.

"Wait."

Andrew takes a notepad from his pocket.

"This is the name and number of a friend. He lives in Norway, a town called Ålesund. Go there if you get stuck. He runs a little travel company. He'll give you a job."

Isobel takes the scrap of paper and stuffs it in her pocket.

"Thank you."

"He's a good guy."

"So are you."

Andrew smiles. He holds her gaze.

"I have to go now."

"I know."

Isobel turns and walks away. She looks back once. Andrew waves, his face solemn.

Isobel doesn't smile, doesn't wave. She moves through the gate, flashing her passport to the officer, and is gone.

23

Sebastian is watching the customers in the motorway services. There is something about the looks he is given, something about the looks they give each other. There is tension in the way they move, a tremble in their hands. These people are afraid.

As he sits there, watching reflections in the black glass, snow falling over the motorway outside, sipping his third coffee, a realisation slowly creeps up his spine and lodges in his head: *All of these people know who I am.*

Ichabod is a coward. He has ducked out of the confrontation. It was always a risk. But Sebastian felt sure the arrogant son of a bitch would show up. He'd want Sebastian to know who he was, before putting a bullet in his head. Sebastian was confident he'd take the bait, but Ichabod is more cautious than he thought.

In the time he's been waiting, eight people have shown up, all dressed for the weather, many carrying bags. They all arrived separately, and now they sit surrounding him, drinking coffee, working hard to be casual.

Sebastian glances across at the various outlets, the restaurant, the Magic Bean café, Burger King. Are the staff part of this team? What about Andrea, still polishing the coffee machine? Is the kid behind the counter at Burger King hiding a gun somewhere in the back of the grease pit? What about the manager at WHSmith or the waitress at the restaurant?

How many am I up against? How bad are my chances?

He should have known better. Nothing about what's happened in the last twenty-four hours has been straightforward or predictable.

Another four men walk through the main entrance. They pause and glance around. One of them looks directly at Sebastian and then quickly looks away. Their faces are blank and they do not speak to each other. All are carrying some kind of bag – a suitcase, a holdall, a rucksack.

What's in those, boys? Sebastian asks silently. Guns? Grenades? Surface-to-air missiles? Why haven't you made your move? Why pretend I don't exist? What are you waiting for?

It should be a simple matter, surely. It only takes one to quietly pull a gun and draw down. Sebastian is a sitting duck. But then maybe they're nervous. He's lived through a lot so far today. They don't want to take any chances. Maybe they're waiting for the rest of their little army to show up. How many will Ichabod send? How many has he got left? This is a small town, not a big city. Surely he'll run out of puppets eventually.

Now his mind is wandering when it should be getting focused. Another thought pops in: What if I'm being paranoid? What if the reason they haven't made their move is because they have no move to make? Sebastian has been sitting here a long while and it's entirely possible that he's spooked himself. But even as he contemplates this, all of his instincts are opposed to it.

The four move away from the door, coming further into the building. They pass by Sebastian without looking at him. He turns in his seat and follows their progress. One heads up towards WHSmith and pauses in the doorway, another goes to Burger King and lingers in front of the counter, but he doesn't order anything. The other two separate and take seats at empty tables.

A guy with a bald head and glasses gets up from the table he was sitting at, his coffee still steaming, and makes his way over to the Lucky Coin Emporium. He takes his bag with him and disappears inside.

Sebastian can feel it drawing closer. Tension. Violence. His heart beats faster and his breath catches in his throat. The pain in his chest flares suddenly, piercing, making him gasp. But then after a few moments everything settles back down, replaced by a curious calm. He becomes conscious of the gun in his pocket. He can visualise the locations and faces of all those who have entered the motorway services since he arrived. Twelve men arranged around him, all unremarkable, perfectly ordinary, except for their intention.

Then, footsteps approach from behind. A young guy, early twenties, hurries passed, making a beeline for the toilets at the far end of the building. He's carrying a briefcase. He slows as he passes the main entrance, as if he wants to run through those doors and escape into the night. But then he moves on, past the restaurant to the toilets.

Sebastian should go for the main exit, escape while he can. But leaving now means running for good. He's out of options. There are no more moves to make.

Sebastian gets up from the table as soon as the guy disappears into the toilets. Everybody is looking at him. The skin on the back of his neck tingles in anticipation. He strolls slowly, pretending to be casual, between the tables and chairs, past the Magic Bean café, between the restaurant and the Lucky Coin Emporium.

Five more men walk in through the main entrance. Sebastian hesitates for just a moment. With his exit cut off he moves towards the toilets, following the young guy.

The men watch him. Everyone is watching him.

They haven't attacked yet because they are waiting for all the troops to gather. Sebastian must have seriously spooked Ichabod for him to send so many. This new group makes a total of seventeen, not counting the staff and the handful that were already in the place when he first arrived. Sebastian takes in the five newcomers in a single backwards glance. All of them are sagging into middle age. They all wear long coats against the weather with suits underneath; BMW-driving businessmen harried by the demands of their jobs, unhealthy with stress, and probably blackmailed by Ichabod. They are pawns to be sacrificed, meat puppets roped to the hand of their deranged master. They tremble in the doorway, sweat standing out on their brows, despite the freezing weather outside.

He doesn't have enough bullets to shoot them all.

Sebastian pushes through the toilet door without looking back. It is tactical suicide, but what choice is there? Perhaps the young guy can tell him how to find Ichabod. Perhaps there is a window he can escape through. As the first door swings shut behind, he barges through the second door into the toilets.

Ten urinals, five stalls with closed doors, and a row of sinks before a long clean mirror. Shining white tiles brilliant beneath the harsh overhead fluorescents; the smell of disinfectant and chemical air freshener. No windows.

The young guy is splashing water on his face at one of the sinks. He looks up as Sebastian bursts in, his ashen face momentarily blank before twisting into unrestrained horror.

Sebastian approaches at speed.

The briefcase is in the sink next to the guy and he grabs for it and backs away but there is nowhere for him to go. His hands tremble with the catches but he manages to fire them up and he pulls a small automatic machine gun from the case.

Sebastian is right in close and he sidesteps and forces the gun up with his left hand while jabbing out with his right, his fingers forward and relaxed. The guy's nose spreads Sebastian's fingers apart and his nails plunge into the guy's eyes. He screams, backing away, knocking the briefcase to the floor and sending spare clips skittering across the tile.

The guy's hold on the gun is slack as Sebastian's fingers sink into his eyes. Sebastian plucks the gun from his grasp without a shot being fired. The guy falls back into the wall at the far end of the bathroom, his eyes screwed up tight, a thin trickle of blood leaking out of the corners. Sebastian slams his forearm against the guy's throat, pinning him to the wall.

The guy is sobbing and his weight sags as his legs give out. The pressure of Sebastian's arm against his neck is the only thing holding the guy up.

"Where is Ichabod?"

"You've hurt my eyes."

"Tell me about Ichabod!"

"I don't know where he is, or who he is."

Sebastian isn't surprised.

"How many are out there?"

"He's sent everyone after you. Everyone left."

"Can I get them to stand down?"

The man laughs.

"We all want you to win. But we can't risk letting you."

"Why don't you stand with me?"

"You don't know the damage he'd do to our families if we lost. No one can take the risk."

"That leaves me fighting guys I don't want to hurt, who don't really want to hurt me."

"They'll kill you if they can. I'd have killed you."

Sebastian takes a step back and the guy sinks to the floor, his eyes still screwed up tight.

Sebastian tries not to think about the size of the force arrayed at his back, knowing that at any moment they could burst through the door, guns blazing. He looks down at the guy and Sergeant Warrington's voice whispers in his ear.

Kill him. You have no choice.

But he knows this guy is no different to him, a victim coerced into playing this ridiculous game. Sebastian remembers Daniel's face, in the darkness behind the warehouse, the way he pleaded, the way he begged for his life.

Sebastian wasn't an executioner then. Can he be one now?

Do I have what it takes? Doubt suddenly floods through his guts. Jesus, how am I going to live through this?

"Stand up."

The guy on the floor raises his head. His eyes flutter open. Sebastian gets a brief glimpse of the red mess beneath his lids and he suddenly becomes aware of the slime on his fingertips. The guy struggles to his feet.

"Turn around."

Sebastian puts the machine gun in the sink and seizes the guy around the neck, cutting off the blood supply to the brain. After a few seconds and a brief struggle the guy slumps unconscious in his arms and Sebastian lets him sink to the floor.

Sebastian plucks the machine gun from the sink and quickly checks the clip. It's a serious piece of hardware, light and compact. Satisfied that it will fire, he scoops up the extra clips, four in all, and stuffs them in his pockets. He takes the pistol from his jacket.

Now he has enough bullets.

As he turns back towards the door he catches sight of his reflection in the mirror above the sinks. For a brief moment he sees a natural born predator, body poised, a hard, cold look in his eyes.

When did this warrior appear in my skin?

But then he hears the rasp of his breath. He sees his chest rapidly rising and falling beneath the jacket. Pain stabs through his ribcage. The warrior that was momentarily there vanishes, and suddenly Sebastian recognises himself in the mirror. Despite the guns, he has an acute sense of his vulnerability. He reaches for the asthma pump in his pocket and takes a deep hit.

This is not going to end well.

Without giving himself time to think, he pushes through the doors and steps out into the main area of the services. For a moment, everything goes still. Employees from Burger King and WHSmith are being ushered through the main entrance out into the night. Sebastian spies Andrea. She meets his eyes for just a moment, her gaze flat and unreadable. Some of the guys already have their weapons drawn; others are clutching bags and suitcases. There are some on this side of the main entrance, others up by WHSmith on the far side of the building. Everybody looks afraid. Sebastian, machine gun in one hand and pistol in the other, faces them down. He could start shooting them now, but with Andrea and the other staff paused at the door, the risk of collateral damage is too great.

For a long moment nothing happens. Then Sebastian moves towards the restaurant. There must be a back way out from the kitchen. He gives one last glance to Andrea. She is being ushered out of the services by the tall manager from WHSmith. She doesn't look back.

Sebastian fixes his eyes on the restaurant door. He can see through the glass partition wall. The place is empty, nobody eating, nobody waiting tables.

With the staff being ushered out of the building it won't be long before the police show up. The clock is ticking.

The silence at his back is broken by the soft click of a weapon, the safety being switched, a round being chambered. Sebastian looks over his shoulder. The last of the employees have disappeared. Those whom remain are puppets, enemies. Sebastian points the machine gun behind and opens fire.

* * *

The air is filled with noise from the machine gun. His blood pounds through his veins, but Sebastian can hardly breathe. Even as he dives he knows how reckless and desperate this is.

He hits the tiled floor just as the clip empties, but there is no let up in the noise as the enemy open fire en masse. The restaurant erupts into splinters, dust and glass. Sebastian scrambles over to a booth as the windows in the partition wall explode, flying glass slicing his hands and face.

He pops the clip from the machine gun and slams in another. Three left. The gunfire stops but his ears are still ringing. Now that he's made it this far he switches back to the pistol. The machine gun is good for covering fire but too inaccurate for what may come next.

He can't stay here. He's a sitting duck and the tables and chairs and these stupid plastic booths are never going to provide enough cover, especially if the aggressors stand up and start shooting at once over the partition wall.

Sebastian looks towards the back of the restaurant, at the door that leads to the kitchen. A fire exit, a window; anything will do.

Vague sounds are beginning to filter back through his ears and he can hear movement, the thud of the enemy slamming up against their side of the partition wall.

Sebastian gains his feet. His legs are like jelly. In a half-crouch he sprints towards the kitchen door.

Gunfire erupts at his back as he bursts through the door, bullets slam into the walls and flecks of plaster hammer against his cheek, but he's through the door and diving to the left for cover.

The firing stops as soon as he's out of sight in the kitchen. The assailants are learning some discipline and control. There's nothing like a battle to produce a steep learning curve.

Sebastian edges back to the door and kicks it open. He fires several shots at the two men just coming into the restaurant, killing them both. They fold to the ground, and he lets the kitchen door swing shut.

The restaurant kitchen is all stainless steel and red-and-white tiles, grills, counters, utensils and ovens. A thick greasy smell mixes with the creeping cordite. There are packets of raw hamburgers and bacon on one counter and large plastic bowls of manky-looking salad on another. A massive sink sits next to an industrial dishwasher and piles of plates and cups are stacked in tall, precarious towers.

Movement from deeper in the kitchen catches his eye and Sebastian creeps towards it, wondering how long it will take for the men outside to risk coming in after him.

A fat chef and a skinny waitress are crouched on the floor at the back of the kitchen looking utterly petrified. For a brief moment Sebastian nearly bursts out laughing;

instead, he levels the pistol at them. The waitress whimpers and the chef says, "Please."

Sebastian suddenly wonders if the gun has any shots left in the magazine.

The chef looks at him aghast; the waitress is fiercely clutching onto his arm. Sebastian tries to think of something to say, but he can't.

"What's going on?" asks the chef.

"They're trying to kill me." Sebastian's voice is barely a whisper, a dry rasp so quiet he cannot even hear himself speak. The pain in his lungs is starting to filter back through the adrenalin flooding his system, and his airways, full of dust, are constricting. He pulls the asthma pump from his pocket and takes a long deep hit.

"Are you going to hurt us?" asks the waitress. Her black eyeliner has streaked down her cheeks. Sebastian doesn't want to be responsible for these two. They might as well have 'collateral damage' written across their foreheads.

"The people out there aren't interested in you," he whispers. "You could probably walk out without being shot."

The chef eyes him warily. Sebastian cannot blame him for being sceptical.

"You just need to call out." Sebastian nods towards the waitress, who starts crying.

"No way, I can't. No way, I can't."

"They're only after me. If they hear a woman's voice they'll hold fire. They've let everyone else walk out."

"Are you sure?" the chef asks.

Sebastian grins. He can well imagine the twisted mask that such demented humour would stretch across his face.

"You won't have a chance if you stay here."

As if to prove his point, bullets suddenly pulverise the door and go slamming into the kitchen, ricocheting off the steel surfaces with a sharp zing.

Sebastian hits the deck and crawls back up the aisle towards the door, scrambling on elbows and knees, as a guy comes bursting through spraying bullets across the kitchen from an automatic rifle.

Sebastian shoots him in the ankle and he drops like a stone. Then he puts another in the top of the guy's head. His body goes limp but his hands twitch.

Sebastian crawls over and retrieves the rifle, taking the opportunity to have a quick scout through the shattered kitchen door. The restaurant is littered with shards of glass, reflecting the lights in the ceiling above in fractured patterns. The tops of a few heads are visible from behind upturned tables, but there are no decent targets, so he crawls back, deeper into the kitchen.

Now he has another machine gun.

Slowly the screams of the waitress filter through the ringing in his ears. The chef is hit in the arm, blood staining his whites. He looks feverish, his big face running with sweat and his whole body twitching. There is little Sebastian can do for him. He crouches down by his side.

"You'll die if you don't get out of here." Sebastian grabs the waitress under the chin and tilts her face up, looking into her eyes. His voice is just a gasp.

"Keep screaming, let them know you're in here. Then get this guy on his feet and walk him out the door."

Awareness floods back into her eyes and she nods her head.

Sebastian leaves them to it. Crouched low and keeping a wary eye towards the direction of the kitchen door, he makes his way over to the far side, avoiding the various pots and pans that are now littering the floor. The fire exit is a big door without a window and a push bar to open it. Sebastian puts his ear against it. Even a vaguely competent aggressor would surely cover the back exits. Opening the door could be a big mistake. The breath wheezing from his chest is loud and he tries to control it, quieten it.

Faintly, he can hear voices from the other side of the door.

A sudden clang makes him spin around, gun raised. The waitress has the big chef on his feet and together they are staggering towards the restaurant, kicking saucepans out of their way. The chef leans heavily on the waitress, his rolling bulk almost too much for the slender girl to bear up. He doesn't look good, but at least he's up on his feet and trying to move.

"We're coming out!" screams the waitress, her voice shaky and on the edge of hysteria. "Don't shoot, please! We're coming out!"

Together they totter along, bumping into counters and sending more pans clattering to the floor.

"Oh God," mutters the girl when they reach the dead guy. His blood has spread in two pools at either end of him, from his head and from his ankle. The chef and the waitress blunder and slip their way through, the girl almost retching. The chef is oblivious, too far gone with shock and pain.

Sebastian spies another door on the other side of the kitchen. It looks like another fire exit. He moves, keeping low, as the waitress and the chef step through the splintered door into the restaurant.

Sebastian backs up against the wall next to the door. He takes another hit from his asthma pump, trying to control his breathing. He closes his eyes, hoping to sense if there is anything on the other side.

He gets no feedback. Fuck it, he's out of options anyway. Sebastian slams down on the bar and shoves the door open.

He darts back behind the wall, expecting the roar of gunfire. But nothing happens. He drops low, and peaks around the door. Beyond is another kitchen, but smaller and with different-looking apparatus. It is the kitchen to the Magic Bean café next door. Makes sense; there can be only two fire exits, one on either side of the motorway. The back areas of the outlets like the Magic Bean and Burger King will all run together, providing access to the fire escapes on either side.

Sebastian darts through the doorway.

Unlike the restaurant, the Magic Bean kitchen is on view to the patrons. At the front is where Andrea stood. In the rear are supplies and utensils.

Sebastian creeps carefully, quietly, through the kitchen. The waitress is still hollering, and hopefully keeping the combatants distracted. He angles over to the far left of the counter, rises ever so slightly and takes a peak.

He has clear lines of sight across the open space of the food court to the Lucky Coin, and into the restaurant next door. Through the shattered windows of the partition wall that sections the seating area of the restaurant, he can see the waitress and the chef blundering through the tables. He can hear the crack of glass beneath their feet as they stumble towards the exit. Below the shattered windows, on this side of the partition, are seven guys, armed with a variety of weapons. All of them have their backs to Sebastian. They're peeking over the half-wall to follow the progress of the waitress and the chef. Sebastian can't see anyone lurking in the Lucky Coin, but he can see the barrel of a large-calibre pistol, poking out from just behind the door.

"Is he still back there?" somebody asks.

The waitress nods her head.

"Is he hurt?" another asks, almost hopefully.

The waitress shakes her head.

Sebastian could spray them all with the machine gun. Kill the lot of them. But he wouldn't get the guy in the Lucky Coin, and he knows there are others, somewhere further back, up towards WHSmith. If he starts shooting now he'll get the guys by the partition wall, but he'll be caught in the crossfire from those that are left.

Sebastian hunkers back down and creeps back towards the rear of the kitchen, hoping for another door leading through into Burger King.

The door is there, closed. Sebastian puts his back to the wall. How long will it take them to realise the kitchens are linked? Could they out-flank me? Sebastian has no way to answer that question. His only option is to open the door.

By now the waitress and the injured chef will have passed through the restaurant. They should be over by the main exit, disappearing out into the snow. Sebastian has only a few more seconds before the distraction will be over.

The hilarity of the situation threatens to engulf him. The urge to burst out laughing is almost too strong to resist. A tiny part of him knows this is the onset of shock. Fear is biting at his heels, threatening to paralyse him.

The sudden desire to laugh evaporates and panic and revulsion swell through his guts, climbing into his throat, burning like bile. He gets dizzy and his vision goes black. The breath gets stuck in his lungs. Fear engulfs him. But in the darkness his Grandpa's question flashes through his mind:

You gonna let them beat you, son?

Gunfire explodes again.

The sudden noise shocks Sebastian out of his downward spiral and instinctively he dives for cover. But then he realises they are shooting up the restaurant kitchen. They don't yet know where he is.

Coming back to his senses, he seizes the opportunity to slam open the fire door.

He darts back out of the opening in case there is someone behind the door. The roar of gunfire is enormous. He leans round the doorway and takes a peek.

The Burger King kitchen looks deserted. He creeps through the door, and forwards through the kitchen towards the counter, past stacks of bread buns in plastic sacks and layers of processed cheese and vacuum-sealed tubs of salad.

At the counter Sebastian rises slowly and takes another peak. The cacophony is subsiding, the urge to shoot up the restaurant running out of steam. After the onslaught, it won't be long before another group makes a run at the kitchen. They'll find the door in the back and catch up with Sebastian all too quickly. He's running out of time. He glances across the open space at the floor-to-ceiling windows opposite. His reflection looks back at him.

He quickly ducks down out of sight. Beyond those windows the darkness is absolute. He moves quickly and silently back through the Burger King kitchen, expecting the additional door on the far side.

Where this one leads he has no idea. Burger King is the last restaurant. There is only WHSmith further along, but they won't a have kitchen. In relation to the motorway running underneath, he's almost all the way across to the other side. The door here must be the second fire exit. It'll put him on the wrong side of the motorway from Kenosha's car, but that's better than dying here. Sebastian goes still and listens.

Silence.

He puts his hands on the bar. Carefully, slowly and as quietly as possible, he presses down. The door is released from the latch and he steps to the side, back up against the wall, as the door swings open.

Something about this one isn't right.

He drops into a lower stance and takes a look: a long grey corridor with another door at the far end. This door stands open and snow billows in from the darkness outside.

And there is a small group of men, all of whom open fire the moment Sebastian peaks around the corner.

He jumps back as bullets streak down the corridor and lay waste to the Burger King kitchen.

The shots will alert the others down by the restaurant. He'll be caught in the crossfire. The corridor may have a door to the outside but he can't shoot his way along it. There's no cover in a rat run.

Acting purely on instinct, with a reckless surge of adrenalin flooding his veins and with hardly a breath left in his lungs, Sebastian leaps across to the other side of the open doorway and sprints up the length of the kitchen to the counter.

A whole group of men are making their way down towards the restaurant, threading their way between rows of tables and chairs.

Sebastian, catching them off guard, lets rip with the automatic rifle.

* * *

Bullets slam through the men and strays hit the windows. One man hurtles backwards through the exploding glass and disappears from sight, falling to the motorway below. Snow billows through the shattered windows, carried by a biting wind. Sebastian turns the guns on everything within sight and tables and chairs and men get torn to shreds.

But in a moment they are shooting back. Sebastian leaps over the counter and sprints out among the tables and chairs. Shots erupt from behind, as the guys at the fire exit come charging up and into the Burger King kitchen.

Sebastian rolls and comes up on his feet, hunkered low, moving across the field of battle towards the shattered windows, shooting between table legs and chair legs at the feet and knees of his enemy.

Bullets are ripping through tables and chairs all around and his only hope is to keep moving and shooting, never staying in one place.

Sebastian is close to the windows now and stray bullets shatter all the remaining glass. He starts retreating, backing up towards WHSmith, keeping the automatic rifle roaring in short controlled bursts until it clicks empty. He loops the strap over his head and lets the gun fall. He raises the machine gun, but before he pulls the trigger a bullet rips through his upper arm and knocks him back off his feet.

Sebastian lands on his back as pain roars through his senses; the whole world seems to be exploding. He can't hear anything, and he's gasping, gasping for breath.

A man comes charging up the aisle taking shots at him with a pistol. Sebastian swings the machine gun up and cries out at the pain in his arm but pulls the trigger anyway. The gun bucks in his hand spraying wildly, but enough shots hit the guy running towards him to put him down.

Sebastian rolls across the aisle, his arm feeling like it's on fire and he turns the machine gun on anything that moves. He hits a few more guys in the legs and they fall, but he misses the chance to take them out completely.

A few guys from the corridor leap the Burger King counter and Sebastian swings the machine gun in their direction, shooting one guy clean out of the air, mid-leap; he goes sprawling across the counter and drops out of sight, leaving a long smear of blood in his wake. The others hit the deck, diving among the tables.

Sebastian turns the machine gun on them but nothing happens. He releases the clip and goes to slam in another but he doesn't have any more. His pockets are empty. He must have lost them somewhere.

He tosses the machine gun and reaches for the pistol. Somehow he's fallen over and he struggles back to his feet. In a half-crouch he goes weaving between the tables, no longer retreating, instead moving towards his enemy.

One guy pops up from behind a table and Sebastian takes him out with a shot to the face, another he hits in the neck and a third in the chest. He catches one guy under the chin and the bullet blows off the top of his head.

Now the pistol is dry firing and he drops it. He grabs another weapon from the nearest corpse, barely even noticing what it is – a pistol of some kind, similar to the previous one – and instinctively he pops the clip, checks there are bullets and then slams it home.

Fast, fast, everything so fast, no conscious thought at all. He's taking aim at everything that moves and somehow he's got them on the run, retreating between the tables, and he's no longer facing a sustained barrage of badly aimed shots. He's killed enough of them to gain the initiative and he's forcing the few who are left back towards the restaurant.

He rises from the barricades of overturned tables, keeping low, moving silently but always moving, never rising from the same place twice, taking them out one at a time.

All he can hear is a high-pitched whine in his head as the gun bucks in his hand and each jolt sends pain shooting down his injured arm. Dust – from all the shot-up tables and chairs and the cordite and the bitter wind coming in through the shattered windows – thickens the air so that he can barely drag enough oxygen into his desperate lungs. Tears spill from his eyes, softening the details so that all he's aiming at are blurred shapes as they move. Somehow this makes things easier.

More shots rip through the tables and splinters slice through his face and knuckles. He takes out three more in quick succession, *boom-boom-boom*, and down they fall, leaving bloody mists in the air.

He hunkers down behind an overturned table with a number of holes punched through the wood. He struggles in his pocket for the asthma pump. With a shaking hand he takes a puff and holds his breath and waits for his airways to expand just a little.

He's close to the shattered windows and there are splinters and glass everywhere and snow gathering among the debris on the floor. He wipes the tears from his eyes and takes a look out of the window. The motorway is a long white streak in the night, fading to darkness. It's mostly deserted, the snow forcing everyone home early and cancelling the rush hour. But there are still a few cars moving and down below, right under the window, the traffic has come to a standstill at the body in the snow. As Sebastian looks down and takes in the twisted limbs and spreading pool of blood, a car door opens and a woman looks up at him. The police will be here any moment. Time is running out.

A shot breaks through the ringing in his ears and goes whistling past his head, out into the night.

Just one shot. The guy is out of bullets.

Emboldened, Sebastian peers over the top of the table. The guy is standing up straight to get a better angle. No doubt he was hoping to take Sebastian out with that one last shot, and now he stands in plain sight, stupidly dry firing his gun. It is the manager from WHSmith, face flushed, sweat cooling on his brow in the cold air. His brown hair is streaked with grey and recedes at his temples. The hand holding the gun is shaking badly. No wonder he missed.

This one poor guy is the face of all the others Sebastian has killed, the face of his enemy, and clearly he is not some moronic henchman, some soulless cliché. This is a guy who works hard for a living and has a family. Backed into a corner and not given a choice. A guy who doesn't want to be here. Sebastian sees the reality of this man, desperately squeezing the trigger of his empty gun, more in hope of ending the nightmare than with any real desire to kill. Sebastian doesn't feel hatred or rage. He doesn't feel righteous or powerful. He doesn't feel anything any more as he stands and takes aim. The man's eyes go wide as Sebastian levels the pistol at his face.

"Please!" He stares down the barrel of the gun.

Sebastian pulls the trigger. His ears are ringing so badly he doesn't even hear the shot. But his injured arm feels it. The pain bursts through his shoulder making him gasp, as the man falls down among the tables.

Sebastian walks away from the windows, crunching over glass that he can feel cracking beneath the soles of his boots. He weaves through the destruction towards the last three remaining combatants. They see him coming, and together they back away. One man, middle aged, blonde hair, his suit covered in dust, chucks his weapon and holds up his hands, tears in his eyes.

"Enough," he says.

His two companions both raise their guns. Sebastian fires at the same time. He hits one guy in the chest before he can shoot back, but the second man hits Sebastian in the head.

Everything goes black. Sebastian falls.

A moment later he comes to. The left side of his face is on fire, wet with blood. The bullet just grazed him, carving a tiny furrow above his temple. A centimetre to the right and it would all be over. Pain throbs through his head, a deafening roar fills his ears. For a moment he doesn't know if he's dead or alive.

Then there is pressure against his shoulder, as a foot pushes against him, forcing him onto his back. The man who shot him thinks he has won. The wound in Sebastian's arm screams for attention. Sebastian rolls onto his back, opens his eyes and fires. His vision is blurred red by the blood in his eye, but with the guy standing over him he can hardly miss.

The man falls and Sebastian drags himself back to his feet. Adrenalin keeps him going, shock is beginning to numb the pain. With his face covered in blood and his arm hanging useless, his airways so constricted he can hardly breathe, deafened by the gunfire with nothing but a roar in his ears, he has nothing left. One way or another, the fight is over.

The man who threw his weapon is still there, hands still raised. Sebastian tries to level his gun, but he barely has the strength to pull the trigger and the barrel is so unsteady it would be sheer luck if he hit him. And the gun is so heavy, and he can only see out of one eye.

Sebastian's arm drops and the gun slips from his fingers. He stares at the man for a long moment. The man looks back, his eyes wide, but blank, already lost to shock.

Sebastian lurches towards the main entrance. He leaves the bodies and the blood behind, pushes through the door and stumbles out into the night.

* * *

He staggers across the car park towards Kenosha's Mercedes. The freezing air is a blessed relief from the dust-filled motorway services, but at the same time it sends even more pain shooting through his lungs, making him gasp. The cold seeps into his wounds in a matter of seconds. His gunshot arm stiffens rapidly. The pain in his head is a steady pounding beat. Down on the motorway, blue lights whirl through the darkness. The police are almost here, although Sebastian cannot hear the sirens. Any second now they'll be coming up the ramp into the car park.

Sebastian folds himself into the driver's seat as quick as he can and starts the engine. He shoves it straight into second, releasing the clutch slowly and gradually pulls away. Good instincts override desperation. The windscreen wipers flick a gap in the snow and Sebastian hits the lights. The car crawls forwards, towards the back way out of the services, a short narrow lane, leading directly into town, bypassing the motorway altogether. He turns out of the car park and drives back into town.

All the streets look the same. Sebastian takes it slowly, carefully. With his good hand he wipes at the blood from his eye but it doesn't seem to improve his vision.

Gradually, the streets become wider, until he finds himself close to what can only be the A2, the main artery that runs through town. There is still some traffic moving carefully along, headlights and streetlights illuminating the freewheeling flakes that go flashing through the air.

Sebastian pulls over in a bus stop. He keeps the engine running and has the presence of mind to turn on the hazard lights. He shuts his eyes and leans his forehead against the steering wheel.

His whole body shakes. Pain bites away at his shoulder, pounds through his head, explodes across his chest. It feels like all his ribs are broken as he sucks in air and lets it out with a gasp.

In the darkness behind his eyes, faces and chests and knees explode silently; men scream in agony, but there is no sound. The weight of the dead forces Sebastian down into the leather car seat. His hands are sticky with blood.

The windows steam up and the world beyond the car fades away. Sebastian is grateful – grateful to be invisible as the guilt and shock and relief and pain bite into his heart.

He cries, and each sob feels like a bullet exploding through his lungs.

24

Kenosha offers a huge tip to convince the taxi driver to wait. The driver, a Sikh guy who seems entirely too big for the car, is sceptical. The snow is still falling and at some point he wants to get home. And besides, why would someone pay such a huge amount for a cab ride?

Kenosha gets out of the car and the coldness rips through his trendy clothes and chills him to the marrow. He had asked the driver to park a little way up past the house, so as not to dent his image too much. But on reflection, he wishes they'd parked in the bloody front garden.

A short but treacherous walk down to the house, and his insanely expensive leather shoes absorb the snow like a sponge. By the time he knocks on the front door he is a shivering wreck, and knows in his heart that this encounter will be filed in the cabinet labelled "Disasters We Do Not Mention In The Pub".

After what seems like an age the door swings open to reveal a handsome man whose height and build is equal to his own.

"Hi," says Kenosha, trying not to shiver.

The man flashes a winning smile, and Kenosha wonders if this lady has hired another escort in addition to himself.

"You must be Kenosha." Ichabod steps back from the doorway and Kenosha gratefully steps inside, shutting the door quickly behind him.

"Man," he says, "some weather out there tonight." Kenosha shrugs out of his jacket and looks for somewhere to hang in up, opting for the knob on the banister at the bottom of the stairs. He turns back to his host, who extends a hand.

"Ichabod."

They shake. Ichabod's grip is strong, his palm cool. Kenosha looks into his eyes and finds the view slightly unnerving. A private smile twitches at the corners of Ichabod's lips, as if enjoying a joke that only he has the punchline to. The handshake draws out and becomes slightly awkward, at least for Kenosha, uncomfortable in the face of Ichabod's scrutiny.

"So you're here to fuck my wife."

Before Kenosha can think of a reply, Ichabod asks:

"Would you like a cup of tea? Talissa will be down in a minute."

Ichabod leads Kenosha through the small lounge and into the kitchen. The television is burbling away to itself. Kenosha wonders if Ichabod actually lives here. The place feels too feminine. He's been in so many single and attached women's homes that he instinctively knows the difference. A man leaves a masculine stain on a place when he lives in it. A woman however, in Kenosha's humble experience, leaves a fragrance.

Ichabod slams the kettle onto the hob and lights the gas. He plucks a couple of mugs off the draining board and goes hunting through the cupboards to find the teabags.

"How long've you been working as a pro?" he asks.

"A while."

"Yeah but how long?"

"Three years," Kenosha lies. He never tells a client anything about himself. But he is not above the occasional story in order to satisfy their curiosity. He views this as part of the service. Some women don't just pay for this cock, they pay for the mystique of having a professional.

"How many women in that time?"

"Lots."

"Ever had two at once?"

"Yup. And got paid twice."

Ichabod turns from the counter and Kenosha grins.

"Seriously?"

"Uh huh."

"Man, I wish I had your job." Ichabod, staring at Kenosha, interlocks his fingers and cracks his knuckles.

"So what's the deal here?" Kenosha asks after a pause

"What do you mean?"

The kettle starts whistling and Ichabod turns back to the worktop. He turns off the gas and pours the boiling water.

"I mean, what are you expecting from me?" Kenosha, looking at Ichabod's back, is thinking that he's never walked into a situation quite like this one. Occasionally a woman will have convinced her man to hire his services. The guy will watch, and perhaps join in. But always the woman opened the door and appeared in control, the guy always nervous. Which is perfectly understandable. But Ichabod doesn't seem nervous at all.

"Ever had an orgy?"

"I've been to a few parties up in London that have ended that way."

"Ever fucked a guy?"

"Nope. Not my thing."

Ichabod turns back and hands Kenosha a mug. He doesn't offer sugar.

"Are you sure?"

"Quite sure."

"Ever got a blow job from a guy?"

"Once." Another lie.

"Was it good?"

"Not really. Women have softer lips."

Ichabod takes a sip of tea, leaning back against the worktop. His thin T-shirt delineates the contours of his body. Kenosha has no idea if he is trying to be seductive.

"So what's the deal?"

"The deal is, you're going to fuck my wife. And you're going to give her everything she asks for. And I'm going to watch. Or I might join in. Or I might just leave you to it and watch the telly. I haven't decided yet. It depends on whether you make me feel inadequate." Ichabod flicks his eyes down to Kenosha's crotch, looks back up and grins.

Kenosha cannot read him at all. He doesn't know whether he is being sarcastic, or trying to hide something genuine beneath a veneer of sarcasm. Overconfidence can be a sign of weakness. But not always.

Kenosha sips his tea. It is too strong, too hot and with too little milk. He also takes sugar, but he is not about to complain. Having Ichabod open the door has thrown him off his stride. Usually by now he is engaged in seducing his client, foreplay with words before actions. But this all seems too domestic, the sexual encounter to follow rendered absurd.

Perhaps that is Ichabod's strategy. Making Talissa wait while he sucks all the charm away, killing the intensity and cheapening the experience. Reducing what some women find intensely erotic to nothing more than a soulless rut with a stranger. Maybe he hopes to dissuade his girl from wanting this again.

"So, Talissa is your wife?"

"One of them."

"You have more than one wife?

"Oh yeah."

"Do they know about each other?"

"Yeah, sometimes I get them all together."

"You know bigamy is against the law?"

"Really?"

Kenosha nods.

"Good job I'm lying then, huh?"

"Right." Confused now, Kenosha laughs and turns away, glancing around the kitchen.

"Oh what? You really think I'm lying?" The tone of Ichabod's voice is suddenly black, steeped with menace. Kenosha looks back, and finds a degree of hardness in those dark eyes, glaring at him from across the kitchen.

"I'm sorry?"

Ichabod's grim countenance suddenly cracks into laughter, so warm and genuine it completely obliterates the ferocity that had carved his features just a moment before.

Kenosha, reeling from such abrupt emotional changes, takes a step back through the kitchen door and slops his tea down his trousers.

"Easy tiger," says Ichabod, erupting into hysterics.

Kenosha wipes at his tea-darkened thigh with his sleeve, embarrassed and positive that tonight will be filed in that never-discussed cabinet.

Ichabod's laughter dies instantly, as if someone threw a switch and turned it off. Straight-faced and serious, Ichabod looks directly into Kenosha's eyes.

"I guess I should pay you in advance?"

Kenosha, reeling, has lost all of his usual tactics and wonders if, when the time comes, he'll be able to perform at all. He nods, as Ichabod brushes past him into the lounge.

* * *

Upstairs, Talissa sits naked at her dressing table, listening to Ichabod's laughter as it bounces around the house. She stares at herself in the mirror. Her body, cleansed and moisturised, looks every minute of its forty-one years. Her small breasts sag lower than the gossip magazines deem acceptable, her belly is too soft and her thighs too big. She hasn't liked her reflection for some years, but just recently it seems as if her body, which has been through so much since Ichabod charmed his way into her life, has decided enough is enough, welcoming age with open arms. She runs her fingers through her long dark hair, wet and silky and glistening under the unforgiving bulbs above her head. One last attribute, still clinging to its youth.

Downstairs, Ichabod's maniacal laughter suddenly cuts off, the absence of the sound more foreboding than the sound itself. Talissa doesn't understand the point of tonight. Why has he hired this man? Another game in which she is forced to participate but is never told the rules. The only thing she knows for certain is that right now Ichabod is downstairs toying with this poor man, moving through his repertoire of emotions, gradually eroding the guy's sense of equilibrium, until he turns into a nervous wreck.

For herself, Talissa knows that whatever Ichabod has in store tonight, it won't be about her. There's a reason he has brought this particular man over. His perversions are never random. There's always a specific target, and for a specific reason.

The days when the games revolved entirely around her are long gone. Her fall from grace happened years ago, her humiliation so complete that once she struck bottom she never got up again. Whatever degradation she may feel during Ichabod's torments is incidental now. It is the other he is focused on. In some ways this makes it worse.

His fixation on her at the beginning at least made her real, a person he wanted to possess and destroy all at the same time. Hers was a will that he wanted control over. Having succeeded, he lost interest in her as a person. With his emotional faculties so twisted, he has confused ownership with love. Now she is just an object, an expression of his absolute power, a tool he employs in the degradation of others.

Looking at her reflection now, Talissa doesn't know which is more tangible: the tired-looking woman in the mirror, or the one sat before it. Nothing but a shadow, she thinks.

"Talissa! Come down here and meet your man!" Ichabod calls from downstairs.

Conditioned to obey, Talissa gets up off the bed and slips into a robe. She takes one last look at herself in the mirror, and falls into the role he wants her to play, glazed eyes, fake smile. She heads downstairs.

She finds them both in the living room. Kenosha is tall and handsome, well groomed, and Talissa is at least grateful that his body will be clean. He is perched on the end of a chair, looking somewhat uncomfortable.

"Here she is." Ichabod stands behind her, slipping his arms around her waist. She is so used to playing the part now, relaxed, smiling. Kenosha will probably think she is doped up to the eyeballs, vacant and pliant and willing to do anything her master commands. Ichabod unties the cord and Talissa's robe falls open. His fingertips brush along her stomach.

Kenosha watches on, impassive. For some reason he was expecting Talissa to be gorgeous, but she looks like most of his other clients, an average body going soft in middle age, a face that once would have been pretty, losing the fight against time, tainted with stress and anguish instead of laughter and happiness.

Ichabod bends and bites Talissa's neck.

To Kenosha, her response is conditioned rather than felt, her false passion fails to ignite in her empty, staring eyes.

"Take him upstairs," Ichabod commands. "I'll join you in a few minutes."

Talissa takes Kenosha by the hand. He stands, allowing himself to be led away through the lounge and up the stairs.

Ichabod watches them go. As soon as they disappear, the bright smile, spread so convincingly across his face, drops like a stone. He sits back down on the sofa, giving them time. He is yet to decide how long to let the game play out. How long before Kenosha starts to fear him? Or should he just take him suddenly, brutally, by surprise? Indecision in these matters is something he has always suffered with. He is decisive in setting these situations up, confident and exact in his manipulations. But once all the pieces are in place, he can never decide how best to finish it. The only thing he knows for sure is that Kenosha must die.

25

The sudden trilling of his mobile phone diverts Andrew's attention from the road. He digs in his pocket, but by the time he extracts the phone the ringing has stopped, the caller forwarded to voicemail.

He concentrates on the road, trying to see beyond the falling snow, the headlights illuminating a swirling tunnel in the darkness.

When he's sure he isn't about to glide into a car in front or slide off into the central reservation, Andrew navigates through the phone, eyes flicking from the screen to the road and back again. The call was from a number he doesn't recognise.

He dials through to his voicemail. The voice tells him he has one new message. Andrew listens to an empty silence for a few seconds, before the automation asks if he wants to delete or save the message.

He knows instinctively that the call had something to do with Isobel. Was this the friend Isobel had spoken of? Andrew hits redial and holds the phone to his ear. It rings for what seems like ages, and then his call is connected.

Silence.

Andrew can sense someone there, someone reluctant to speak.

"Hello?" he ventures. "Someone there just tried to call me."

"Who's this?"

"Who are you?" Andrew asks back.

A pause, then:

"A friend gave me this number."

"Would that friend be Isobel?"

"Where is she?"

"She's gone away."

"Where?"

"Overseas."

There is a big sigh. Andrew cannot tell if the person on the other end is pleased by this information, or angered by it.

"Is she safe?"

"Of course."

"When did she leave?"

"Not too long ago."

"Were you there? Did you see her go?"

"What the fuck is going on? She looked a mess, and she was scared. Is that anything to do with you?"

He is approaching the junction back into town. Up ahead are the motorway services. Blue lights cut through the blizzard and the warbling of police sirens increase in volume as he draws closer. Looking up at the services spanning the motorway as he passes underneath, he can see that all the windows have been shattered. Police and an ambulance are surrounding something on the other side of the central reservation, but the crash barrier is too high for him to see.

"What are those sirens?"

"Some kind of accident," Andrew replies distractedly. The scene is surreal, like the opening salvo from a disaster movie. The snow, the police, the accident that doesn't add up – a prelude to something bigger, something catastrophic. Andrew fixes his attention on the slip road coming up.

"What do you want?" he asks down the phone.

"I needed to make sure Isobel was alright."

"Why wouldn't she be?"

"It's complicated."

"It always is."

Andrew nudges the indicator in preparation for the exit ramp. An ambulance goes hurtling past in the other direction, snow billowing up from the wheels, the roving blue lights thrown into the night.

Andrew senses the person on the phone is about to hang up.

"How do you know Isobel?"

"I don't. Not really. I just met her yesterday."

"And why did she suddenly decide to leave the country?"

"It's complicated."

"Of course."

"The less you know the better, believe me."

"Perhaps I could help."

"With what?"

"With whatever's going on." Andrew takes the exit and drives cautiously up the slip road.

"What's your name?"

"Andrew. Who're you?"

"How do you know Isobel?"

"We're…" Andrew pauses, suddenly unsure what to say. Lovers? It sounds so wrong. "We're friends. Mates."

"Uh huh."

"And you?"

"And me what?"

"How did you meet Isobel?"

"I gave her a lift. Last night."

"I saw her last night too."

"This was late."

"It must have been."

Silence, and then Andrew says:

"Where was she going?"

"I don't know."

283

"Where did you drop her off?"

"I didn't. She knocked me out. Since I woke I've been fighting for my life, against people I used to work for. I think. I took Isobel hostage to get answers and realised these same people were using her the way they used me." The deadpan delivery of the words betrays no hint of emotion.

"That sounds…"

"Impossible? Yeah, tell me about it. It's not been a good day."

Andrew plants his foot firmly on the accelerator, the car picking up speed. He is on the link road now, leaving the motorway behind, coming back into town.

"Is it over?"

"No."

"Will Isobel be safe?"

"Provided nobody knows where she's gone."

"Good."

"Do you know?"

"I wasn't with her when she bought her tickets. I don't know her destination."

"That's probably for the best."

Controlling the car around the roundabouts in the snow is tricky with one hand holding the phone. Andrew's car begins to drift and he takes his foot off the gas.

"Look, I'm gonna roll the car if I don't get both hands on the wheel. Perhaps we should meet."

"Why?"

"I can help. Whatever it is, I want to know. I want to help Isobel."

"You must be a good friend."

"The best."

There is silence from the other end of the phone. Andrew wonders if the mysterious caller will bite. The voice sounds so empty, so drained of emotion.

"You have no idea what you're asking."

"Perhaps."

"It's best if you stay away."

"Isobel described you as a friend, which makes you my friend. I can help."

"I've lost count of the amount of people I've killed today."

Andrew remains silent. How is he supposed to respond to that?

"Do you still want to help me?"

"Yes. Where shall we meet?"

"Your town, not mine. You tell me."

"Do you know St Mary's Island?"

"Near the tunnel?"

"That's right. There's an Odeon down there. Park up and walk beyond the cinema towards the marina. I'll hook up with you there."

"How long?"

"I'm just coming back into town. I'll be there in about fifteen minutes, provided I don't slide off the road."

"Right."

Then Andrew asks:

"What's your name?"

"Sebastian."

The line goes dead.

Andrew chucks his phone onto the passenger seat, at last getting both hands back on the wheel.

* * *

Sebastian cuts the call and chucks the phone on the dash. The number Isobel had given him has yielded another potential ally, but still he is suspicious. What could Isobel have told him? He feigns ignorance on the phone, but could he know more?

Sebastian is so tired he's struggling to think it all through, his thoughts vague and half formed. This guy on the phone could even be one of them. He could've caught up to Isobel and killed her. But then, why would Isobel have his number?

Sebastian doesn't bother following this line of thought. There's no point and he's too far along to start worrying about consequences now. He just wanted to know Isobel was safe.

Sebastian's only real concern is the state he's in. His body is alive with twitches and shivers, the pain from his arm chews away at his thoughts. His whole left side is wet with blood. His lungs feel like they've been punctured and each breath whistles loudly in the tight confines of the car and sends a stabbing through his chest. Although he's wiped the blood from his left eye his vision still hasn't returned and there is a hammer going in his head. His legs feel like jelly. He's so tired he can barely move.

A car cruises past, the rumbling of its engine cutting into his thoughts. Sebastian looks up as it glides slowly by, forging its way through the snow. A few moments later its rear lights are swallowed by the blizzard. The quietness that follows is deep.

Sebastian contemplates staying right where he is. Tip the seat back and stretch out. Sleep. Why not just give it up? After the battle at the services, surely they'll call it even and everyone can go their separate ways. As idyllic as that thought sounds, Sebastian knows in his bones it'll never happen. He's caused too much trouble for Ichabod to let him fade away. And unless he finishes this, he'll spend the rest of his life looking over his shoulder, wondering when the attack will come. That's no way to live.

Sebastian turns the key and the Mercedes roars into life. Kenosha will never forgive him for keeping the car the whole day. He'll never get the blood out of the seat. But Sebastian just hopes he'll be in one piece to return it.

He's too heavy on the pedal and the car doesn't go anywhere, the engine revving and the wheels spinning.

Ease back, he says to himself. Get a grip, calm down, slow down. Sebastian takes a moment, trying to refocus his scattered brain, trying to get his hands steady.

This time he eases the Mercedes out from the bus stop and gets rolling along the A2. The windscreen wipers thump and swish the snow. The clock on the dashboard says 21:52. He can hardly believe he's been living this nightmare for barely twenty-four hours.

Sebastian wonders what Isobel is doing. Is she on a plane, or a train? Going somewhere hot or cold? Does this Andrew know more than he's letting on? What kind of a guy would willingly get himself mixed up in bullshit like this? An adrenalin junky, or some Special Forces nutjob who can't live without action? A psychopath? There is of course a more realistic answer.

"Maybe he loves her," Sebastian mutters to himself. Maybe he just wants to do what he can to make sure she's safe. His opinion of the guy goes up a notch, but it doesn't really quell his apprehension.

The pub on the corner at the bottom of Canterbury Street is blasting some cheesy eighties tune into the freezing night. Light spills from the windows and there are people slipping and sliding around out the front, hurling snowballs and falling over. Seems like a great place. As Sebastian turns left onto Dock Road he looks at the snowballers and they all seem to be staring in at him. He wonders if any will reach for a phone and call ahead.

The turn at the bottom of the road causes his arm to shout in pain. Pretty soon he won't be able to use it at all.

He should go to the hospital, but as Isobel is a nurse and she got him into this in the first place, he's not sure he'd trust anyone there. Perhaps he should head back to Kenosha's. But the tart would likely try and kill him for not bringing the car back. Fuck it. He's come this far, why stop now? He's strung out. He knows it. Even his thoughts are reckless. But for hours now this thing has had its own momentum.

Sebastian swings the car around the roundabout at the bottom of Dock Road, his poor arm screaming. He cruises down towards Dockside and the Odeon, alone on this dark road. He makes a left. Lights from the Encore Hotel spill out across the snow covered road. A few people are sat at the bar watching sports on the television. It looks warm and safe in there.

The dockyard is too quiet. Great swirling clouds of snow go billowing through the streetlights, looking far more ominous than Sebastian ever thought possible. He turns into the car park in front of the Odeon, driving by the foyer, glancing into the light at the people milling around, clutching popcorn and drinks.

He finds it hard to conceptualise such normality, such a simple, ordinary thing to do, going to the movies, or drinking at a bar and watching the football. Yesterday he could understand such things, but now, with a small army of dead men between that life and where he is now, the idea of ever doing something so normal again seems impossible.

Sebastian pulls into a space and turns off the engine. The large characterless warehouse of Dickens World sprouts from the side of the Odeon like a corrugated metal tumour, together the two structures form a gigantic monument to soulless, charmless architecture.

Two half-built towers, some developer's idea of an expensive apartment complex, loom up behind the Odeon and disappear jaggedly into the blizzard, revealed and hidden as the wind-driven snow billows around and through the twin skeletal structures. The sight is apocalyptic. Sebastian stares for a few minutes, his mind empty at last.

A few people walk out of the Odeon, pulling coat collars up around their necks and wrapping their arms tightly around themselves.

He shoves the door open and gets out into the freezing night. His whole body aches and his left arm is numb. The moviegoers are heading towards him, talking and laughing.

Sebastian turns away from them, hoping they won't notice the blood. They look at him, their expressions darkening.

What must I look like to them? Sebastian shuffles by the front doors to the Odeon and again looks inside. One of the screens has just emptied and there is a flood of people spilling into the foyer.

On the far side of the building is a road leading to a small boatyard and the marina. He leaves the light and life of the cinema behind. His boots crunch loudly through the snow. He stuffs his hands deep into his pockets and tucks his chin into his chest. He's freezing, shivering, but it's more than just the weather. He lurches on, feeling like he might fall down at any moment.

The marina is a forest of thin masts, rising from a multitude of yachts at anchor, bobbing on the swell. The wind howls through the rigging, producing a high-pitched shriek that sends shivers down his spine. He stumbles along on this deserted stretch of road, the fast black river on his left and that eerie scream setting his teeth on edge.

Sebastian turns and looks behind to see if anyone is following, but all he sees are his footsteps in the snow being erased by the wind. He stops to watch, a deep sense of foreboding swelling through him as the mark of his journey is casually swept away.

I can't win this fight on my own.

It is a thought that comes to him fully formed, a realisation so sudden and so clear that his already tormented breath catches in his throat. Injured and without allies he has no chance.

Perhaps Andrew will be his salvation.

* * *

A dark figure waits up ahead. He is tall and imposing, his hands stuffed in the pockets of a long black coat, the type of coat that could conceal a shotgun if its wearer were so inclined.

Suddenly, this feels like a really bad idea. Sebastian pauses. The figure remains still, the tail of his coat whipping around his calves.

"Andrew?" The wind snatches Sebastian's greeting and hurls it out across the river. The figure cocks his head.

"Andrew?" He tries again, his voice just a croak.

The man in the coat comes forwards, his footsteps crunching in the snow. One hand draws loose from a pocket and Sebastian is tense, waiting for the gun to appear. But the man's hand is empty, held out, palm up, waiting for Sebastian to shake.

"You look bloody terrible." Andrew's large face is kind, concerned, as his squinting eyes look Sebastian up and down. "In fact you look dead."

"It's been a long day."

"Let's walk." Andrew turns and makes for a narrow path by the river wall, heading away from the marina, across a small bridge and onto St Mary's Island.

Sebastian looks out at the black water, snow stinging his eyes. The far side of the river is lost in darkness.

"That's Upnor over there. There's a small castle and another marina. I take it you're not from around here," says Andrew.

"London."

"What brings you down?"

"Work."

Their footsteps crunch through the snow. They leave the marina behind. To the right is a large patch of wasteland, waiting for the developers to move in. In the distance Sebastian can see lights, houses. He can imagine people dozing in front of the television, making tea in the kitchen, or snuggled warm beneath a duvet.

"How do you know Isobel?" he asks.

Andrew turns and looks at him, his hands again buried in the pockets of his coat.

"I met her at the hospital. She patched me up." He grins. "I got battered at kung fu."

Sebastian offers a weak smile. That makes sense. Andrew carries himself like a fighter, standing straight despite the wind and the cold.

"Are you tough?" It must sound like an odd question coming from someone in his state, as if Sebastian were looking for a protector, which perhaps he is.

Andrew laughs. "Nope. There's a big difference between training in class and real life. My *sifu* tells me I'm not aggressive enough."

"That's not such a bad thing."

Again Andrew looks him up and down.

"Is Isobel safe?" Sebastian asks.

"Yes."

"You're sure?"

"I drove her to Ashford International. She left for somewhere in Europe."

"Somewhere?"

"She didn't tell me and I didn't ask."

That's a relief at least, one less thing for him to worry about.

"Was she alright?"

"No. She really wasn't. She's scared and a little crazy. I mean, she's always been a little crazy, but this was different."

"She's been through a lot today," Sebastian says quietly.

Up ahead is a short pier creaking in the wind. Just beyond is a large skeletal structure, like a crane, preserved from some previous industrial era. It rears up fifty feet or more and fades into the blizzard.

"What is that?" Sebastian asks.

"No idea. Some relic. Something to do with the dockyard. This whole place used to be heaving with boats, one of the largest dockyards in the country. St Mary's Island was home to some kind of toxic waste. The people who live here now can't grow vegetables in their back gardens."

"Sounds like an urban myth."

"Maybe it is."

What is this? Presented with a guy in Sebastian's condition, Andrew should be reaching for the phone to call an ambulance or running a mile. The conversation seems entirely too mundane for the situation. Sebastian cannot make sense of it. But there is a part of him that is grateful. Normality is a virtue to cling to at this point, however brief it may last.

The way ahead is darker. The lights stop at the weird structure. The path narrows and the river wall comes to an end. The river is a black fury just a few feet away.

"Where are we going?"

"This path runs all the way round the island. It's usually quiet and we can talk."

"You come here a lot?"

"I live here. Just over there." Andrew points across the wasteland towards the lights in the distance. I'd say we go straight back, but my wife'll be up. Probably best if she didn't see you in... umm..."

"You mean covered in blood with a bullet in my arm?"

Andrew looks out across the river, as if embarrassed. Sebastian can sense he so desperately wants to know what's going on, but he's too polite to ask. It's ridiculous. Sebastian is badly injured, struggling to stay up on his feet, cold and tired, probably in shock, and grappling with varying degrees of guilt and fear. He can hardly breathe, let alone indulge a delicate sense of propriety.

"Your wife? So Isobel's your bit on the side?"

"My wife and I are together for financial reasons. You know what it's like."

Sebastian doesn't, but nods anyway. So he's been seeing Isobel. But their relationship is more than casual, otherwise Andrew wouldn't be standing here now.

"Do you have kids?" Sebastian asks, trying to gauge how much he has to lose.

"Yes. Two. But my wife is more of a parent than I am."

He's still looking out at the river, standing ramrod straight in the blizzard. He reminds Sebastian of Sergeant Warrington, just taller and without the attitude.

They arrive at a bench set back into some bushes at the edge of the waste ground. Andrew sits down facing the river and Sebastian gratefully collapses next to him. They look out at the rushing water, the snow, and the faint blocky shape of Upnor Castle on the far side of the river. The blizzard swallows all the ambient noise and they sit in the silence, in the darkness.

Sebastian is freezing, shivering. His arm hangs dead at his side. He can't even wiggle his fingers. The cold snatches air from his lungs and he can hear himself wheezing. He's in no condition to take the fight back to Ichabod. All he can do is hole up and rest, get some sleep and find some strength. Is Andrew the person to provide that help? Sebastian hopes so. Right now he's too tired to care about the danger he may bring to this poor man's door. In some ways, it's too late for him already. Ichabod will already know about him. Sebastian wonders how he can tell Andrew this. How do you tell a man his life is about to change?

* * *

Andrew has never seen another human being in such a wretched state. One side of Sebastian's face is a black mask of blood, the other is ghostly white and glistening with sweat, despite the cold. His eyes are sunk so deep in their sockets Andrew can barely see them at all. Hunched and shivering, Sebastian is on the verge of collapse. How has he endured so much?

"What are you doing here?" Sebastian suddenly asks.

"What do you mean?"

"Why did you want to meet me? What are you offering?"

"I'm not offering anything. I want answers."

"Isobel was mixed up with some bad people. I doubt you know her half as well as you think you do. I got mixed up with the same people and last night they tried to have me killed. They're still trying."

Andrew nods. "Okay," he says, "that was succinct, and told me fuck all. Who are these 'bad people'? How much do you know about them?"

"I don't know much. I used to work for them, driving stuff around, nothing significant. I've never met the main guy, only ever spoken to him on the phone. Isobel never met him either. He controlled her, forced her to do things."

"Like what?"

"I don't know. But it's been going on for ages, years, and it's fucked her up."

Andrew is silent for a moment, thinking.

"So in a nut shell. Someone's trying to kill you, but you don't know who and you don't know why. And Isobel has been blackmailed by this person for years and somehow you two hooked up to find this guy."

"That's about it. Except this guy has an army of people he's sent after us, and I know his name."

"His name?"

"Yeah, Ichabod. Although there might be a second guy, who Isobel calls Mr Punch. She doesn't believe Ichabod and Mr Punch are the same person."

Andrew looks away from Sebastian and out over the river. Clearly Sebastian doesn't know much.

"If you weren't in such a state I'd say you were crazy. Have you got help?"

"What do you mean?"

"I mean help. Friends, people you can turn to who'll back you up?"

Sebastian shakes his head. "One mate has helped me out, but I think I've used up all my favours there."

"What about in London? You must have people there?"

"I know lots of people, but none I'd count on to back me up in a fight, and none I'd trust to keep their mouths shut."

"What about the police? You could go to them."

Sebastian laughs, a bitter sound, short-lived, which answers that question more clearly than words ever could.

"Why don't you run?"

"I have asthma. Since I was a kid. Running was never an option for me."

"You know there's a fine line between being principled and being stubborn."

"My granddad brought me up. He was a career soldier. Tough old bastard. He encouraged me to face everything, no matter what. If you start running, you'll never stop."

Andrew spends a few moments thinking about this. He nods to himself and stands up.

"You're crazy, and stupid. But you've got courage, and I can respect that." Andrew inclines his head, a brief acknowledgement of Sebastian's misplaced virtues. "You best come on back to the house."

Sebastian shuts his eyes and sighs with relief. He struggles to his feet and holds out his good hand. Words won't express his thanks. All he can offer is a sincere handshake.

Andrew shakes with one hand, and pulls the knife from his pocket with the other. He yanks Sebastian forwards and stabs him in the belly, his movement swift and practiced, his thrust powerful and his intention pure and undiluted.

Sebastian sags as the blade is withdrawn. Andrew spins Sebastian around, his big left hand coming up under Sebastian's chin, tilting his head back and with one fluid movement he cuts Sebastian's throat and shoves his body forwards into the river.

* * *

He moves so fast Sebastian doesn't even see it. He's so tired, and Andrew is ruthless.

So ruthless.

Sebastian watches the snow blowing over the river. He can feel his guts pushing at the hole in his belly. There's no pain. Sebastian's throat is open before he thinks about fighting back.

He's falling now, the river rising to engulf him, his blood running into her swift currents. Despite everything, despite all he's done, all he's survived and the ferocious way he fought back, against this man he never stood a chance. Isobel didn't betray him; he knows this. Andrew seduced her, he cared about her, he loved her; and Isobel believed him. Just as Sebastian believed him. This man is the strategist, the power behind Ichabod's throne.

Andrew.

Mr Punch.

Sebastian flashbacks to Grandpa, sat in the rocking chair by the window. Grandpa tells him to stand up, to fight back, to face forwards, always forwards. Never back down. Never run, no matter what. You can't run, son. It's not an option for you. You must always stand and fight.

Grandpa would be proud.

He tries to draw one last breath before going under, but it blows back out through the split in his neck before ever reaching his traitorous lungs. He tries to swim, but his one good arm is so far away. He tries to kick, but his legs are too heavy.

Sebastian's thoughts are getting smaller, his mind filled with so many images, so many memories of the life before this day.

He's lost. The realisation finally comes. After everything, the bad guy still won. Against some evils there is no defence. All those people he killed in his struggle to survive. Such a price to pay for failure. They all died for nothing. But don't we all? In the end.

Darkness.

Only darkness at the end.

* * *

Andrew watches as the black river carries Sebastian away. In just a few moments he is gone, carried into darkness by the rapid current. He'll be found at some point, but Andrew isn't worried about that. He bends down and washes the blade in the river before putting it back in his pocket. The wind whips his coat-tails around his legs. He looks out across the river for a moment, before turning and striding back along the path, past the old crane and over the bridge. When he gets to the car park in front of the Odeon he unlocks the Audi and slips behind the wheel. He takes out his phone.

"Yeah?" asks Ichabod.

"What are you doing?"

"Just entertaining the friend."

"What?"

"Me and Talissa. This guy is fun, man."

Andrew sighs. More and more Ichabod is becoming a liability.

"I told you to finish that quickly."

"Where are you?"

"At the cinema."

"Oh yeah? What'd'ya see?"

"It's over Ichabod. He's dead. It's all finished. Your little game has cost us everyone we had control over in this town. It'll take years to rebuild."

"Hmm... What?"

Andrew can hear noises down the phone, sounds like a woman having an orgasm, and Ichabod is clearly distracted.

"Kenosha's there now?"

"Oh yeah, he's here now."

"I'm coming over."

Andrew chucks the phone on the passenger seat and turns the key in the ignition. He pulls out of the car park. Just one last thing to do before this day is done.

Part 3

26

It takes Andrew a short while to get through the tunnel under the Medway and out to Talissa's place on the Hoo Peninsula. He glides to a halt in front of the little detached house. Ichabod's BMW is parked in the driveway, and there is a taxi parked a little way up the road, it's hazard lights flashing.

Andrew gets out and walks up the garden path to the door and rings the doorbell. He waits, for what seems like an age. The wind tugs at his coat and the snow billows around his face.

Eventually the door creaks open a fraction and Ichabod's ice blue eye presents itself at the crack.

"Open the fucking door."

"Don't be mad." Ichabod pulls the door wide and looks at his friend, immediately realising that this time he has pushed too far.

"You're really angry," he says.

"What's with the taxi up the road?"

"What taxi?"

"There's a cab parked just up the road."

"Dunno. Nothing to do with us."

"Your man still here?"

"Yeah, him and Talissa are getting along famously."

Andrew sighs. "Where's his car?"

Ichabod looks beyond Andrew's shoulder, out to the street.

"Don't know."

"How'd he get here, Ichabod?"

"I don't fucking know."

"Could it be that cab's waiting for him? D'yer think?"

"Yeah. Maybe."

Andrew grabs Ichabod by the throat and forces him back into the house. He slams him up against the wall in the hallway with incredible force. Ichabod smacks the back of his head against the wall and sags. Andrew holds him up, his face in close.

"You're causing far too much chaos for our friendship to survive. Go get rid of the taxi. Just tell him to leave. Do it now. No questions, no arguments. Do exactly what I say."

Andrew lets go of Ichabod's throat. Ichabod sags to his knees, gasping for air. Andrew stands over him. The ferocity has gone, replaced by an unnerving, preternatural calm.

Ichabod crawls along the hallway to the door. He gets to his feet and staggers down the garden path towards the waiting taxi.

Andrew heads deeper into the house. He's already committed the license plate of the taxi to memory. From upstairs comes the steady rhythmic creaking of the bed, and the occasional gasp and groan.

Andrew goes into the dining room and takes a seat at the table, with his back to the wall, facing the door. He takes the knife from his pocket and lays it on the table. He waits, ramrod straight, eyes unblinking.

The front door shuts gently, and a moment later a sheepish looking Ichabod appears in the doorway. He hesitates before coming into the room. Andrew's mood, which is a rare presence in itself, is dark indeed.

"Now take the knife and do what should have been done hours ago. No fuss, no games. Just go upstairs and kill him."

"Here in the house?"

"Here in the house."

Ichabod, reduced to a meekness that would have Talissa stunned, picks up the knife from the table.

"Don't fuck about, Ichabod. You and I need to have a talk."

Ichabod nods like a chastised child.

* * *

During the climb up the stairs, Ichabod's mood becomes black. He hates the way Andrew dominates him, makes him feel like a fuck up. So what if I've played a little? That fucking miserable cunt needs to get more fun out of life. Ichabod's rage is quick to ignite and difficult to extinguish, fuelled all the more by the acceptance of his own shortcomings. He knows that without Andrew he would never survive in this world. He doesn't have the head for strategy, or the self-control required to see things through. His desires always get the better of him.

Why can't I be more like him? Ichabod asks himself.

Because then I wouldn't be me.

He reaches the landing and lascivious sounds halt his introspection and turn him onto the scene: Talissa on her back and Kenosha on his knees between her legs, smoothly thrusting away. Talissa's eyes are closed, her mouth slightly open. Her small hands grip Kenosha's knees. Ichabod watches the rippling muscles in Kenosha's body. The candle-lit bedroom is stifling hot. Before Kenosha arrived Ichabod had turned up the central heating. Both their naked bodies glisten beneath a sheen of sweat.

"I'll let you both in on a little secret," says Ichabod from the bedroom doorway.

Talissa opens her eyes.

Kenosha turns. He doesn't notice the knife in Ichabod's hand.

"At some point, people who hate being humiliated always start to enjoy it."

* * *

Kenosha notes the subtle shift in atmosphere. A sudden chill. His rhythm falters. Again he wonders at the wisdom of coming out on this dreadful night. He looks down at Talissa. Her expression is slack, her eyes open and staring at the ceiling, as if she's been plucked out of the moment entirely.

Kenosha turns back to the doorway, but finds Ichabod standing right next to him at the side of the bed. Kenosha is startled for just a moment.

Then Ichabod grabs a fistful of his hair, wrenches his head back and drags the blade across his throat.

Kenosha's eyes go wide.

* * *

Ichabod steps back as blood erupts, pumping from Kenosha's neck in a long powerful arc.

Beneath him, Talissa is suddenly drenched red. For a moment she is frozen in horror, looking up at Kenosha as his blood pours into her face. She whips her head to the side and screams.

Kenosha falls forward, his chest heaving, trying to draw breath. There is a whistling noise from his throat.

Talissa thrashes beneath his weight, struggling to get out from under him. The rich, pungent odour of his blood makes her retch. Its wetness. Its heat. She drags herself from under Kenosha's slippery body and falls off the bed, collapsing in a bloody heap on the floor, gasping and spitting and shaking.

Kenosha struggles, crawling across the bed, fighting to live but failing, his strength fading quickly.

Ichabod drives the blade into the back of Kenosha's neck, just about severing his head.

Kenosha's struggles cease immediately, although his limbs spasm, his fingers beating an irregular rhythm against the red, saturated sheets.

Ichabod leaves the knife lodged in the bones of Kenosha's neck and walks back downstairs.

* * *

Ichabod enters the dining room to find Andrew sat at the table, looking back at him. Two mugs of tea are sitting on the table, wafting thin spires of steam.

"It's done," says Ichabod, sitting down.

"How much mess did you make?"

Ichabod waves away the question.

"Talissa will clear up."

"Will she?"

Ichabod sips his tea and looks over Andrew's shoulder at his reflection in the dark patio doors. There is blood on his face, but he doesn't bother to wipe it away.

"Is it still snowing?" he asks.

"Who cares?"

"There's a field out the back. We should go and dig trenches like we used to years ago. Only this time we can have real guns."

"And who would we shoot, Ichabod? Everyone we used to employ is dead."

"Yeah. Who'd have thought Sebastian would be so tough?" Ichabod grins and takes another sip.

"You think this is funny?"

"Not funny, but it's been the most exciting day we've had in ages."

Andrew's veneer of calmness begins to crack.

"Exciting?"

Ichabod grins again. Andrew wants to ruin that handsome face once and for all, break those perfect teeth, rip off those lips and spread that nose so wide it splatters across those bony cheeks.

"You are this close to being in trouble."

Ichabod can sense the tension in his friend. He knows how dangerous Andrew can be.

"I'm sorry, alright? I had no idea it would get so out of hand."

"Out of hand?"

Ichabod hides behind another sip of tea. He places the mug down on the table and stares into its depths.

"We have lost so much in the last twenty-four hours. About twenty years worth of work. Do you know how much control it takes to put a gun in a man's hand and send him out to kill? Do you think we can just find that sort of leverage again? Our life's work Ichabod, destroyed because of your weakness for humiliating that bitch upstairs."

"No one's ever fought back before," Ichabod says quietly.

"What? What did you say?"

Intimidated, Ichabod turns away. For the first time, a real tinge of fear bites at his heart.

"Tell me what's going on here, with that cunt upstairs."

"What do you mean?"

"Why bring him here? Why let him fuck her? I don't get it, Ichabod."

"I don't know. I get bored. I can't help it."

"Help what?"

"I get bored."

"You've had no discipline in your life. Your mother spoilt you and your father was a second-rate academic with a chip on his shoulder who taught you nothing except arrogance. You've had no boundaries."

"You've always kept me in line."

"It's getting harder. I'm losing the will for it. These psycho games are out of control. You've completely undone us this time."

"People will fall back in line."

"You think? We've lost all our influence. All our power."

"You are our power. People are terrified of us, and you especially. Those that know us will do whatever we say. You know it. I get that you're angry with me, and I know I've fucked up. But this isn't the disaster you're trying to make it out to be. In fact, if anything, it'll work in our favour."

"How?"

"Because Sebastian beat everybody he went up against. But still we've won. What kind of message does that send? People will be even more scared now, and fear is all we need. You said that."

"Except all our meat puppets are dead. There's nobody left to be afraid of us."

"Rubbish. We think we're secret but we're not. We're an urban legend. Everyone knows something. Everyone's heard whispers. And when we come calling everyone will shit their pants and fall into line."

They sit in silence for a few moments, drinking their tea like regular friends.

Andrew watches Ichabod intently. For most of his life he's been responsible for him. He never planned it this way; it's just a role he instinctively played, like all the other roles he's adopted to preserve his standing in the world.

But now he's wondering just how far loyalty can stretch. At what point should he cut his losses and throw his wayward accomplice into the river? After a lifetime of working together, would it be hard to do? Would he even hesitate?

Ichabod is uneasy beneath Andrew's intense scrutiny. Looking into his eyes has always been an unnerving experience. An entire world of calculations churned away in there, a machine-like intelligence, cold and distant and remote. But Ichabod had always believed Andrew felt some warmth towards him, that they were genuine friends. Now, though, he isn't so sure.

"Where's the bag?" Andrew asks.

"What bag?"

"For fucks sake. The cargo, Ichabod. Remember that?"

"Oh that. It's in my car, in the boot."

"So you do have it?"

"No, I donated it to science."

"Sarcasm doesn't suit you, Ichabod."

"Neither does sanity, restraint and fat whores." Ichabod grins, trying to lighten the moment.

"Isn't Talissa a fat whore?"

"No, she's a ruined whore. There's a difference."

"Is that why you keep her around? Pining for the memory of what she once was?"

Ichabod is genuinely surprised for a moment, amazed at his friend's misunderstanding.

"Talissa was abused by when she was young. She was so vulnerable when we met. Almost perfect. But she was a product of her dad and I wanted her to be a product of me. Talissa is an ongoing process of destruction. She's intentionally ruined."

"Why?"

"Why what?"

"Why do that? What's the point?"

"Because."

"Because what?"

"Because I was jealous. Because I still am."

"You're twisted."

"It's part of our dynamic. You're the cold one, I'm the perverted one. It's how people tell us apart."

"Now they'll know us as the two who almost got beaten by a courier."

"They'll know us as the two who faced a real challenge and triumphed."

"Such an optimist."

"Always." Ichabod grins, finally starting to relax.

Andrew sighs again, and Ichabod realises he isn't completely safe yet.

"I know this time it's bad," he says, looking down into his mug.

"I'm not going to kill you," Andrew says quietly.

Ichabod looks up with surprise.

"I'm not going to kill you," Andrew says again. "But every single part of me is screaming that I should. I should butcher you here and fade away. You've turned this entire town upside down. We need to bury ourselves in the normal routine for at least a year. Do you understand?"

Ichabod is silent, scared even. Andrew has never talked to him this way before.

"What do we do now?"

"We go to ground. That's all we can do. Tie off any loose ends, close everything down, disappear into a normal life for a year, maybe two, then start again."

"Loose ends? You mean your girl, what's her name, Isobel?"

"She's gone. We don't need to worry about her."

"What did you do?"

"Nothing, she caught a train into Europe."

"Does she know who you are?"

"Of course not."

"I never did understand why you got involved with her."

"An opportunity I couldn't resist."

"No, I mean why you started fucking her."

"That wasn't planned, but it was an interesting situation to pursue."

"And she has no idea?"

"None. That's what I mean by keeping a low profile. But not you. You've got to show everyone how fucking insane you are."

"Where did she go?"

"To Europe. I don't know where."

Ichabod is surprised.

"You've actually let her go?"

"She's still within reach."

"Can't resist your cock, huh?"

"Something like that."

They fall silent for a moment, looking at each other across the table. Then Ichabod says:

"What other loose ends are there?"

"You. And your bitch upstairs."

"Me?"

"Yes you, Ichabod. We can't very well leave you here. You're too well known. Sooner or later someone will mention your name to the wrong people. You'll have to leave."

"Where will I go?"

"I don't know yet. South America maybe."

"What about Talissa?"

"She's been your Achilles heel for far too long. Whatever you've got going on with her, it clouds your judgement and you make too many mistakes. Time to end it."

310

Andrew can see that Ichabod doesn't like this idea.

"Don't even start whining about it. If you don't sort her out, I will."

"She could come with me."

Andrew brings his hand down hard on the table. So hard he bounces both mugs onto the floor. Ichabod jumps in surprise. He can't hold Andrew's gaze.

"You're hanging by a thread." Andrew's voice is empty of malice, of anger, of any recognisable human emotion. It is the *voice* that has sent so many into the darkness.

Ichabod shrinks.

"Alright," he says quietly. "I'll do it."

"Tonight. When we're done here. No games, no ceremonies. No fucking about. Shove the knife in her heart, watch until the light goes out of her eyes, and then we torch this place and drive you straight to the airport."

"What about the snow?"

"The roads are passable. Some people think the world stops when it snows, but it doesn't."

Ichabod sits quietly, his hands resting on the table. The thought of losing Talissa fills him with sadness. He still has such a long way to go with her, so much still to subject her to. To simply snuff her out is such a waste. Surely he can be more inventive than that? Andrew wouldn't begrudge him one final act of love.

Ichabod looks up to meet his friend's empty eyes. Andrew has been staring at him with the same cold intensity for a long time now. Ichabod cannot recall seeing him blink, not once.

After all these years, the man is still a mystery. I wear my heart on my sleeve, Ichabod thinks. But you are an absolute blank.

"Why do you do this?" he suddenly asks.

"What do you mean?"

"You don't seem to take any pleasure from our business. It can't be the money because you don't spend any of it. It can't be the violence, because you're too efficient at it. You don't play."

"An enlightened man will always question the nature of his self. But I'm not enlightened, Ichabod. I don't question. I strategise, yes, but the 'why' is of no interest to me."

"A psychologist would call you a sociopath."

"A philosopher would call me a misanthrope. So what?"

Then, from the corner of his eye, Andrew sees movement. His eyes dart to the doorway as Talissa, wearing a blood-covered robe, shuffles into the room.

Talissa holds the knife, clenched fiercely in both fists. She pauses in the doorway, taking in the two men sat calmly at the table. Her eyes slide from Andrew's face to the back of Ichabod's head.

Her blank expression twists into a horrible mask of pain and hate, and with a high-pitched and murderously unhinged shriek she charges forwards with the knife held high.

Andrew doesn't move.

He doesn't even blink.

27

There is a heavy red mist. A distant noise, like an animal shrieking, coming closer, growing louder.

Talissa snaps back into her mind. The noise is coming from her own contorted, blood-covered lips. Her eyelids peel open, the red mist speared by a ray of white light, becoming broader, thicker. Her eyelashes are heavy with gore.

She lies on the floor, in the corner of her bedroom, face turned to the wall, shrieking.

And then she stops.

She stares fixedly at the join in the skirting board in the corner of her bedroom, not wanting to close her eyes, not wanting to turn and face the carnage.

She can sense Kenosha's dead body on her bed. She can sense the blood-drenched sheets. She can feel his blood drying on her skin. She can taste it on her lips. She can smell it, in the air, on her hands.

Talissa struggles to stay in the moment. Her mind desperately wants to find a safer place. A trip down memory lane looking for a pleasant retreat, somewhere that isn't haunted by the image of men.

But there is nowhere in her past where men have not left some kind of stain on the tapestry of her life; first her father, who abandoned her before she even knew his face, then Carl her stepfather, and now Ichabod. Her whole life spent retreating from the spectre of those that would do her harm. Always running, never confronting.

You're such a fucking victim! Her mother's voice, whispered in her ear.

Talissa slowly gets to her feet. Still facing the wall she waits a moment, her eyes going dark and her head swimming. After regaining her equilibrium, she turns and confronts the grotesque abattoir that used to be her bedroom.

Kenosha's inert body lays on its front, the knife still buried in the back of his neck. Talissa looks at it pointedly for a moment, its absurd reality somehow confirming the scene.

Talissa takes one haltering step, and then another, towards her dressing table. Her legs are weak. She collapses on the stool. She leans on the small table and looks at herself in the mirror.

She takes a box of tissues from a drawer and wipes at the blood on her face. But it has seeped into her pores and stained her skin; too deep for tissues, she'll need soap and water.

But that can wait.

She looks deep into her eyes, trying to find the courage for what comes next. She knows it must be there. Her mother always had it. It has to be there. But all she sees is a frightened and thoroughly beaten woman.

And in that she finds her resolve. The recognition of what she has become, of the changes that Ichabod's madness has wrought. She was pretty once. Although plagued by her demon stepfather, her face never betrayed the boogieman within. But Ichabod set a far more ambitious agenda than rape. So much for the hopeful dreams of a young woman, giving her heart to a prince. Ichabod never whisked her away on a white horse, he chained her to a dungeon wall and watched while others raped and destroyed her.

A shallow spur it may be, but it is all she has.

Talissa, taking one final look at her miserable self, gets up and retrieves her dressing gown from the floor beside the bed. She slips it around her shoulders, heedless of the blood that stains it.

She takes a moment, building her courage. Then with a firm hand she grabs the hilt of the knife and wrenches it from Kenosha's neck. His head rolls at a sickening angle, barely attached.

Talissa turns away quickly, knowing that if she lives through the next half hour, she'll revisit that gruesome sight for the rest of her life.

28

Ichabod turns in his chair at the sound of Talissa's shriek. But she is already on top of him, driving the knife into his face.

For a moment, his mind freezes on the impossibility of this. Why has Talissa, his meek and tormented little love, turned so savagely against him?

The image of her enraged face, tears cutting tracks through the blood on her cheeks, stays with him, even as his eyes are skewered on the blade and his world goes dark.

Talissa, stabbing frenziedly, screaming with each thrust, looses an unrelenting torrent of suppressed rage and hatred from deep inside, delivered through the merciless blade, carving her fury into the very bones of Ichabod's skull. She feels the impact of her strikes through the blood-slick hilt of the knife, carried along her arms into her shoulders.

Ichabod, his face no longer a face, lurches to his feet. The tortured tapestry of his mind spits only one recognisable word from the turmoil:

Unfair! Unfair! Unfair!

But his plea is unspoken. He's no longer capable of forming actual words, just a high-pitched wail coming from deep within his throat as Talissa redirects her attack, stabbing him in the chest, the neck, the gut, the blade still held in a two-handed grip, her arms driving forwards and back.

Ichabod collapses back against the table, then drops to the floor. Talissa follows him down, her attack still ferocious. Ichabod's hands wave in space, a last, futile attempt to stop the knife, even as his life ebbs away. Talissa continues, unrelenting, the blade chewing up Ichabod's face and body until he is nothing more than a butchered carcass.

Crying now, Talissa's fury gives way to exhaustion, fear, relief. The blade gets stuck between Ichabod's ribs and she struggles to wrench it free, her body now spent. She wrestles with the hilt, but gives up and collapses on the floor, her breathing ragged, gasping through sobs, shaking.

Talissa crawls away from the spreading pool of blood, the robe open and hanging around her shoulders, her modesty long since abandoned to her furious attack. Her shaking hands go to her face and cover her eyes.

"That was entertaining."

The voice sends a chill down her spine, making her shiver.

Talissa looks up from her hands at the man sitting calmly behind the table. She saw him when she entered the room, but his presence didn't register, she only had eyes for Ichabod.

He sits perfectly straight and composed. He doesn't appear remotely bothered by the carnage he's just witnessed.

"You're Talissa. We've never met, but I know everything there is to know about you, so I can understand your actions."

Talissa always knew there was someone else, someone behind Ichabod, pulling the strings. Ichabod was too unpredictable, too impulsive, to survive in the world without someone constantly keeping him in line.

"Why don't you pick yourself up off the floor and have a seat?" Andrew gestures to the chair on the opposite side of the table.

Talissa stares at him from the floor.

With his foot, Andrew nudges the chair Ichabod was sat in. Talissa drags herself from the floor, staggers over to the chair, wrapping the robe around her as she goes. Her bare feet squelch through Ichabod's blood. She sits down and stares across at the man opposite. She puts her hands on the table in front of her, palms down.

"It's interesting," says Andrew, "just how much some people will endure before lashing out."

Talissa doesn't speak. She looks at her hands, deeply aware of the twitching body by the side of her chair.

"I was deciding whether to kill him myself. He's made some mistakes today that have cost me dear. It's not the first time, but it's the worst fuck-up he's ever made. I was just asking myself if I felt anything for him. I couldn't decide if I would be sad if he were dead. I wondered if I would feel guilty." Andrew reaches across the table and places his fingers under Talissa's chin, gently pulling her head up so her eyes meet his.

"I couldn't decide if I had any feelings for him whatsoever. And then you came in, and you know what?"

"What?" Talissa's voice is barely a whisper.

"I don't feel anything. You just hacked up my oldest friend, you might say my brother, and I don't have any feelings about it."

Talissa, looking into his eyes, has no problem believing this. There is an empty blackness inside this man. If she weren't so exhausted she would be terrified.

"I've always struggled to understand. So much effort goes into forming attachments. But nothing is impervious to time. Sooner or later, everything you invest your emotions in will disappear. People betray you, or die.

Objects become obsolete and break. All this energy, all this effort, and all you do is set yourself up for a fall. I never understood it. I still don't."

He looks at her as if expecting a reply. Talissa simply shakes her head.

"You don't agree? You think I'm wrong?"

"I… I don't know what you're talking about."

Andrew sighs. "What I'm trying to say is that despite what happens next, it's not because I hate you for butchering my friend. In many ways you've done me a favour."

Talissa is silent as this sinks in.

"You know what has to happen now."

"Why does it have to happen?"

"You've seen me. That's all it takes."

Talissa shakes her head. "I'm not ready."

Andrew smiles, but not with his eyes. "Unfortunately, that means nothing."

"Can I have a moment?"

"Of course."

Talissa sighs deeply. After so much, it comes to this. She always believed that she would die at Ichabod's hands. She always thought that one day his rages would be too much. He'd go too far or just grow bored of her.

But now?

Now she's won her freedom, at long last. She's defeated the nightmare in her life, just like her mother defeated Carl. What cruel irony to endure so much before release, only to loose again moments later. Talissa, despite her tiredness, despite all the violence of this dreadful day, feels her resolve harden.

She doesn't want to die yet. She isn't ready.

"Excuse me," she says, standing up. She ties the robe around her tightly, and bends down and wrenches the knife from Ichabod's inert body. If she can take one, then she can take the other.

Talissa stands up straight and faces Andrew, bloody knife in hand.

"I'm not ready to give up yet."

"That means nothing. Only in Hollywood do the good guys win. This is the real world."

"We'll see."

"You beat Ichabod because you attacked by surprise and from behind. Why do you think I sit with my back to the wall, facing the door? You can't defeat me the same way. So, how do you propose to escape with your life?"

Talissa knows his words are true.

"Indulge me. I'm curious. How will you live through the next five minutes?"

She takes a step back towards the doorway, away from the table. Blood oozes thickly between her toes. She hardly notices; her attention is fixed on the blank, unmoving man at the table.

"I see. You're not going to fight. You're going to run. A wise choice. But the odds are stacked against you. Few can outrun me, and you're not even wearing shoes. But you never know, right? I might lose my footing and fall over, maybe even bash my head against a rock, and then you'll be free." Andrew nods encouragement.

Talissa takes another step backwards.

"I'll give you a thirty-second head start. May the best man win."

Talissa turns and bolts from the room.

Andrew betrays his promise. Instantly he is up from the table and flying across the room in pursuit.

Talissa, now in the kitchen, fumbles for a moment with the backdoor, then flings it open and plunges out into the night.

The coldness strikes the breath from her before she's even cleared the square of light thrown from the doorway. She races down the garden, ploughing through shin-deep snow, her bloody robe falling open and whipping behind her like a cape. Arms pumping. Lungs screaming. Falling snow blows into her face and stings her eyes.

I will live, she thinks. *I won't give up.*

She risks a glance over her shoulder and cannot believe how close he is. She gasps in disbelief and drives forwards even faster.

At the end of the garden she hurls herself over the low wall into the field beyond. She catches her bare feet on the top of the wall and lands heavily, knocking the air from her lungs. But instantly she is clawing her way back to her feet, oblivious of the bloody footprints trailing behind her.

Staggering, slipping, but onwards, into the darkness of the field, away from the light, Talissa keeps running, the knife clutched fiercely in her fist – a last, desperate defence. Losing all sense of direction, all coherent thought, blinded and freezing, she has no idea where she is going or how she really intends to escape. Panic in her heart forces her to run, nothing more – just to run, from the devil chasing her, from the devil she's just defeated, from all she's witnessed, from all she's responsible for.

She can sense him, just a few steps behind in the real world. The others are lunging from her past. Her father. Her stepfather. Ichabod. Always she is running, never standing her ground, never fighting back.

Talissa looks over her shoulder again. He is just an arm's length behind. His face betrays nothing, no expression, and no indication of exertion. His eyes bore into hers, unblinking despite the snow whipping into them.

He's inhuman, she thinks, crying out in frustration, turning away from him, unable to look at him.

Snow. Blizzard. Nothing but a blanket of whiteness in front, nothing but darkness behind, as the wind erases her bloody footprints, erasing this chase from the world before it's reached its conclusion.

Talissa, knowing that she cannot outrun him, knowing that she made a mistake racing into the field, has no choice but to fight. Running has never saved her; maybe standing her ground will. She tightens her grip on the knife.

Acting on instinct far more than design, she lets her legs go slack, twisting her body round as she drops to the ground and lashing out with the knife, hoping to surprise him, hoping he'll rush headlong onto the blade, impaling himself in the gut.

It's a desperate but not ill-conceived plan. As Talissa spins and sinks she sees her target right there, hurtling towards the blade.

The tip of the knife is just centimetres from his gut.

Talissa has a moment for her breath to catch before the blade sinks in, the realisation that she's done it, that she's going to beat him.

But then the impossible; he is leaving the ground, rising upwards, spinning over her head and she cranes her neck to follow his somersaulting progress.

Talissa screams in frustration and disbelief, as Andrew lands with poise and grace, silently in the snow. He turns to face her. He shakes his head.

"WHAT ARE YOU?" Talissa screams at him in rage, her words lost to the wind the moment they leave her lips.

He doesn't answer, doesn't blink. Against some evils there is no understanding. There is no defence. He walks towards her through the driving snow with his coat blowing around him.

Talissa staggers to her feet and raises the knife. Andrew doesn't pause, doesn't even look at the knife. Talissa senses the relentlessness of his will, his strength, his resolve.

She takes a faltering step backwards, his mere presence now enough to sap the defiance from her heart.

"Please." She feels the strength going from her legs. Her robe hangs from her shoulders, her bloodied body shivering in the freezing cold.

"Please!"

He's right on top of her and she lunges at him with the knife, her last, final, desperate attempt at survival.

Talissa barely sees his reaction, so swift, so smooth. Pain flares through her wrist up into her arm as he blocks her lunge, the knife propelled from her hand, sailing away and lost in the snow.

She takes another step backwards.

His advance hasn't faltered. Unceremoniously, he punches her brutally in the throat.

Talissa drops to her knees.

The world goes black.

She's dead before she hits the snow.

29

Andrew looks down at Talissa. His hands do not shake. His breathing is no different to what it was inside the house. He looks upon her exposed body in the whiteness, the blood black on her pale skin, her open empty eyes filling with snow. He looks down on the woman who endured so much, and he feels nothing.

He goes looking for his knife, his acute senses knowing roughly where it landed. Finding it, he slips it into the pocket of his coat. He goes back to Talissa and scoops her body into his arms. He doesn't use the robe to hide her modesty. There is no dignity for anyone in his heart.

He strolls back through the field, carrying Talissa's dead weight as if it were nothing. When he reaches the wall at the bottom of her garden he simply hurls her body over it onto the other side. He takes a quick look behind. There is nothing but the falling snow, white fading to darkness. He knows that the power station is back there somewhere, out in the estuary, but nothing else. The white field is silent, the snow reducing visibility. It's doubtful anyone was watching.

He leaps elegantly over the wall, picks Talissa up and walks back to the house.

He dumps her in the dining room next to Ichabod. He pauses for only a moment, looking down at his friend. He is curious about his own detachment. They'd been together since they were kids, and he knows he should be feeling something about this loss. He knows there should be some sense of grief, or relief. But when he looks down at his friend's destroyed face, unrecognisable now after Talissa's fury, he feels absolutely nothing. He bends down and retrieves Ichabod's keys from his pocket, getting blood on his hands, which he wipes on a dishcloth in the kitchen.

He goes outside, leaving the front door open and unlocks Ichabod's car. He opens the boot and looks in at the cargo.

Its size.

Its weight.

He doesn't smile at his triumph. He simply hauls the bag from the boot and carries it out to his own car at the curb. He beeps it open and chucks the bag on the back seat.

Back at Ichabod's car, he pulls the petrol can from the boot and walks back into the house. He douses the two bodies, then walks into the kitchen and turns on all the gas burners on the hob. Back in the dining room, the smell of petrol and gas a heady cocktail, he strikes a match. The two bodies blaze.

Andrew picks up the empty petrol can. He shuts the front door, puts the petrol can back in the boot of Ichabod's car and slams it shut.

For a moment he turns and looks at the house. There are no signs of the fire yet, but it won't be long.

There is no sense of relief at the day finally being over. There is no sense of satisfaction at retrieving the cargo. For Andrew, there is only what happens, and how he deals with it. Everything else is blank.

He gets in his car and turns the key in the ignition. The Audi roars to life and drives away from the house as the glow from the fire appears in the open front door.

His mobile beeps. He takes it from his pocket and checks the text message:

Thanks for your help.
I'll miss you.
This is my new number
xxx

Behind him, the gas ignites and Talissa's house explodes, filling the darkness with noise and light.

Andrew doesn't flinch; he doesn't even look in the rear-view mirror. Instead, he saves the unrecognised number on his phone, then he sends a message back.

At the end of the street he makes a left, heading back into town. The burning house is now just an amber glow in the darkness behind him. The day is over, Ichabod gone, Sebastian defeated, and all loose ends tied up. It is time to move on.

Andrew dials another number.

His wife answers the phone.

"Hey you," he says, his voice suddenly full of warmth. "Are you still up?"

* * *

Isobel is in a window seat, looking at her reflection in the glass as the Eurostar train barrels through the night. Beyond, the dark countryside of France rushes by.

Although exhausted, she nurtures a tenuous sense of hope. Optimism is such a fragile state of mind, and new to her after so many years trapped in a web of darkness. For the first time she can sense a future, a place further along the path that might be safe, a place where Mr Punch is but a dark, half-remembered dream.

She wonders if Andrew might join her there.

Isobel pulls the scrap of paper he gave her from her pocket. The name of his friend, *Anders Madsen*, is written in Andrew's precise script. She thinks about Norway and the town of Ålesund.

Then her new phone beeps with an incoming text message.

Missing you back.
Keep your eyes peeled for that beach house.
I can hear the waves already.
xxx

Isobel smiles. She puts the phone away and closes her eyes. Sleep comes quickly. She does not dream.